Critical acclaim for Melissa Senate

The Breakup Club

"Senate's latest has her trademark quick
pacing and sympathetic, lovable characters,
proving once again she's one of
Red Dress Ink's brightest talents."
—*Booklist*

"One of the many gifts Senate brings to the writing
table is her ability to establish equally compelling
stories for four fascinating characters. That she
does so with humor and insight adds to
the pleasures of this novel."
—*Romantic Times BOOKreviews*

Whose Wedding is it Anyway?

"Melissa Senate's third novel wittily debunks
the idea of a perfect wedding."
—*Marie Claire*

"Unexpected twists in the story distinguish Senate's
novel from the pack of bride-to-be books."
—*Booklist*

The Solomon Sisters Wise Up

"Senate's prose i
—*Bost*

"If you're in the mood
female bondinç
—*W Network*

See Jane Date

"A refreshing change of pace."
—*Publishers Weekly*

"The story unfolds like a brightly wrapped bonbon.
It's tantalizing and tasty."
—*Sacramento Bee*

"This Cinderella story provides plot and dramatic
tension, but what makes it more than a fairytale
is that Jane's daily life...captures the very real
loneliness of being a contemporary, urban single."
—*Washington Monthly*

"You could almost imagine a star like
Renee Zellweger being interested in
playing a character like this."
—*Entertainment Weekly*

Love You to Death

Melissa Senate

RED
DRESS
I N K
TM

First edition January 2007

LOVE YOU TO DEATH

A Red Dress Ink novel

ISBN-13: 978-0-373-89546-5
ISBN-10:   0-373-89546-1

www.RedDressInk.com

Printed in U.S.A.

Love You to Death

Acknowledgments

As always to my great editor, Joan Marlow Golan.
Extra thank-yous to Margaret Marbury for her
continued and constant support, Selina McLemore
for the cover and good cheer, Sarah Rundle for the
PR, and the entire RDI team for all their hard work.

To my agent Kim Witherspoon and Alexis Hurley,
thank you, thank you, thank you.

XOXOs to Lee Nichols, Sarah Mlynowski,
Lynda Curnyn, Alison Pace and Kristin Harmel.

Special thanks to Levi Robinson for answering
my questions about law enforcement.

To Adam for talking me through every book.

And to my precious Max for being who he is.

For my mother

Chapter 1

According to my half sister Opal, all of twenty-five and a self-professed expert on men now that she was engaged, everything you needed to know about your boyfriend, fiancé or husband you learned on your first date.

Did he talk about his mother? Guess who'll rule your life in a few years?

He blabbed on and on about his job without taking a breath? Even with reminders, he'll forget your birthday.

Couldn't keep his eyes off the hot blonde at the end of the bar? Maybe he'll only lust for other women in his heart like Jimmy Carter. Maybe.

Was he rude to the waiter? And you said yes to a second date?

"Abby, do you wanna know what your problem with men is?" Opal had said last week during breakfast at the diner. (The Foote sisters—which included my other half sister, Olivia—had made a pact to get together the first

Saturday of every month without fail and had failed until this month, mostly because it was January and everyone had made resolutions to be more family oriented.) "Your problem with men is that you don't pay close enough attention on that telltale first date. One of many cases in point—the linebacker. His commitment issues must have come up fifteen minutes into your first date!"

The linebacker was Charlie. We broke up two years ago at Olivia's wedding. Why? When all the single women (myself included) had lined up for the bouquet toss, Charlie, a former defensive linebacker for Notre Dame, had charged from our table (where he'd consumed four Jack and Cokes) and taken a running dive for the airborne clutch of pink roses, knocking over me, two bridesmaids and my recently divorced aunt Annette.

"Wow, Abby, he *really* didn't want you to be next," Opal had commented later in the emergency room as we waited for Aunt Annette's ankle to be wrapped.

Opal had the tact of a four-year-old, which was why I paid attention to *her*. When all was said and done (and a lot had been said that night), the linebacker *hadn't* wanted me to be next.

I had. Until that night anyway. (Charlie hadn't even stuck around the E.R. long enough for my aunt to be released!) Had his obvious commitment issues come up on our first date? If they had, I'd been too googly-eyed over him to notice.

"Forget the football player," Olivia had said. "He was the

definition of *passive-aggressive*, but he was no Ted Puck. "*Ted* was your worst boyfriend, Abby. I'd be surprised if he didn't start making out with the waitress on your first date!"

Ted was my most recent ex-boyfriend. And I'd loved him the way you love The One. But I clearly hadn't been paying attention on our first date because I'd missed whatever blinking neon sign indicated Caution: Will Cheat On You At Your Own Birthday Party With A Woman He'll Bring And Say Is His Cousin Mary.

That was six heartbreaking, humiliating months ago. And it had taken me that long to agree to go out with a new guy. Mostly because, this time, I knew exactly what I was looking for, and he wasn't easy to find: Clark Kent. A mild-mannered, kind, polite guy who'd morph into someone else (and a superhero, instead of, say, a big fat jerk) only if the world's future depended on it.

My Clark Kent, a quite cute tax attorney named Henry Fiddler, whom I'd been dating for one so-far-so-good month, was at this very moment driving us closer and closer to Olivia's house, where thirty or so relatives and friends of the family were waiting to meet him. No— waiting to see what insane thing *he'd* do. Because as the whole family knew, "Abby sure can pick 'em!"

My relatives weren't really gathered to meet my new boyfriend. The occasion was my newborn nephew's bris. But Olivia had started a hoo-ha by telling everyone that not only was I finally dating again, I was actually bringing the guy to the party.

"Good God, what if he knocks into the mohel during the circumcision!" Olivia's husband had worried aloud to more than a few relatives. "I wouldn't put anything past a boyfriend of Abby's!"

A little harsh, but unfortunately true. If the men I got involved with didn't make absolute jerks of themselves in front of my family and friends, à la the linebacker and Ted Puck, they turned into martians, like my college boyfriend who, at a dinner to celebrate my father and stepmother's twentieth wedding anniversary, answered the first three questions directed to him—such as *So, what's your major?* and *Did you also grow up in Maine?*—in pig latin. We broke up before dessert was served.

Why? Why, why, why? Was it them? Me? Hazards of dating? Or was I just a magnet for every jerk and nut job in New England?

"Didn't you read that book *He's Just Not That Into You?*" Opal had asked after the pig latin incident. "The only reason guys agree to meet your family when you're dating is because they want a blow job later. It has nothing to do with how serious they are about you or the relationship. But then there they are, meeting your family when they're just not that into you, and they freak out and start talking in pig latin."

Or they fracture your aunt's ankle. Or they cheat on you at your own birthday party with a woman they brought and said was their cousin. Mary. (Her name was more likely Angelina or something sexy like that.)

"And then ten minutes later," Opal had continued, "the relationship is over. Because he just wasn't that into you to begin with!" She'd gone on and on about the excuses women (specifically me) make for men who "just aren't into them." I'd tuned her out, but maybe she'd been onto something.

I glanced at Henry—nice, normal, polite Henry, of the rimless eyeglasses, Dockers and oxford shirt. Did men who "just weren't that into you" agree to meet your entire family after dating you for only one month? Even when they knew for a fact (because you had yet to put out) that there was zero chance of oral gratification later? Did they pick you up promptly at noon on a Sunday during football season for said family function with a bouquet of lilies for you and one for brand-new mother Olivia? Did they say you looked "so, so beautiful" in your pale yellow sweater and flippy brown suede skirt, which you shouldn't really be wearing when it was flurrying outside?

No, no and more no. And besides, jerks did not wear Dockers. Unless…they were the clichéd wolves in sheep's clothing.

I slumped in my seat, which Henry had prewarmed for me with a flick of a button in his Subaru Outback— good-guy car if there ever was one. I had to have faith— in my taste in men, in mankind—that Henry was not another Ted Puck. Or Charlie. Or Riley. Or Tom. Good Lord, I could go back to first grade.

"Abs, you have nothing to worry about," Olivia had assured me last week. "Henry couldn't possibly be another Ted. Ted was king of the assholes. There's only down from there. I mean, up. I mean there couldn't possibly be a worse guy out there than Ted Puck. Forget the past. You're dating again, which is great. I'm sure Henry is a great guy."

He was! Is! I *had* paid attention on my first date with Henry. He hadn't committed any of the first-date crimes Opal and Olivia had counseled me to watch out for. He didn't stare at the waitress's chest. He didn't talk about his exes. He didn't refer to his last girlfriend or his mother as a bitch. He didn't excuse himself to check in with his parole officer.

Everything would be fine. Henry would not freak out at the bris and suddenly start singing "Hava Nagila" at the top of his lungs and doing the accompanying kick-dance, bumping into the mohel and scarring young Oscar Grunwald for life.

As snow flurried on the windshield, Henry, two-hands-on-the-wheel, drove us carefully up I-295 toward Olivia's house in Freeport. He was so cute for a nerd! Truly attractive. Tall and lean, but muscular, broad shouldered. Almost black hair. Blue eyes. Roman nose. And one delicious dimple in his right cheek, at which I was now staring. Not only was he Clark Kent, he was a young Christopher Reeve!

Everything would be okay. Repeat. Repeat.

Henry was singing along to the radio in an *American*

Idol-reject voice that made me smile, but he suddenly snapped off the radio midsong and took a deep breath. "Abby, there's something I need to talk to you about. Okay, I'm just going to say this." He eyed me for a moment. "I wouldn't mind knowing where we stand. I mean, here I am, about to meet your whole family…"

I smiled and turned to face him, relieved that I could be googly-eyed over his Clark Kent face, those gorgeous blue eyes, without worrying that he was a jerk-in-hiding. Jerks did not want to know where the relationship stood! Well, unless they were control freaks. Henry, who'd given me total control of the radio, was not a control freak.

Maybe later today, after the bris, we would go back to one of our apartments and I'd finally say, "Yes, yes, yes, make mad passionate love to me," or something like that. After each of our nine dates, I'd said a chaste good-night to Henry at my apartment door—well, if three-minute killer kisses that left him panting could be considered chaste. But I could finally rip off his clothes without worry. He just *might* get orally gratified! He *wasn't* another Ted Puck! I did not have crappy taste in men! I did not need years of therapy! I mentally went through my lingerie drawer. Should I wear the black lace? Or maybe first-time white?

I decided on the white. "Wow, Henry, that is so refreshing to hear," I said. "Usually it's the woman who wants to know where the relationship is going, and—"

"I mean *sexually*, Abby."

Oh.

He glanced at me. I stared straight ahead at the snow-flakes being obliterated by the windshield wipers.

"We've been seeing each other for over a month," he said. "We've gone out, what, like ten times? And all we've done is make out like we're in high school. Middle school, even."

"Or like I just got out of a bad relationship and don't feel ready to jump into bed," I said. "Henry, I like you a lot. *So* much. But sex is a big deal to me, and I just want to make sure—"

"Make sure what?" he interrupted. "That we're headed for marriage? Abby, it's been a *month*."

I was getting less googly-eyed by the second. "I'm not talking about *marriage*." Did I say anything about marriage? "But yeah, it's only been a month and I'm gun-shy, that's all. If it's any help, I'm incredibly attracted to you. Saying no isn't easy."

He laid his hand on my thigh. High up. "So say *yes*."

I grabbed my coffee from the holder separating our seats and sipped at it to have a buffer. "I'm just not there yet, Henry."

"Maybe tonight?" he asked more hopefully than jerk-fully. "I'll have met your whole family. That should help you feel closer to me, won't it?"

Oh, God. Why was Opal Foote always right?

Stop pressuring me! "I really don't know," I said. "I only know that I'll know when I know." You blew it, Henry! You have no idea how close you came.

He moved his hand from my thigh to the steering wheel. "Okay." He glanced at me and smiled. "You're hard to resist, that's all. Okay?"

Barely. Barely okay, buster. It was nice to be wanted. But back off!

"So tell me about the party we're going to," he said. "It's a 'Come see the new baby' thing, right?"

Good. A change of subject. "Officially it's a bris, but yeah, it's the first opportunity for the whole family and friends to meet baby Oscar."

He laughed. "Oscar? Like the Grouch?"

'Fraid so. As if we didn't have enough *O*'s in our family, Olivia married an Oliver and they named their baby, an adorable nine-pounder with slate-blue eyes and wisps of blond fuzz, *Oscar.* Olivia and I are less than a year apart (more on *that* later), but our lives are light-years apart. For instance, my tiny apartment in Portland is the size of her master bedroom, which overlooks three garden-lush and wooded acres, and I couldn't imagine naming my baby Oscar, but according to Olivia, it's the new Ben/Sam/Max of the playground set and quite popular in England. All I can think of is an old man scratching his belly or—like Henry—that grouchy green *Sesame Street* monster popping out of a garbage can and singing, "I love trash."

I laughed, too. "But our Oscar is much, much cuter."

"I hope *so,*" he said, that delicious dimple popping. "So what's a bris?"

He didn't know what a bris was? I knew he wasn't Jewish (I'm half Jewish, half Methodist), but I thought everyone knew what a bris was. Seconds into my explanation, the car swerved slightly into the slow lane, and we were beeped by another car. Henry's knuckles were white on the steering wheel, and he slowed down to pull over onto the shoulder of the highway.

"Snow flurries are so deceiving," I said. "The roads must be getting—"

Henry put the car in Park and turned to face me full-on. "Wait one minute. You're telling me that they circumcise the baby right then and there? In the *living room?* With everyone *watching?*"

He'd almost lost control of the car because of the word *circumcise?*

"Well, yeah," I said. "But there's no *they* attacking the baby with an ax, Henry. Just a mohel. A nice, normal-looking man in a yarmulke. It's a ceremony. A Jewish tradition on the eighth day of life. What did you think a bris was?" I added, trying to smile.

He seemed barely able to lift his shoulders to shrug. "A *mole?* What's a *mole?* Is he a medical doctor? This mole is going to surgically remove the foreskin of an infant in front of everyone? And then you're all going to eat lunch?" He slumped over the steering wheel for a moment, then took a deep breath and eased back into traffic.

Mohel, Henry. *Moh-el.* I didn't think now was the time to correct him.

A second later he slurped at his own coffee and tugged at his collar, and half the contents of the cup ended up on his nice gray shirt. "Oh, shit."

"I'll dab some club soda on it when we get to Olivia's," I told him. "I'm sure it'll come out."

He shook his head. "I can't meet your entire family with a giant coffee stain on my shirt. Let's stop at L.L. Bean. I'll buy a new shirt, change into it there and we'll be in and out in five minutes. We're a little early anyway."

I glanced at my watch. It was almost twelve-thirty, and we were expected at one. Olivia's house was only a few minutes' drive from L.L. Bean, which was two minutes up the road. "Okay, good idea," I told him.

He parked, and we headed past the giant duck boot into the store. L.L. Bean was open twenty-four hours a day, seven days a week, 365 days a year (yes, Christmas, too!) just in case someone needed a tent in the middle of the night or a monogrammed tote bag at the crack of dawn. As we walked past the canoes to the men's clothing department, I eyed Henry to see if he was still uncomfortable about the bris, but he seemed focused on finding a good shirt. He stopped in front of a table stacked with crisp oxfords, grabbed three and headed for the fitting rooms.

I touched his arm. "Henry, about the bris—you don't have to watch, you know. You don't even have to be in the room. You can suddenly have to use the bathroom. Then it'll just be a party. Okay?"

He smiled and dashed into the changing room.

I waited by a rack of plaid pajamas, exactly the kind my father had always said he wanted for Christmas, year after year. For the past three Christmases there was no Dad; we'd lost him to a heart attack (hence the pact the Foote sisters had made to be closer), but Olivia and Opal and I still placed his presents under the tree as usual—the pajamas from me, the sherpa-lined moccasin slippers from Olivia and the terry bathrobe with the serious moose on the pocket from Opal. I had no idea how long we'd continue this odd tradition. Or what my stepmother, Veronica, did with my father's gifts.

I also had no idea what was taking Henry so long to try on a shirt. Five minutes had come and gone. I glanced at my watch. Six. Seven. At the ten-minute mark, I eased closer to the men's fitting room and called out, "Henry?"

No response.

"Henry?" I tried again.

No response.

A salesclerk emerged with an armful of jeans. "No one's in there, miss."

"My boyfriend is trying on shirts. Tall, dark hair?"

"Oh, yes. I saw him. He went into a fitting room, but left a minute later."

Huh? "What do you mean, he left? I've been standing right here." Had Henry come out and not seen me over the stack of plaid pajamas and Shetland sweaters? Was he looking for me by the cash registers?

My cell phone rang as I peered around. Henry's number appeared on the tiny display. "Henry, you are such a guy!" I teased into the phone as I headed toward the checkout line. "You're lost, aren't you? I'm right by the cash registers, near the pond. Come find me, okay? We're running a little late now, and—"

"Abby, I'm really sorry," he interrupted, "but I can't. Okay? I'm sorry."

"You can't *what*, Henry?"

"I just can't," he said, his voice a pitch higher than normal. "I can't do any of it. The no sex. The living-room circumcision. People eating lunch while a newborn is screaming bloody murder. I can't do it."

Oh, good Lord. "Henry, honestly, you don't have to *watch*. You can go into another room with the other squeamish types." But you can totally forget about sex now!

"I can't, Abby," he repeated for the tenth time. "I just can't. I can't!"

"Fine," I snapped. *Wuss!* "I'll meet you by your car. Just drop me off at my sister's and we'll talk about this la—"

"I'm already on the highway, Abby," he interrupted. "For what it's worth, I'm really sorry."

Click.

What!? "But you have my nephew's gift and the honey cake!" I shouted to dead air. Was I on *Punk'd*? Was Ashton Kutcher going to jump out from behind the monogrammed tote bags? Not that I was a celebrity. "Jerk! Superjerk!" I yelled at my phone while people nearby stared at me.

I slunk back over to the pile of plaid pajamas, mentally listing what Superjerk had driven off with, aside from my dignity and the sideshow boyfriend my entire family wouldn't get the chance to gawk at. There was the four-foot-tall fuzzy stuffed monkey I'd spent an hour deciding on, plus an adorable and expensive outfit from Baby Gap. There was the traditional Jewish honey cake that was almost impossible to find in the state of Maine, and the four bottles of Coke and Diet Coke that Olivia had asked me to bring. And then there was my umbrella to stop the snow flurries from turning my I-spent-an-hour-with-a-blow-dryer, pin-straight, shoulder-length hair into a frizz puff. I glanced down at my beloved brown suede lace-up boots with the three-inch heels. The ones I also shouldn't have worn when it was flurrying outside. The ones that already pinched.

"I am going to *kill* him!" I muttered.

The salesclerk, adding jeans to a table, eyed me under his glasses. "Can I be of any assistance?"

You can assist me in the murder of Superjerk. I shook my head and stomped off toward women's shoes for a pair of cheap sneakers and expensive wool socks to keep blisters at bay. Then it was down to the kids' department for a two-second perusal before I ran to the checkout with an adorable faux shearling baby bundler with bear ears. Then up to the café for a whole cheesecake and a pecan pie. Hopefully no one would want any Coke. Or Diet Coke.

Four blocks into the half-mile walk to Olivia's house,

the flurries turned into fat, wet flakes. To ward off tears, I practiced an amusing anecdotal version of the story to tell around the buffet table, *(Heh, get this—he couldn't handle a little ceremonial snipping, so he ditched me in L.L. Bean!),* but it turned out there was nothing amusing about it.

Great. Now I was tearing up on the sidewalk like a moron. I repositioned my packages to dab under my eyes so that mascara tracks wouldn't compete with the frizz-puff for scaring away small children. Of course, the cheesecake, fighting for space with the tall boots in the shopping bag, upturned onto the ground. A car honked, and I jumped, but it turned out to be Opal and Jackson.

"Abby, sweetie, those sneakers totally don't go with that outfit," Opal said, grimacing at my feet. "And hello, what's with those hiking socks?"

I'd never been so happy to see Opal in my life.

Chapter 2

"Next date you go on, I'm coming with you," Opal said as we rang the bell to Olivia's house. I'd filled her in on where my new boyfriend was. Which was probably back home by now. With my monkey and Coke collection. "When the guy sneezes into his pasta or stares at the waitress's chest or drones on about his bad childhood and then asks you for a second date, I'll be there to tell him *no.*"

"You won't have to," I said. "Because I'm never dating again." Ever.

Jackson, Opal's surfer-dude of a fiancé, walked behind us, carrying the four-foot-tall plush rhino Opal had bought for Oscar. I wondered what Henry was going to do with the monkey. "Once," Jackson said, "before I met Opal, I didn't date for, like, a whole week. That was rough."

"I'm talking *forever,* Jackson," I said. I'd had it. No more. Done. Finis! I would devote myself to my work, even though it didn't require devotion. I would read the classics. I would volunteer. Take Latin. Or piano. I would do anything but date.

A young man in a Clark's Catering T-shirt welcomed us in and took our coats and gifts, and I polite-smiled my way through throngs of people I'd seen once or twice in my life, the last time being Olivia's wedding. My father's side of the family was small and not from Maine, so the relatives I saw most often were my mother's. And my mother's family and the Foote family had shared the same space *twice* since the divorce—my high school and college graduations. Since I was clearly never getting to the altar, they wouldn't have to worry about bumping into each other on the dance floor at my wedding reception and clawing at each other.

Olivia rushed up to me with Oscar cradled in her arms. She looked absolutely amazing, despite having given birth a week ago. Shiny blond bob with swingy bangs. A little mascara and lip gloss. Cute silver hoop earrings with tiny dangling pearls. Banana Republic outfit unstained by spit-up. I couldn't pull myself together like that, and I didn't even have a pet or plant to take care of. Also throw in three separate notebooks in her possession at all times, one to note time/color/consistency of Oscar's poops, one for Oscar's nutritional intake and one to document any new developments. Such as: *burped twice after 4:00 a.m. feeding instead of once!* I'd misplaced my new day planner already and it was only the beginning of January. Olivia glanced around me. Behind me. "Where's Henry?" she asked. "I'm dying to meet him."

"We broke up," I said, poaching a miniature chocolate cream pie from a tray on the buffet table. Delicious. Chocolate really *could* make you feel better. "Yum, these are good."

She tilted her head and eyed me. "Broke up? Between the time I spoke to you this morning and now?"

While I soothed myself with yet another mini pie, Opal launched into the entire sob story for me, including the $142 I'd had to spend on items like socks.

I expected a *How dare he! Someone go teach that punk a lesson!* But instead, everyone in hearing distance began berating me for picking another jerk.

"Where do you find these losers?" guffawed Olivia's husband.

"Dear, you really need to start watching Dr. Phil," said an aunt.

"What Abby *needs* is to find a man like her father," my stepmother, Veronica, said, setting a tray of potato blintzes on the buffet. She kissed me hello on the cheek, her perfume overpowering. "Now, *there* was a good man."

True, except for the cheating-on-my-mother part. When she was at home with a newborn. My father had gotten around the six-week rule by having sex with Veronica, his administrative assistant, and getting her pregnant. Which was why I had a half sister less than a year younger than myself. Had he pulled a fast one on Veronica, as well, impregnating her attractive replacement at Foote, Finnegan and Bowman, Oncologists? No. He'd fallen head over heels in love with Veronica, to whom he'd been happily married for twenty-four years. That made it harder to be as angry at him as I'd wanted.

As the "telephone" version of my latest breakup made its way around Olivia's house ("Abby caught her new boyfriend having sex with a salesclerk in the fitting room in Wal-Mart! A *guy* salesclerk!), various relatives and friends of the family produced seven nice-single-young-men from Veronica's and Oliver Grunwald's sides of the family. They were marched up to me no matter where I went in Olivia's huge antique farmhouse. One was introduced moments after I'd taken a huge bite of a potato blintz. I'd been so startled by the nice-single-young-man's braces (was he even eighteen?) that I dropped the blintz, laden with sour cream, on my sweater.

The introduction was always the same. "Have you met Abby? Isn't she lovely? She works at *Maine Life* magazine as the 'Best Of' editor! Ronald/Michael/Jonathan, don't you own your own business? Abby can declare you the best plumber/attorney/moron in the state!"

Nope. Been there, done that. Including the Best Moron, even if that one was only in my head. (Unfortunately, *Maine Life* was not a snarky magazine.) Anyway, no one was a bigger moron than I was. I'd been bamboozled by a guy—Riley—who'd dated me in the first place only so that I'd put him on the "Best CPAs in Portland" list. I'd named him one of the best only after he'd gotten me quite a refund, though.

If my system sounded a little shady, it really wasn't. There were no criteria, other than my own taste. If I ate dinner in a random Chinese restaurant and loved the moo shoo pork, I named it Best Moo Shoo Pork in the next issue. The guy who dug me out when I was stuck in a snowdrift last winter? Best Good Samaritan. Restaurants, stores, businesses—you name it—sent me invitations to sample them in the hopes of landing a spot on one of my lists. Finch, my boss, had given me the column after grudgingly agreeing that my answers to reader mail, which were printed in the magazine's letters section, generated bagfuls of more reader mail. *Where's a good place to get my nails done? Where's the best place to hike? Where's the best place to literally and figuratively dump your girlfriend when you learn what a bris is on your way to a bris?* Readers wrote in to say they'd tried my recommendations and agreed 100 percent. There were a few—we're talking three or four—*what, are you, crazy?* letters a month, but though I couldn't pick The Best Men in Maine, I had a knack for picking the best anything else for the female demographic. Anyway, after Riley I vowed no more boyfriendotism.

Braces was still talking. Turned out he was nineteen and a sophomore at Bowdoin. He'd just finished telling me that he "dug" older women when Olivia saved me with an "Abby, can you help me with Oscar?" and led me to her bedroom. "Figured we could use a little break from wall-to-wall people," she said to me as we slipped inside. As she shut the door behind us, I was relieved to find that I wasn't being summoned for diaper duty. Opal was in the rocking chair, the fat Sunday newspaper on her lap, a mimosa in her hand and a plate of crudités on the tiny round table next to her. Olivia headed over to the window and rocked Oscar, his sleepy eyes finally closing. I sat on the ornate wrought-iron bench to Olivia's dressing table and mentally oohed and aahed at my baby nephew. *See, Henry, no newborn screaming bloody murder! He's sleeping like a baby!* The bris had taken all of two minutes, and Oscar looked happy and peaceful.

At the rate I was going, I'd never have an Oscar. Someone was clearly poking a voodoo doll version of me with a stick and chanting, *No love for you! No future family for you! Only superjerks for you!*

"You okay?" Olivia asked me.

I nodded. "I'll be fine. One of these days."

"Abby," Opal said, pointing a hummus-laden carrot stick at me, "no one ever treats me like crap. You know why? Because I don't *take* crap. Repeat after me—I will not take crap!"

"But this was invisible crap," I said. "Henry was a great guy until he turned into an asshole. So was Ted." Crazy as that sounded, it was true. God, I'd loved him. Six months later my heart still squeezed when I thought of Ted.

"Great guys don't turn into assholes," Opal said, her two-carat engagement ring gleaming on her finger.

"Sometimes they do," Olivia said, staring out the window.

Uh-oh. I glanced at Olivia, hoping that all was well in the Foote-Grunwald household. "Olivia?" I asked. "Is everything—"

Olivia smiled at me. "Everything's fine. Really, hon. I'm just hormonal. And starving." She nuzzled Oscar's fuzzy head. "Want to hold him so I can eat?"

"Of course," I said. I'd held Oscar once, in the hospital when he was hours old, but there'd been doctors and nurses around to save his life if I did something wrong, like drop him on his head. Olivia settled him in my arms. He moved his tiny mouth, but he continued sleeping peacefully. I liked the way the small weight of him felt. "Olivia, why don't I stay after the party, help clean up and babysit for a few hours? Take some time to yourself."

Not that I had any experience with newborns. The thought of that wobbly neck scared me. As did the poop diapers. And being in the same house with Oliver Grunwald, whose every sentence began with, "Do you know what your problem is? I'll tell you," as though *he* were Dr. Phil and not a mortgage broker, made me itchy. Apparently I wasn't asked to be Oscar's godmother because Oliver thought my bad taste in boyfriends would preclude Oscar from growing up with a good male influence in his life, should Olivia and Oliver perish. But Olivia was clearly overwhelmed, so what was an unbearable brother-in-law and a little poo in the name of helping my sister?

Olivia smiled at me. "Thanks, Abby, but that's okay. I'll definitely take a rain check, though. Count on it."

Whew.

"Olivia, I totally would have offered to come help, too," Opal said, flipping through the weddings-and-engagement section of the newspaper, which rivaled my love life for Opal's favorite topic of conversation at any get-together. "But I'm going headpiece shopping with the head case after this."

The head case was Opal's mother-in-law-to-be, whom I'd met at the engagement party, and who was less a head case and more a carbon copy of Opal, only thirty years older.

Next month, soon after Valentine's Day, Opal and Jackson were marrying at a posh inn in Prouts Neck. I was a bridesmaid and had to wear a wig for the wedding. Brunettes weren't permitted in Opal's bridal party. Yes, you heard that right.

"How gorgeous are my pictures going to look!" Opal had said several months ago when she told me I had to wear a wig for her wedding because I wasn't blond. "The bridal party is all blond and the ushers are all dark haired. That's *hot*. You're not upset, are you, Abs?" she'd added, fake pouting. "I really, really want you to be in the wedding, but I really, really want a blond theme."

Opal was obsessed with Paris Hilton and had adopted one too many of the socialite/actress's trademarks. Like the "that's hot," the crazy fashionista clothes, the oversize sunglasses collection and several giggling blond friends. All she was missing was a tiny dog to carry around. And the Hilton money. She had the height and bony frame and the unusual-beautiful face. Her eyes (which were really blue but were now tinted-contacts emerald-green) were huge, and her nose too long, her mouth too wide and her teeth too big. Which, with the long and silky light blond hair, made her look like a model. Olivia was striking, too, but in a different way. Her "pretty" was intimidating in its even-featured, lightly enhanced, expressive efficiency.

Anyway, being blond for a day sounded pretty good.

"God, would you look at this bride's dress?" Opal said, holding up the wedding section of the newspaper. "What was she *thinking?*" She shook her head and continued ripping brides to bits. Then she sucked in her breath and quickly folded the paper and put it away.

"What?" Olivia asked.

"Nothing," Opal said, slowly shaking her head at her sister and darting her eyes to me.

"Opal, if you're going to be so obvious, you might as well just tell me," I said, bracing myself.

She gnawed her lip, then unfolded the paper and handed it to me while carefully taking Oscar out of my arms.

Puck-Darling
Ted Puck and Mary-Kate Darling are delighted to announce their engagement…

I screamed and flung the paper away as though it were a big, hairy bug; it fluttered down to the floor. *I will not look. I do not care.*

I snatched up the paper. I looked. I cared.

Ted, a cheating jerk, and Mary-Kate, a cheating slut, are planning a December wedding. A little embellishment there.

I glanced at the picture of the happy couple. Ted looked gorgeous, of course. Mary-Kate Darling looked…darling. So her name *was* Mary. Well, Mary-Kate. And it was startling to see, now that I was seeing her for longer than the five seconds it had taken her to shoot out of my bedroom, that she looked a lot like me. Long, straight, dark brown hair. Pale brown eyes. Cheekbones, but a round face that made her look like a nicer person than she clearly was.

Ted looked so happy in the photograph—eyes bright, million-dollar smile, arm casually slung over Mary-Kate's bony shoulder. But he'd looked just as happy in the one photograph of us that I had. After our breakup I'd spent weeks staring at that picture, trying to figure out how we went from happily walking Clinton, Ted's black pug (named for his favorite president), along Portland's Eastern Promenade the morning after we slept together for the first time, to what happened on the night of my twenty-eighth birthday six months ago.

That glorious morning in the park, when I'd felt so in love, we'd run into my friend Jolie, out snapping photographs of seagulls at the crack of dawn for a class she was taking. Jolie wasn't a master photographer; Clinton hadn't even made it into the shot. But she had captured the brilliant blue Casco Bay in the background, the sailboats dotting the water, and me, glancing up at Ted, who'd just said something funny.

Three months later at my birthday party, my hands had to be pried off Ted's neck, so great was my adrenaline-and-anger-enhanced grip. My mother, who'd come all the way from Florida for my birthday as she did every year, had reached for her tube of pepper spray and managed to spray me in the eyes instead of Ted, which was how Ted had escaped past Olivia and Opal—not that they were doing anything but standing there gaping. Mary-Kate—who'd been kneeling between Ted's legs, his black pants and gray Calvin Klein boxer briefs pulled down to his knees—had shot out of the room, pulling her skirt down over her hips and her tiny tank top back down over her huge bare breasts. She was out the front door before anyone could even blink.

Later, when Jolie and Rebecca had shooed all the guests away and brought out the birthday cake Rebecca had made from scratch (she's a pastry chef), I didn't even have the energy to blow out the two edible pink candles, which were in the shape of a two and an eight. When I finally went to bed, I found a lacy black bra that wasn't mine under the pillow. It smelled like Chanel No 5.

Yes, happy birthday, Abby!

"Jesus, will someone tell me what it is?" Olivia asked, staring from me to Opal.

I handed her the section of newspaper. "Guess who's

marrying his cousin?" I said, tears coming from out of nowhere. I was a regular crybaby today.

Olivia scanned the announcement and handed it back to me. "He's a jerk and she's a jerk and they deserve each other."

Opal nodded. "I'm sure she'll come upon Ted getting a blow job from the nanny in a couple of years. No doubt." She glanced down at Oscar, sleeping peacefully. "You didn't hear that, little nephew."

I glanced at the photo of Ted and Mary-Kate. The headline, Puck And Darling.

Opal's premonition did make me feel a little better. "Thanks," I said, crumpling the paper into a ball and throwing it toward the little wicker garbage can under Olivia's dressing table. "Have a nice life!" I yelled at it like an idiot.

"Hey, I wasn't done with the wedding section," Opal griped.

There was a knock at the door. Veronica. "Picture time!" she trilled. "Foote girls family photograph."

I stood up, but then realized she didn't mean me. She meant herself and her daughters. She had a hand on each of their shoulders and was guiding them toward the door.

"And Abby, too, of course," Olivia said quickly.

Veronica smiled a beat too late. "Of course! Abby, too!"

That was me, *Abby, too.* She took Oscar from Opal, and we all headed into the living room. Veronica positioned the four of us by the sliding glass door to the backyard, and my aunt Marian snapped the photo, then Veronica called for pictures of the Foote sisters, this time smiling at me on time. "Say cheeseburgers!" Veronica trilled, which was what my father always used to say when taking pictures.

"Shitburgers!" Opal said through a grin.

I smiled. Since puberty, Opal always shouted *shitburgers!* instead of *cheeseburgers,* despite being punished time and again. The first time it had come out of her mouth (which had been washed out with soap moments later), Opal was twelve; Olivia and I were both fourteen (we overlapped for a month). We were celebrating my father and Veronica's thirteenth wedding anniversary, and Veronica called for pictures of the Foote girls. Opal, already wearing Isaac Mizrahi clothes (albeit from Target), knee-high leather boots and supersized black sunglasses, stood grinning on my right, holding her fingers in a V over my head. On my left, Olivia, a future PTA president in her taupe twinset and pearls, stared moodily at the floor. I was the tiny, brown-haired, brown-eyed monkey in the middle between the two beanpole blue-eyed blondes, the easy answer to *Which girl in the picture doesn't belong?*

The answer to why I was invited, year after year, to my father and stepmother's anniversary dinner was much, much harder to figure out.

A second after the "say cheeseburgers" and the click, my dad noticed his eldest daughter had Opal's fingers over her head. There was a mock-weary "Opal!" which led to a fit of giggles from The Immature One, as I called her then, which sent Veronica (or Demonica as my friends called her, quite undeservedly, as she wasn't really *mean*) clickety-clacking on her high-heeled shoes into the living room. Though Veronica was more hostess-polite than nice, she definitely wasn't wicked-stepmother material. Still, she'd always reminded me physically of a made-over Wicked Witch of the West. Which was funny because I was often told, especially every Thanksgiving, when *The Wizard of Oz* came on, that I looked just like Dorothy, minus the braids. And the skipping. And Toto.

Veronica had then snapped at Opal for ruining the shot ("we're going to miss our dinner reservations!") and at Olivia for not smiling. "Why can't you both act more like Abby!" she'd complained to her daughters, sliding the sunglasses on top of Opal's head and squeezing Olivia's frown into an upturn that didn't last.

"You mean boring?" Opal asked, snickering.

My father moved the camera from his face and sing-songed, "There's a twenty-five-dollar Tar-*gzay* gift card for any Foot-ay girl who smiles when I say 'bacon-double-cheeseburgers.'"

On her first day of seventh grade, Opal had told her teachers that her last name was pronounced Foot-ay, as in French, and not Foot, as in feet (it *is* pronounced *foot*). My father thought that was cute. Because my name was

Abby, and not even Abigail, I hadn't been able to go around telling people my name was Abby Foot-ay.

"Ha! Abb-ay Foot-ay! That does sound pretty stupid!" Opal had agreed.

"*You* sound pretty stupid," Olivia had shot back.

The Foot-ay sisters did not get along so well back then.

Anyway, the bribe worked. Opal had smiled from earring to dangling earring. Olivia, who'd been saving up for an iPod, forced cheer. My smile was school-pictures stiff, but my father and stepmother liked that kind of smile for family albums.

"Perfect!" my dad had said. "Just perfect. Okay, say bacon-double-cheeseburgers!"

"Shitburgers!" Opal had yelled simultaneously with the *click!* and then had been dragged off to the bathroom to eat some Zest.

The two photographs are side by side in my The Teen Years album—the left side representing the real moment, the truth of my family, which was why it was my favorite photograph, and the right side representing the manufactured, the *cheeseburgers*, when we all wanted to say *shitburgers*.

"Where's that new boyfriend of yours?" my aunt Marian asked as she lowered the camera. "I'm dying to meet him. I hope he's a nice young man, unlike that last one you dated. Or the last one. Or the last one."

Shitburgers.

Chapter 3

I learned many boyfriends ago that an easy way to feel better (slightly better, anyway) after a breakup, even if the breakup was a godsend because the boyfriend was clearly a superjerk in hiding, was to *look* good. And so, on Monday morning I didn't drag myself to work with bed head and the blues. I blow-dried my hair pin-straight, put on mascara and the pinky-red lipstick Opal had once given me. I slipped into my favorite outfit—a black wrap dress that managed to be both office appropriate and hot-date appropriate—my favorite shoes (glen-plaid tweed), and I looked much better than I felt.

Of course, a torrential downpour began halfway into my twenty-minute walk to work. My umbrella, which was usually in my tote bag at all times, was instead in the backseat of Superjerk's car. I was dripping wet. My fabric shoes were soaked. My hair clung to the sides of my head.

The moment I walked through the double glass doors of *Maine Life* magazine, Marcella French, our obnoxious receptionist, pointed and laughed. Marcella was enjoying the perks of a flirtation with Gray Finch, editor in chief of *Maine Life* and everyone's boss on the small staff, so she felt free to ridicule whomever she wanted. Just wait till summer intern season started. Forty-year-old Marcella would be toast.

Henry's face was the first thing I saw when I set foot inside my tiny cubicle. No, not his face-face. A photograph of his face. Ugh! Why had I put up that stupid picture of the two of us on our second date!

I'd had the photo in my desk drawer for weeks, but last week, after a particularly sweet date, I'd pinned it up on the bulletin board to replace the empty four-by-six space that Ted's photo had left six months ago. I glared at it, at Henry's stupid smile, at his dumb dimple. The picture had been taken on our second date as we boarded a dinner cruise around Casco Bay. A photographer was snapping everyone's photograph in front of a buoy, and if you liked the shot, you could pay to have it in a paper frame. Henry and I were all awkward smiles and unsure of what to do with our hands. So we both settled for school-picture smiles and hands clasped in front of our stomachs. Since it was our second date, we felt compelled to say yes to the photograph, which was $14.99.

At least *Henry* had paid for the picture. I glared some

more at his face, then grabbed the mini darts set that my coworker Shelley had given me for Secret Santa last month. I aimed in the vicinity of Henry's heart. Or lack thereof.

"Bull's-eye!" I said.

Shelley's head appeared over the gray fabric "wall" that separated our cubicles. Her wildly curly brown hair bounced on the top of the divider. "Uh-oh. What happened?"

My second dart landed on Henry's nose. "I am going to kill him, that's what happened. That jerk ditched me in—"

"Abby Foote?"

I swiveled around at the unfamiliar voice to find a familiar face. The face of all faces. A face ten years older than the last time I'd seen it, but yes, it was him! Benjamin Orr! The love of my teenage life. Well, secret life. I—and countless other girls—had been secretly in love and lust with Ben Orr for two years in high school. He probably couldn't match my name with my face, despite having been in two classes of mine. Ben Orr had been captain of everything, from the football team to Mathletes. I'd been the Amazing Invisible Girl.

He stood just outside my cubicle with another man, fiftyish. His dad? Perhaps they had a Best Of request. Best-Looking Guy in Maine? Best Body?

"Yes, I'm Abby," I said, unable to take my eyes off Ben. He was tall—six feet. Broad shouldered. Dark, dark hair to match his dark, dark eyes, which were so intense, so intelligent, but sparkling. He had such fair skin. He'd

been drop-dead cute at fifteen and sixteen. He'd graduated to drop-dead gorgeous.

Both men reached into the breast pockets of their suits
and pulled out gold shields, their gazes going from the dart
in Henry's nose to me and back again.

They were the police? I jumped up. "Did something
happen to my mother? Opal or Olivia? Veronica? Oh
God, Oscar—did something happen to Oscar?"

"You didn't mention the brother-in-law," the older
one said. "Why is that? Do you want to kill him, too?"

Huh? I glanced at Shelley; so did both cops. Her eyes
widened at me and she ducked back down.

"Excuse my partner," Ben said, cutting the other man
a look. "He hasn't had his fourth cup of coffee yet. We're
not here about your family. We're here about Ted Puck."

Ted Puck? What about Ted Puck?

Ben eyed me. "I'm Detective Benjamin Orr of the
Portland Police Department. This is my partner, Detective
Frank Fargo. We're investigating the murder of Ted Puck."

What? I staggered back, my butt hitting the knob of the
drawer on my desk. I opened my mouth, but nothing
came out. Murdered? *What?* What? No. There had to be
a mistake. They must be talking about a different Ted
Puck. I straightened. "The Ted Puck I know is fine. I just
saw him yesterday. I mean, his face. His engagement announcement was in yesterday's paper."

"That's the one," Detective Fargo said, jotting something down in a tiny spiral notebook.

I stared from Ben to Fargo, unable to speak, unable to shut my mouth, which had dropped open. Ted Puck was dead? *Dead?*

"In fact, Miss Foote," Fargo said. "I believe Ted brought his fiancée, Mary-Kate Darling, to your birthday party six months ago when you and Ted were a couple. You caught them in a sexual act, according to witnesses."

There was a sudden silence in the offices of *Maine Life* magazine. Unusual. Which meant everyone had stopped in midsentence to listen.

Ben glanced around. "Is there somewhere we could go to talk more privately?" he asked. "A conference room?"

"You can use conference room A," Gray Finch, my boss, said, appearing behind the detectives. "Second door on the left. I'll have my admin bring coffee." He paused. "Officers, our Abby isn't in any kind of trouble, is she?"

Fargo smiled. "I sure could use that coffee."

Finch's eyes widened and he glanced at me, then hurried off.

"Lead the way, will you, Miss Foote?" Fargo asked.

I would have led if I could've moved. I stared down at Fargo's shoes. Scuffed black Rockports like the ones Henry wore.

"Whenever you're ready," Ben said, and I looked up at him.

"I'm just—" I shook my head. "I'm just so shocked."

"I'm sure you are," Fargo said. "Why don't I lead the

way. Second door on the left, the man said. We cops are trained to listen carefully," he added, tapping his ear.

Now *my* eyes widened. I trailed behind him; Ben trailed behind me. I felt my coworkers' gazes on me until I opened the door to our small conference room. Fargo sat at the head of the long table. Ben sat adjacent. I sat across from Ben. I could smell someone's cologne.

"Let's start at the beginning," Ben said, flipping open a small spiral notebook. He clicked his pen, and I jumped.

"You sure do startle easy," Fargo said.

Easily, I wanted to correct. I didn't.

Ben smiled at me. "We'd like to ask you a few questions. Is that all right?"

I nodded.

"Your hair's dripping," Ben said, reaching into his breast pocket for a pocket of packet tissues. He held it out to me.

"Uh, thanks," I said, squeezing the ends of my hair with the tissue, which disintegrated into shreds immediately. My hair was coated in tissue guts. Ted Puck was dead. Benjamin Orr was sitting across from me. Talking.

"You and Ted dated some months ago?" Ben asked.

I nodded.

There was a knock at the door. Fargo said, "Yeah," and Marcella opened the door and peered in, her round blue eyes ever rounder. She held a tray with two mugs of coffee, a pint of milk and sugar packets. She set down the tray, then slowly backtracked from the room, clearly hoping to eavesdrop.

"You can close the door on the way out," Fargo snapped, and she bolted.

Ben took his coffee black. "So, Abby, you were telling us about your relationship with Ted. When did you start dating and when did you break up?

"Um, we broke up in July. On my birthday. The seventh. We started seeing each other in April."

"Why did you break up?" Detective Fargo asked. "We think we know," he added with a snicker, "but we'd like to hear it from you."

"Um," I said. And that was all that would come out of my mouth.

Fargo raised an eyebrow. "According to witnesses, Ted brought Mary-Kate to your twenty-eighth birthday party, introduced her to you and your family and friends as his cousin from out of town, and then you, along with your mother and half sisters, came upon the two of them participating in a sexual act in your bedroom, which—" he flipped a page in his notebook "—was supposed to be off-limits to guests."

My entire faced burned. "Um, who told you that?"

Fargo ignored my question. "You must have been very angry at Ted," he said, tapping his pen against his notebook.

That was an understatement. At the party I'd taken my mother and sisters to my bedroom to show them the gift Ted had given me when he and his "cousin" had arrived. Just a half hour earlier Ted and I had gone into my bedroom. *Close your eyes and hold out your hand,* he'd said. And when I opened my eyes, there was a small wrapped jewelry box on my palm. The size of a ring box. I'd almost fainted. If he'd asked me to marry him right then and there, after only three months of dating, I would have said yes. But inside the box were earrings, not a ring. Diamond earrings, though, which had said so much to me about what I meant to him, how he felt about me. Big present. Big love.

Of course, later, the earrings were determined to be cubic zirconia, worth around $9.99 at Wal-Mart.

Ted then suggested a quickie, but I was afraid of getting caught, so I'd promised him a longie later. A half hour later, when I opened the door to my bedroom, my mother and Olivia and Opal standing behind me, so excited for me, there was Ted, sitting up against the headboard of my bed, his jeans unzipped and his "cousin" facedown in his naked lap.

I heard my mother's and Olivia's united gasp, Opal's "you pig!" and all that came out of my mouth was "But she's your cousin!" My mother reached for the pepper spray, and I lunged for Ted's neck.

Ted, six foot two, 180 pounds of muscle, escaped unharmed. He called from his cell phone a half hour later. "She's not my cousin, okay? Look, I shouldn't have brought her. I shouldn't have even gone to your party. But I didn't want to disappoint you, so I figured I'd hang for an hour and then make an excuse to leave. I was planning on telling you tomorrow that I'd met someone else, but…for what it's worth, I'm really sorry about what happened. So I didn't hurt you while I was prying you off me, did I?"

No, Ted, you didn't hurt me at all. Really. Not a bit.

And what was with guys and *for what it's worth?* It was worth *nothing.*

Fargo was staring at me. Ben was still writing in his notebook. I'd told them the whole sorry story.

"So a few minutes ago, in your cubicle, you mentioned that you saw Ted yesterday," Fargo said, his shellacked gray hair glinting. "Where and when?"

"No, I meant I saw his face—in the newspaper," I explained. "The wedding section."

Fargo's gray eyebrows slanted. "So now your story is that you *didn't* see Ted yesterday in person. You didn't go over to his apartment to, say, congratulate him on his engagement?"

I shook my head.

Ben took a sip of his coffee. "How'd you feel when you saw the announcement in the paper?" he asked.

I shifted my gaze to him, grateful to avoid Fargo's moving eyebrows. *I don't know! Why are you interrogating me?* I shrugged.

Fargo leaned close. "The court reporter can't hear a shrug. You really should start practicing speaking up now for when you're on trial."

I felt every ounce of energy drain from my body. Whoa. Wait a minute. "Are you saying you think I tried to hurt Ted?"

"Tried to hurt?" Fargo repeated. "Honey, the guy is *dead.*"

"Abby," Ben said. "May I call you Abby?"

I nodded.

Ben offered a smile. "We're just investigating all leads."

I stared from Bad Cop to Good Cop. My lower lip trembled, and I decided to ignore the bad one. "Um, Detective Orr, you probably don't remember me," I began, "but we went to high school together. Go, Rangers!" I added like an idiot.

Ben tilted his head slightly and stared at me. He shook his head. "I can't place the face. But it was a big school, and my family moved out of state before my senior year."

Yeah, a big school with 164 graduating seniors. That I hadn't registered on his radar wasn't a surprise.

"Well, what I mean is, you *know* me," I said to Ben. "You don't *know me* know me, obviously, since you don't remember me, but we grew up in the same town, walked the same halls—"

"Miss Foote," Fargo interrupted. "Do you want to know who I went to high school with? One of the most infamous serial killers in Massachusetts history."

Oh.

Ben flipped a page in his notebook. "Abby, can you tell us where you were yesterday evening, between the hours of seven and nine?"

"Home," I said. Under the blankets. "I went to a family party at my sister's house until around three, then I went home."

"What did you do at home?" Fargo asked.

"Nothing, really," I said. Which was true.

Fargo raised an eyebrow. "Nothing—from three until you arrived at work this morning? That's most unusual."

"I had a tough day," I said. "I watched TV and then went to bed."

They wanted to know what I watched, so I had to tell them I spent two hours glued to a Lifetime movie about a woman who finds out at her husband's funeral that he had two other wives. Then it was reality TV. A little CNN. And then I pulled a pillow over my head and tossed and turned for a few hours until I fell asleep.

"Did you talk to anyone on the phone?" Ben asked.

I nodded. "I called a couple of friends, but they weren't home. And then Opal—my half sister—called around seven."

"How long did you talk?" Ben asked, turning a page in his little notebook.

"We were on the phone for at least a half hour," I said. "And then she called back an hour later and we spoke for another fifteen minutes. About her wedding, mostly." Opal had initially called to ask if I'd mind wearing a butt-length wig with heavy bangs instead of the shoulder-length blunt cut she'd already chosen for me. An hour later she called back to say her mother-in-law had nixed the idea of butt-length hair for a bridal party member.

"Did you talk about Ted?" Fargo asked.

"A little. She asked if I was okay about seeing the engagement announcement, and I said I was."

"Were you really?" Ben asked.

I nodded. "We broke up six months ago. I moved on. I was even seeing someone new."

"Was?" Fargo asked, those eyebrows slanting at me again.

"We broke up," I said. "Yesterday. Before the party." I explained about the bris. I tried to make it sound amusing-anecdote.

"Really!" Fargo said, smiling, shooting a gaze from me to Ben. "You sure do get dumped a lot."

"I…" I started, but again, nothing came out of my mouth. I felt my cheeks burning.

"So let me see if I have this straight," Fargo said, scraping his chair against the floor as he moved closer to me. "Six months ago Ted cheats on you at your birthday party. Your family and friends are witness to this humiliation, *adding* to the humiliation factor. You finally start seeing someone new, and yesterday you get dumped again on the way to a family party, once again humiliated in front of your family. You go to the bris, everyone's ragging on you for picking another jerk, and then your half sister shows you Ted's engagement announcement in the newspaper. Then you go home all alone and watch a movie and talk sporadically on the phone, during which time Ted is mysteriously murdered. Do I have that right?"

"Well, I don't know that I'd put it quite like that," I said, "but that is the gist, yes."

"This new ex-boyfriend's name?" Fargo asked, shaking his head. Slowly.

A minute later, the names and numbers of Opal, Olivia and Henry in their notebooks, the detectives finally stood.

"Thanks for your time," Ben said, those dark, dark eyes unreadable on mine. "We appreciate your help."

"Oh, and Abby," Fargo said, one hand on the conference-room door, "don't leave town."

Chapter 4

"Who could have done it?" my friend Jolie asked, handing me a cup of tea. She sat down next to me on my couch and settled my mohair throw around my shoulders.

I shrugged, my new response to everything. I sipped the tea, vaguely appreciating that Jolie had remembered the Sweet'n Low and overtly appreciating that my friends were here. Jolie, a paralegal, whom I'd known forever—since first grade. Rebecca, a pastry chef, whom I'd met in college (she and Jolie had become good friends through me). Shelley, *Maine Life*'s fact-checker and my cubicle neighbor since I started there three years ago. And Roger, *Maine Life*'s copy editor, whom I rarely spent time with out of the office, but who I considered an office friend.

Shelley and Roger sat on floor pillows against the wall facing the sofa, both picking at their take-out lunches that were balanced on hardcover books on their laps. The

smell of Shelley's tuna hoagie was making me a little sick.
Roger was on his second hamburger. Jolie, who ate three
bites of food per day, nibbled baby carrots, the least of-
fensive smelling food there was. Rebecca sat at my tiny
dining-room table, eating a salad from a plastic container.
They'd each brought me two kinds of lunches—comfort
food and a decadent treat. The counter between my mini
kitchen and my mini living room was covered with everything from grilled cheese and fries to a turkey club to
an entire chocolate cake. It was good to have good friends.

When they'd arrived soon after noon, they'd all been
as dumbfounded by the news as I was. I'd talked so much
about Ted during our three-month relationship that they
felt they knew him, too. They'd all met him.

"I can't believe he's dead," each one of them had said
at least twice since arriving. It had been my refrain from
the moment the detectives had left me alone in the conference room two hours ago. I'd sat there, unable to move,
even when the nosiest of my coworkers (most of them)
had rushed in and bombarded me with questions, thanks
to Fargo's indiscretion in the hallway about my catching
Ted cheating at the party.

Do they think you did it?

But you're so petite!

*I'll bet he had a long line of girlfriends he cheated on—it could
have been any of them!*

*How was he killed? Shot? Stabbed? Bludgeoned? Pushed
into the bay?*

It occurred to me that I had no idea how Ted had died. *I hope it didn't hurt* went strangely through my mind.

"Did you do it?" a coworker—Marcella, of course—had dared ask.

"Of course she didn't do it!" Shelley had snapped as she'd rushed into the conference room, elbowing staffers out of the way, with Roger lumbering behind as usual. "Give the girl some air!" she'd muttered as my coworkers continued to stare at me. She'd taken me by the hand and led me to my cubicle. Roger had followed, biting his lip, also as usual.

Shelley had sat me down in my guest chair, disappeared for two seconds and returned with her pink wool hat, an umbrella and her pink-and-red wool scarf. She put the hat on me and pulled it down over my ears, then stood me up, slid my arms through the sleeves of my puffy down coat, zipped me up and wrapped the scarf around my neck. Then she slid my tote bag on my shoulder.

"Go home," she said. "I'll tell Finch that someone you know was killed and that you need the day off—tomorrow, too, probably. Don't worry about a thing or think about a thing. I'll handle whatever flow of yours is necessary here. Will you be okay getting home? I can walk you if you want."

I shook my head. "The air will do me good," I said. "I just need to process."

My coworkers were hovering outside my cubicle. Shelley and Roger shooed them away much the way Jolie and Rebecca had shooed away my party guests after the Ted debacle.

"Roger and I will be over the minute the clock strikes twelve," Shelley said. "That's just two and a half hours. Call me if you need anything, okay, hon?"

I nodded. Finch had a thing about lunch being one hour between the hours of noon and two only. You couldn't leave before twelve or return after two without having your Christmas bonus negatively affected.

The moment I'd hit the air I'd started running. It had been drizzling, and I'd stopped under an awning to catch my breath and call Jolie and Rebecca with the news. I'd also left messages for Opal and Olivia.

On the way to my apartment I'd stopped at a kiosk to look at the newspapers. No headlines about Ted's death. I was sure it would be on the news, though.

It was. The five of us stared at my thirteen-inch television as the noon news reported, "Police need your help in the investigation of the murder of Ted Puck, a young investment banker whose body was found by workers early this morning on the far end of the Wharf Pier.... Police don't suspect robbery was the motive, as his Cartier watch and wallet full of cash and credit cards were not taken. Anyone with information is asked to call the Portland Police Department at 555-1444. More tonight…"

Jolie turned off the television and sat back down. "Did the detectives tell you they had any leads?" she asked me. As a paralegal, albeit a corporate paralegal, Jolie, in her crisp black suit with an ivory silk blouse peeking out from the jacket, was asking all the questions. No one else even knew where to begin, other than *He's really dead? As in* dead *dead?*

"Me," I said. "I seem to be their lead. The humiliated ex-girlfriend!"

"That's insane," Shelley said, tuna sandwich midway to her mouth. "You won't even step on bugs!"

"And the most insane part?" I said. "One of the cops is someone I knew in high school." I turned to Jolie, who had listened to me moon about Ben for two years. "Ben Orr."

Her mouth dropped open. "You're kidding! Is he still gorgeous, or fat and bald?"

"Still gorgeous," I said.

"Wait a minute," Shelley said, putting down her sandwich. "If you know one of the cops, everything will be okay. I mean, he's gotta know you're not a murderer!"

"He didn't seem to care one way or the other that we went to school together," I said. "And he didn't even remember me."

"But you were madly in love with him for two years!" Jolie said. "How could he not remember you?"

"Because (a) it was ten years ago," I said. "And (b) he didn't know I was alive then."

Jolie gnawed her lip. Rebecca was smushing chickpeas in her salad. Roger sat shaking his head. And Shelley seemed to be racking her brain.

"I'm sure Shelley's right," I said. "By tonight, they'll

have investigated other people, and they'll have suspects and have gotten evidence back from the lab, or wherever evidence goes, and Ben will have confirmed that we went to high school together—not that that means anything."

Rebecca took a sip of her Diet Coke. "You know, speaking of suspects, maybe Ted's new fiancée caught him cheating with someone at *her* birthday party." She cocked her thumb and ring finger together. *Pow,* she mouthed.

We all stared at her. Five foot two and teeny-tiny with pixie blond hair and round blue eyes, Rebecca Rhode, creator of cakes and pies, wasn't the blast-'em type.

"Well, maybe," she said. She'd recently discovered her boyfriend was cheating on her with his ex-girlfriend. It was a sore subject. When it had first happened, Jolie had marveled (privately to me) that Ted had done the reverse. Converse? Anyway, that he'd cheated on me with his *future* girlfriend.

Jolie squeezed my hand. "I'm sure the police will catch whoever did it. Especially because it wasn't a random robbery. Someone killed him for a reason, and it was likely someone he knew and had pissed off."

"Or whoever killed him didn't have time to take his watch or rummage for his wallet," I said.

"Did he have any enemies?" Roger asked, ketchup from a French fry dripping onto my hardwood floor. I stared at the tiny bloodred spot and felt queasy.

"Aside from you?" Shelley teased.

Roger blushed and nudged Shelley in the ribs. Roger had a crush on me. On my first day at work three years ago, he asked me out. He was nice, but so tall (six foot four) and lumbering and timid that I couldn't be attracted to him. Also as a copy editor, he had a bad habit of correcting grammar in conversation. He kept asking me out and I kept telling him I didn't mix business with pleasure. Finally I told him the truth, gently, that I just wasn't attracted to him, but that I really valued him as a friend, which was true. He'd been beside himself when I'd come into work moping and dejected after the Ted debacle. *How could any guy cheat on you? What a jerk!* But then he'd say, *If you were my girlfriend, I'd cherish you,* and I'd want to leave his company immediately. I wanted to be cherished. Just not by Roger.

"Oh, God," Rebecca said. "Is that blood?"

All eyes darted to where Rebecca was staring. Roger mopped up the spot with his napkin. "Sorry. Ketchup. You know what I think? I think that anyone who'd do what Ted Puck did to Abby on her birthday is the kind of person who'd have a lot of enemies. A jerk is a jerk is a jerk. I'm sure Ted treated everyone like shit."

That was probably true. Ted didn't seem to have many friends. I'd met a cousin once, who lived a few towns over. Ted's parents had been killed in a car accident six years ago. And he had no brothers or sisters.

"Once we hear how he died, we'll know if it was a man or a woman," Jolie said. "Unless he was shot. Both women and men shoot. But women tend to stab, whereas men tend to strangle or use baseball bats."

We all stared at her.

"I watch every cop show there is," she explained.

And then it was nearing two o'clock, and they all had to get back to work. There were hugs and kisses and much encouragement to *call me if you're freaking out.* Roger gave me the world's most awkward hug, mostly because I was five foot three and he was six foot four. Shelley refused to take back her hat or umbrella.

I stared at the mountain of food on the counter between my kitchenette and the living room. I couldn't imagine ever being hungry again. I wanted my friends to come back and stay with me until—until when?

I took a deep breath, grabbed my photo album and flipped to the Ted page. There was just the one photo.

I am so in love with you, he'd said a month into our relationship. *I don't want to see anyone but you.* Granted, we'd been in bed and had been about to make love for the first time, but he wouldn't have said it if he hadn't meant it, would he? I mean, we were already naked. He was already going to get what he wanted.

How did he go from *I am so in love with you* to falling for someone else two months later?

"I'm sorry about what happened to you," I whispered to the photograph. "But I assure you that no matter how much you hurt me, I didn't do anything to hurt you."

Then again, he probably already knew that. Unless he was blindsided. Shot in the back.

I wasn't sure I wanted to know the details.

The phone rang. Opal.

"Omigod, Abby," she said. "The police are asking all sorts of questions about you!"

"Like what?" I asked, trying for nonchalance.

"Like exactly what time I spoke to you last night," she said. "Exactly what time you left the bris. Exactly how you seemed after catching Ted cheating at your party. All I told him was that you were madly in love with Ted, that you wanted to marry him, even though you'd only been seeing each other for three months, and that you were *so* humiliated when you walked in on him getting a blow job from some Angelina Jolie type at your own birthday party. I mean, who wouldn't be, right? When he asked if I thought you killed him, of course I said no—but I added that if you did, I'd totally understand why."

This was my alibi?

"Omigod, Abby, my mom is flipping," she said. "And so is Oliver. And Olivia is so worried about you. The cops have been at her house all morning."

"At Olivia's house? Why?" I asked, sitting up ramrod straight.

"She said they said you said you were at a party there yesterday. They're looking for evidence, I guess."

I got past the *they said you said she said* and focused on

the word *evidence*. "Evidence of what, Opal?" And how did they go from checking my alibi to looking for evidence?

"If Oliver's gun was taken!" she whispered.

I shot up. "Oliver has a *gun?*"

"So you didn't know that?" she asked. "I'll call back the detective and tell him that."

"I didn't know," I said. "But I don't think my saying so will make a bit of difference to the police."

So Ted had been shot to death?

"Opal, did you tell the detectives that I knew Oliver had a gun?"

"Um, I don't know," she said. "I might have said that you probably knew. Oliver said he bought it when Olivia got pregnant. For protection," she added. "And when the cops asked Oliver to check if it was still there, it was. Oliver said it was exactly as he'd left it the day he brought it home, locked in a secret drawer in his office desk. But the cops took it for evidence, anyway, and now Olivia and Oliver are freaking out."

"Because Oliver killed Ted?" I asked, trying to make sense out of that one.

"No—because they think you might have taken the gun, killed Ted, then returned it in the middle of the night."

Wait a minute. "*Who* thinks that, Opal? The police or Oliver and Olivia?"

Silence. "Um, the police and Oliver discussed that possibility."

Oh. My. God.

My legs felt funny, and I dropped onto the sofa. "Well, there's something called ballistics," I said. "When the bullet that killed Ted doesn't match the bullets in Oliver's gun, the police will investigate someone else who supposedly had reason to want to kill Ted, and I'll be cleared."

"You sure know a lot of gun lingo," Opal said.

"I watch *Law & Order,* Opal."

"That'll make a good defense," she said earnestly.

"Opal, I didn't kill Ted!"

"I know," she said quickly. "Oh, um, Abby, Jackson just got here. I have to go. Talk to you later, okay?"

"I'll probably save my one phone call for my lawyer," I said.

Silence.

"I'm kidding, Opal."

Silence. "Weird that you can joke at a time like this, Abby. Um, okay. Bye!"

The phone rang again. It was Detective Fargo.

"Just making sure you didn't leave town," he said. "Bye now."

So much for being cleared.

Chapter 5

Buzz! Buzz-buzz!

Please be Jolie or Rebecca, I thought, running to the intercom at my apartment door. It wasn't yet five o'clock, though.

"It's Detective Orr" came the deep voice. "I'd like to ask you a few questions."

I buzzed him in, then glanced at myself in the hallway mirror. I'd changed from my look-better/feel-better outfit into a white tank top and yoga pants. Should I dress more appropriately? Perhaps the not-trying-too-hard look was best, so as not to appear even more suspicious. I pulled the elastic band out of my hair and finger combed. I had no idea what cold-blooded murderers looked like, but for some reason I assumed their hair didn't look like Charles Manson's.

Knock. Knock.

I opened the door, and Benjamin Orr filled the doorway. I stared at him, unable to believe the guy I had thought about 24/7 as a teenager was now standing a foot in front of me, looking like a god. He was so close. So—

"I'm sorry to disturb you at home," he said. "But I would like to ask you more questions."

I glanced behind him. "No partner?"

"He's investigating other areas. May I come in?"

I held open the door and he stepped inside my tiny foyer. He took off his black wool overcoat and hung it on my coatrack, then followed me into the living room.

"So I'm not the only suspect," I said, my shoulders relaxing for the first time. "I just made a pot of coffee. It's French vanilla, though."

He nodded. "I'll take it. Thanks."

I was surprised that he followed me into the kitchen, which wasn't big enough for one person to turn around in, much less two. He stood in the archway, watching me. No—that wasn't quite accurate. He was watching, period. Perhaps looking around for a gun hidden inside the toaster oven or the cookie jar—not that I had one. As I filled two mugs, he turned and leaned against the side of the archway. Now he could watch me and take in my entire living room.

"I might as well just tell you, Detective Orr," I said, "that—"

"Call me Ben," he said. "I checked. We did go to high school together."

No kidding.

"You haven't changed at all," he said. "From your yearbook picture."

I scowled. "I looked like a prepubescent boy in that photo."

He laughed, but I wasn't kidding. I'd been short and skinny, without a curve. My hair had been a weird length between my ears and chin. And you could have played backgammon on my chest.

"What I was going to say, Ben, was that I heard you took my brother-in-law's gun into evidence. I didn't even know he had one."

"It wasn't the murder weapon. We knew that just by looking at it. But we wanted to take a closer look at it regardless. Do *you* own a gun?" he asked.

"Nope," I said, holding out his mug of coffee. "I've never even touched one."

"Then how were you planning on killing Henry Fiddler?"

"What?"

He'd so startled me that the coffee shook over the edge of the mug. He took it from me, then grabbed a napkin from the counter and blotted my hand and the mug. He sipped. "Very good," he said, leaning back against the counter ever so casually, as though we were old friends. "I usually don't go for flavored coffee, but I like this."

"Back to that question," I said, trying to rip open two packets of Sweet'n Low at the same time. My fingers wouldn't work. "About Henry?"

He set his mug on the counter, took the Sweet'n Low

from me and shook them into my mug, then grabbed a
spoon from the dish drain and stirred for me. He handed
me the mug. I couldn't even manage a thank-you.

Out came the notebook from his pocket. "According to
a salesclerk at L.L. Bean, Abby, you said, 'I am going to kill
him.' In reference to Henry Fiddler, who ditched you in
L.L. Bean. You reiterated your intention of killing him this
morning. My partner and I heard that with our own ears."

"No! I was just…" But it sounded stupid even to me.
*It's just an expression, Officer. You know, people say they want
to kill people all the time. But they don't do it!*

Thing was, some did. Obviously.

I needed to get out of this kitchen. I moved past Ben.
I felt his eyes on my back as he followed me into the
living room.

"Under the circumstances," he said, "we did need to
alert Mr. Fiddler to the threat you made against him. He's
under protective detail."

"What? But that's crazy! I'm…" Once again, what was
I possibly going to say? I sat down on my sofa and stared
at my feet.

He sat on the chair across from the sofa, sipped his
coffee, then put down the mug and faced me full on.
"Abby, I'm going to be straight with you. You seem like
a very nice person. You have a nice family. Nice friends.
A good job. I think anyone who knows you would understand that sometimes perfectly sane, perfectly nice people
snap. You finally started dating again, and what happens?

Your new boyfriend breaks up with you. Then you see the engagement announcement. You snapped. It's okay to say so, Abby."

I gaped at him. "You can't be serious!"

"I'm dead serious," he said, his expression backing up his choice of words.

Do not hyperventilate. Breathe. Breathe. Breathe. "I didn't kill Ted," I said.

He sat back, silent.

"And I have no intention of killing Henry!" I added. "I just said it because I was angry at him for ditching me the way he did in L.L. Bean. People say it all the time! They don't *mean* it."

"Where I come from, Abby, which is the Portland police station, they do mean it. Saying you're going to kill someone is a threat. But I do have good news for you, too. The phone calls you made to your friends and the two you received from your sister put you home during a large portion of the time frame in which Ted was killed. Still, it's humanly possible that you managed to shoot Ted and get back to your apartment within twenty minutes."

This was crazy! "I didn't kill Ted," I said again. "You have to believe me."

"I believe in evidence. Motive. Means. Opportunity."

"Don't tell me there's evidence," I said. "There *can't* be. Unless someone is framing me!"

"I can't discuss the case with you," he said. "Unless it pertains directly to you."

What did that mean? Apparently it all pertained to me.

"Could someone be framing me?" I asked. "Did you find something of mine near Ted?"

"I'm not at liberty to say."

"You're just at liberty to scare me to death?" I asked.

"I'm not trying to scare you, Abby. I'm just following up. That's all."

"Are we done?" I asked. Ironic. All I'd wanted for so long was to be having a long, involved talk with Benjamin Orr. *Now* all I wanted was for him to leave me the hell alone.

"Not yet," he said. "I need a list of all your boyfriends, in order, plus all your dates—blind dates, one-shot dates, one-night stands."

Oh, brother. "Why?" I asked.

"It's just all part of the follow-up," he said.

I crossed my arms over my chest. "Do you ever answer a question?"

He smiled. "If I can."

Huh. Now I didn't have a question. "I've never had a one-night stand," I said. "And I'm not a serial dater."

He eyed me. "I'll need full names, phone numbers and addresses if you have them, and when the relationship began and ended. Annotate as you see fit," he added. "Anything you'd like to say about the relationship would be helpful. I'll need the list by tomorrow morning." He stood.

"Um, about this list," I said. "How far back should I go? The past few years? College?"

"You can go back to kindergarten if you had a boyfriend then," he said.

"You're not serious. You want to know about the crush I had on Raymond Phipps in kindergarten?"

"I remember Raymond Phipps!" he said, smiling. "He used to beat me up once a week."

I really did have bad taste in men. Starting in kindergarten.

"Anyway, yes," he said. "List everyone."

Great. This was going to be embarrassing.

"Thanks for the coffee, Abby." He headed toward the door and retrieved his coat.

I followed him. "Ben, for the record, I didn't kill Ted. I didn't even *want* to kill Ted."

"Duly noted," he said, opening the door.

"By the way," I said, "what's going to happen to Clinton, Ted's pug? Is his fiancée taking him?"

He nodded.

There was no way Mary-Kate was a dog person.

"Thanks for your time," he said. "I'll be in touch. Oh, and again, Abby, don't leave town."

My penchant for picking heartless heartbreakers really had begun in kindergarten, when I developed a mad crush on Raymond, a thin blond boy who had the best lunches in the best TV-character lunch boxes. There would be a sandwich, always something good, like bologna on white bread with mustard, one slice of American cheese and a Hershey bar—a whole one, not a miniature—an apple or orange, a thermos of Hi-C and a small bag of potato chips. My mother packed a protein, a carb, a vegetable and a fruit every single day in one of those dull soft mini coolers. After holidays I would find one piece of my Halloween candy, doled out for an entire year.

Anyway, age five was a toughie for me. I'd understood in a way I hadn't before that my father didn't live with us because he lived with another family, with another mother and other children, one of whom happened to be in my class. Every morning, Olivia who was a very nice five-year-old, reported in about the morning at our dad's house. "Daddy woke up me and Opal and then he made eggs and pancakes and then he gave us each two kisses and a special quarter for our piggy banks." Much later I found out that Veronica had instructed Olivia to give me the morning reports so that I wouldn't feel left out.

Veronica had to know that *left out* was the first thing I'd feel. I'd known my stepmother for my entire life, and I still didn't understand her.

Anyway, the more left out I felt, the more fixated I became on Raymond and what was inside his lunch box. A few weeks into my secret, silent crush on Raymond, he yelled, "Would you quit looking at me already? If you want a potato chip, just ask. *God!*"

My first humiliation. Everyone had laughed at me. Except Olivia. I remembered that.

"I heard he pees in his bed," she'd whispered to me.

And just like that, my crush was gone. If only adult crushes were that easy to snap out of.

I sat down at my computer and started a Word file: *Abby Foote's List of Romantic Involvements.* I couldn't call it a boyfriend list, since I couldn't call many of the guys I'd dated *boyfriends.* I added Raymond's name, then *Kindergarten. Got over him when I heard he was a bed wetter.*

Stephen Fingerman. First grade. First boy to have a crush on me. Did disgusting boy things, like stretch out his eyes and eat bugs. I fell hard. Ignored me when new girl from Russia joined our class. Last I heard, Stephen was preparing paperwork to marry a Russian mail-order bride.

Dylan Gold. First boyfriend of early teen life. Broke up with me in the cafeteria of my school, right in front of Olivia. He sidled up next to us, squeezed his tray between ours and said to me, "I can't go out with you anymore because I like your friend. There, I said it, okay."

My heart dropped. So did the cellophane-wrapped tuna sandwich I'd just taken from the rack. He liked Jolie? She was really my only friend at this school besides Olivia, who really wasn't my friend then.

"So will you find out if she likes me?" Dylan asked, his gorgeous blue eyes suddenly puppy-dog hopeful.

"Are you on some kind of drug?" Olivia said to him. "Ask her yourself."

Dylan added onion rings and French fries to his tray. "I would, but I don't know where she goes to school or where she lives or what her name is."

Huh? "Which friend are you talking about?" I asked.

"The tall blonde with the hot boots with all the laces," he said. "I saw you guys at the mall last weekend and I can't stop thinking about her."

Olivia's mouth dropped open. "You're talking about my sister, Opal. And she's *twelve.*"

Dylan turned red. "Oh. Well, she doesn't look it."

Olivia rolled her eyes. "She *stuffs,* okay?"

He eyed my chest, then Olivia's, then shrugged and headed on down the line.

"That was your boyfriend?" Olivia said. "Nice guy."

"We were only going out for a few days," I said, then half lied about a stomachache.

Transferred later that year to private school, I added to the brief version I wrote for Ben. For all I knew, Dylan and Ben were best friends from Little League or something.

Marco Cantinelli. Dated for one month in college. Lost my virginity to him my freshman year. So did my roommate. And our entire floor.

Jonathan Alterman. Dated for one year when I was a college junior. The pig latin king. Last I heard, was living on kibbutz in Israel.

Slade. Just Slade. First boyfriend postcollege. He didn't talk much. Would not kiss on the lips, like Julia Roberts in *Pretty Woman.* I dated him for one month anyway and loved every minute of it. Told me he was moving to Alaska to fish, but I saw him in various Portland hot spots for years afterward.

Charlie Heath. Dated for six months, two years ago. Broke up after he injured my aunt during bouquet toss at my sister Olivia's wedding. Did not respond to letter from my aunt Annette containing bill for the deductible portion of her E.R. bill. Never saw him again.

Tom Greer. Dated for four months until December of the year before last. He broke up with me via e-mail at work. *I can't make it to your company Christmas party tonight, sorry. I've met someone else. You know I can't handle confrontation.*

Riley Witherspoon. Dated for two months. Really liked him. Dumped me in February after issue declaring him Best CPA in Portland hit the stands.

And then there was Ted Puck in July. You know what happened there.

And Henry this month. (Ditto.)

What happened to Ted was all over the evening news. I couldn't *not* watch it. There weren't many more details, except that there were no witnesses. He'd been shot to death around eight o'clock last night, but he hadn't been found until early this morning by the workers.

No witnesses. He'd been completely trapped, with no one around to help. What had Ted been doing down at the end of the pier on a cold January night anyway? There was nothing down that far but boats, and Ted didn't own a boat. Perhaps he'd been meeting someone who did own a boat? Had been out for a jog? Ted was a runner. Was he meeting someone? Why down there? Why not in a restaurant? Or a bar? If he'd been having an affair, he couldn't very well rendezvous on the street. In the cold.

He hadn't been robbed, so there was no way it was a random shooting. He'd gone down there for a reason, and had been shot to death. Maybe he'd gotten involved in something shady, like gambling. Or drugs. But Ted was a banker on the up-and-up, as far as I knew. Or maybe he was a cheater in love *and* in business? He was very likely booby-trapped, set up.

I doubted the good detective would be spending so much time on me if Ted's BlackBerry had contained any notations about meeting someone down at the pier last night. Nothing on his calendar and nothing on his voice mail, home machine or e-mail—I was sure. Nor anything suspicious about Ted's coworkers or business associates or his habits, whatever they were. Ben and his partner seemed very thorough. Unless, as I suspected, Ben was tracking me and Fargo was investigating all other areas of Ted's life.

They were focusing on me because I, as the spurned girlfriend, made the most sense. So maybe they should be focusing on Ted's *other* spurned girlfriends. I had no idea who they were, but I had no doubt they existed in the hundreds. Both unfortunately and fortunately, Ted didn't kiss and tell.

"Women always ask, but they don't really want to know," he'd said during our early dates when I asked him, ever so coyly, about exes.

I *needed* to know. Perhaps that was information I could get from Ben. Yeah, right. Mr. I Can't Discuss The Case. There had to be ways to track down former girlfriends.

But first I needed to see where Ted was found. Maybe it would jog my memory of something he'd said, a reference he'd made. Or maybe it would just make me very, very sad.

I called Jolie to ask if she'd meet me at the pier.

"You have no idea how you're going to react," she said. "Don't go alone. I'm working late, but I can go with you tomorrow if you really want to see it with your own eyes."

Rebecca basically said the same thing.

But I needed to go *now*. As I tried Olivia and Opal, I had no doubt both would make up crazy excuses. No one answered at Olivia's house, which meant she was screening, since she had caller ID and was definitely home at six o'clock at night. Opal answered her cell phone, but was at a rehearsal dinner for her rehearsal dinner. (Very likely a first.)

Shelley to the rescue; she immediately said she'd cancel her plans with Baxter. "We're just going to hang out at my apartment and watch TV—*again*," she complained. "He never wants to go out! Anyway, I'll meet you down there, Abby. But I don't know if it's a good idea. What if there's blood?"

But there couldn't be blood because of all the rain. It would just be the same old beautiful pier with the same old beautiful boats docked for the winter. Except it couldn't possibly be beautiful anymore.

Turned out I was wrong; the pier was still beautiful. The lights shone on the dark water, and the boats bobbed. I stood at the base of the pier, squinting down the length of it. There wasn't much to see. There was some yellow tape. That was all.

"Abby!" came Shelley's voice from up the block. She waved and jogged over, her wild brown curls bouncing all over the place in the wind. "It's so cold," she said, rubbing her gloved hands together. "And it must have been this cold last night. So what was he doing out here?"

I shrugged. "That's what I've been wondering. Maybe he was involved in something illegal. Why else would he be hanging around the edge of a pier in the dead of winter? He must have been meeting someone."

Shelley nodded. "Whatever it was, the police will figure it out. So don't worry about all their questions, okay? They're just doing their job."

"I can't believe he's really…gone," I said, staring down the pier. "Jerk or no jerk, he was so full of life, with grandiose plans. It's so hard to believe that he's just *no more,* just like that."

"You really loved him, didn't you?" Shelley said, slipping her hand through my arm.

I nodded.

"You know what drove me nuts?" I said. "That Mary-Kate looked so much like me. If he was going to pick someone to cheat on me with, to fall madly in love with, couldn't he have picked a tall blonde or a redhead? If he was going to pick a woman who was practically my double, why not just stick with me in the first place?"

Shelley nodded in commiseration.

"Eh, that's stupid," I said. "Lust and love are about chemistry. Not a checklist, like long brown hair and big boobs. He fell for her, plain and simple, because of who she was."

"Don't excuse what he did," Shelley said. "Yeah, he fell for someone else. But the way he handled it was absolutely disgusting. He was a pig, Abby. But you're right. He fell for her because of who she was—a slutty, cheating pig! I mean, who goes to someone's party and gives that someone's boyfriend a blow job on that someone's bed?" She shook her head. "If I hadn't been there, Abs, I don't even think I would have believed it."

"Yeah, you and the forty people at my party," I said. "Anyway, I'm glad Baxter wasn't there that night. At least there are a few people who don't know the story, weren't there to witness my utter humiliation with their own eyes."

She glanced at me sheepishly. "Uh, I did sort of tell him about it. I'm sorry."

"It's okay. That's what a boyfriend is for, right? Speaking of which, I really appreciate that you canceled your plans. Not many women do that."

"I never want to be one of those women," she said. "Baxter would like me to be, but I can't. *He'd* cancel on *me* in a second if a friend needed *him,* but he really wants me to always be available for him. He wants me to move in, but I don't know. If we're going to live together, why not just get engaged? And if we're just going to sit around and watch TV, why bother at all?" She gnawed her lip. "I don't know what I want."

"What does Baxter want?" I asked.

"He says he loves me like crazy but wants to wait until he's at least into his residency before getting engaged. He wants to give me a huge wedding. And since my parents are gone, he'd have to pay for it." She took a deep breath, as she always did when talking about her mom and dad. They'd been killed in an accident almost five years ago.

When my dad died three years ago, soon after I started at *Maine Life,* Shelley was the only coworker who came to the funeral. She sent a beautiful card, flowers, even homemade lasagna, her specialty. We'd been close friends ever since. Our dads were buried in the same cemetery, and we often went to visit their graves together.

"Well, I'm never going to have a relationship last long enough for moving in," I said. "Six months was my longest since college."

"It's not your fault," she said.

"So I just have bad taste in guys?" I asked.

"Maybe," she said, squeezing my hand. "Or maybe you're only twenty-eight and haven't met the right guy."

"Thanks," I said. I hoped that was it.

"Let's skip this and go get pizza," she said. "I don't think looking at where it happened is going to give you any closure. It'll just make you think of it. What if you have nightmares about it?"

I shook my head. "I need to see where it happened." But when I tried to step forward, I stayed rooted to the spot.

"Hon, you don't have to do this," Shelley said, her brown leather glove on my shoulder.

"I do. I just need to make it real for myself so that I can believe it's not just some surreal nightmare."

"Okay, let's go," she said.

We headed up the long pier. I could see the yellow "crime scene" tape at the end. I could also see someone standing there, not moving, not doing anything.

I froze. "I think that's Mary-Kate Darling," I whispered to Shelley.

As the woman bent to place the bouquet on the ground, I could see that it *was* Mary-Kate. She stood up and stared out at the water for a few moments, then snatched up the bouquet, ripped off the petals and threw them down at the ground. Because of the wind, the petals scattered all over the place.

Shelley and I eyed each other.

"That was weird," I whispered.

"Very weird," she said.

Mary-Kate then flung the green stems on the ground and turned and started running. She froze when she saw me, her expression pure hatred, then she ran.

I turned and watched her until she disappeared onto Commercial Street.

"She didn't exactly look like the grieving widow," I remarked.

"More like the black widow spider," Shelley said.

Chapter 6

In the morning I found Ben's card in the empty candy dish on the console table in my foyer. I hadn't realized he'd put it there. Maybe he'd forgotten that he'd already given me one yesterday morning in the conference room. Yeah, like he forgot anything. I called, eager to let him know about Mary-Kate and her petal tantrum, but he wasn't in.

Because he was on his way to my apartment, of course. Not five minutes after I called, he buzzed.

"Got that list for me?" he asked. He stood in the doorway. As usual, every thought went out of my head at the sight of him. He was that good-looking. That *hot*.

I nodded. "Come in," I said, stepping aside.

He didn't take off his coat or his gloves. Hopefully because he was in a rush to go out and catch the killer, not because he was going to haul me "downtown" to the station.

I handed the list to him, and he scanned it. "What

exactly are you going to do with my list of romantic involvements, anyway?"

"I really can't discuss an ongoing investigation," he said. "Speaking of which, I understand you were at the crime scene last night."

Interesting. So Mary-Kate had reported in? Considering that she'd been the one acting suspiciously, I was surprised. Then again, maybe she was smart. Maybe she was covering her tracks, alerting Ben that she'd been there as the grieving fiancée, while making sure he knew I, as the spurned ex, had been there, clearly to hunt for any evidence I might have left behind. Like an earring or a scarf.

"I just needed to see where it happened," I said.

"Do you know that most killers return to the scene of the crime soon after?" he asked.

"No, I didn't know that," I said, my legs turning into rubber. "And if you know I was at the scene of the crime, you must know that Mary-Kate Darling was, too. Since I assume she reported my presence there."

"Mary-Kate was Ted's fiancée," Ben said. "It makes sense that she'd want to see where he was last living and breathing. For closure, for self-torture, I don't know."

I stared at my shoes. "I loved Ted, too," I said. "I mean, not lately. But I loved him until he—"

"Cheated on you with Mary-Kate?"

I nodded. "When someone you love does something so awful to you, it's easy to fall out of love. Not so easy to shake the hurt. But that was six months ago. I got over Ted fast."

"By dating Mr. Fiddler," Ben said. "Who then ditched you in L.L. Bean rather than witness a bris."

"This is just embarrassing," I said. "And it's possible that Mary-Kate killed Ted. Maybe she caught him cheating on her, and she flew into the rage you accused me of flying into. Maybe Ted dumped her, and she was the spurned woman who killed him. Why isn't that a plausible theory?" I told him about the flowers.

"So perhaps she was angry. Grief affects people in different ways, Abby."

"I know all about grief," I snapped.

"In any case, Mary-Kate Darling has an airtight alibi for the night of the murder," he said. "You don't."

"Where was she?" I asked.

"I can't discuss that with you, Abby. It wouldn't be professional, and it's also not relevant. She's not a suspect."

"Am I?" I asked.

"You're a person of interest," he said.

"Have you investigated Ted's other ex-girlfriends?" I asked. "Maybe one of *them* snapped."

"Abby, I can't talk about the case with you. What I can do is assure you that we are investigating all areas. I'm not focused on you at the expense of other potential suspects."

That was a relief.

"Thanks for the list," he added, folding Abby's Romantic Involvements into his breast pocket. "I'll be in touch."

And then he was gone.

"How can I find out what Mary-Kate Darling was doing the night Ted was killed?" I asked Jolie and Rebecca later that night. They'd come over to cheer me up.

"You do what lawyers do when they need information they can't just ask for," Jolie the paralegal said. "You track down the info in newspapers or online. Do a Google search for Mary-Kate. Or just read some of the news articles about Ted's death. I wouldn't be surprised if she was interviewed and mentioned what she was doing the night he was killed."

Jolie handed me her *Portland Daily News*. There were two articles about the murder.

In a heartbreaking twist, Ted's fiancée, Mary-Kate Darling, had been registering for wedding gifts at Crate and Barrel when the murder took place. "I can't believe I was dithering over china patterns when Ted—" she said, breaking down in tears. "When my beloved Ted was killed," she finally managed to say amid heart-wrenching sobs.

How airtight could that alibi be? It wasn't as if a sales-clerk had been mooning over her for two hours. Why couldn't she have slipped out to commit a little murder and then rushed back to finish choosing salad bowls? Anyone who'd cheat with someone else's boyfriend at that someone else's own birthday party was coldhearted enough to be a cold-blooded killer.

I loved Crate and Barrel. Every time I walked into the store, I felt like someone who had a love life. There was something about all those glasses, all those vases and candles and interesting pillows, that said *couple living together*. It was eight o'clock at night; the store would be closing in an hour, and it was packed. With couples living together. I'd never seen so many guys in a store in my life. Well, except Sharper Image.

A month into my relationship with Ted I'd gone to Crate and Barrel to find a birthday gift for Opal, and I'd been unable to resist playing registry. There were brides-to-be walking around with their sheets of paper and pens, picking up forks and studying them as though they were the most important aspect of married life.

I'd picked up a glass and studied it. A bride-to-be had smiled at me. "Ooh, are you thinking of those?"

"Yes, I think Theodore would love them."

She laughed. "Michael would hate these. Way too girly, he'd say."

For those five minutes I was a bride-to-be. A woman with a crappy track record, but in a good relationship of one nice month. Things had been looking up. I'd cut myself a break and let myself pretend I was one of them, even if I didn't have the paper or the pen. Or the ring. Or, say, a grip on reality.

I headed over to the registry computer and typed in *Darling and Puck.* Eight sheets came out.

Huh. Maybe she *had* been there for three hours.

"Excuse me," I said to a salesclerk who was straightening candlesticks on a display. "I'm looking to buy a gift for this person." I held up the registry. "I was wondering if you could help me choose—"

The guy put his hand on my arm. "I am so sorry to tell you this, Miss, but didn't you hear? The groom was *murdered*."

"Yes, I know," I said. "I'm a friend of the bride's, and I thought I'd buy her something that she wanted for their life together, something to commemorate what they would be sharing. Something more for her, or perhaps decorative. I think she'd like that."

I sure wouldn't.

"That's a lovely idea. Let's see," he said, glancing from the registry sheets to displays. "She did register for that adorable old-fashioned alarm clock, the one with the pug on it."

That was actually a relief. Maybe she *was* a dog person. A pug person, at least. Clinton might be in good hands.

"Wow, she really picked out a ton of stuff," I said. "She must have been here for hours."

He nodded and began straightening glass vases. "Oh, she was. I helped her for most of it. She said she wasn't too good at this kind of thing."

"I hope she took a break for coffee or something. Three hours of straight shopping isn't easy on anyone, even an excited bride."

"You'd be surprised. Some brides are in here from opening to closing. But come to think of it, I did see her leave about an hour after she arrived. Then she came back about a half hour later. She probably went for coffee."

Bingo. Got you, cousin Mary! You're toast.

"Probably," I said.

Or she might have, say, slipped out to murder her fiancé for no reason I could think of right now.

I couldn't wait to tell Ben!

Chapter 7

I was still sleeping when Ben buzzed the next morning. Either he had ESP or he had another round of questions. Why he had to come at seven in the morning was a question *I'd* ask *him*. Probably to catch me off guard.

I buzzed him in and had just enough time to brush my teeth before he knocked. As I headed to the door, I glanced at myself in the hall mirror. Once again he was getting the real me. My pink velour sweats and a freshly scrubbed face.

His eyes went straight to my Winnie the Pooh slippers, a gift from my dad.

"The floors are cold," I said, giving Winnie's ears a little shake.

He didn't smile. In fact, he looked downright…grim. "I need to talk to you."

My smile faded. "I need to talk to you, too," I said fast.

"And me first, okay?" Because if he was about to arrest me, the news about Mary-Kate just might keep those big silver bracelets off my wrists. "It's about Mary-Kate Darling. I think you'd be very interested to know that she left after the first hour of registering for gifts at Crate and Barrel the night Ted was murdered. The clerk who was helping her said she came back a half hour later. The timing checks, Ben. She could have slipped out and killed Ted."

He took off his coat and held on to it. "It's looking more and more likely that *you* slipped out and killed Ted, Abby. Would you like to know why?"

"I really wouldn't," I said. "Would *you* like to know why?"

He crossed his arms over his chest. "Yes, I would."

"Because this is such a colossal waste of your time. I didn't kill Ted. I didn't even think of it. Not for a second."

"Well, then," he said, "maybe you can explain this *coincidence*—two of your former boyfriends, recent former boyfriends, were the victims of attempted murder."

He might as well have punched me hard in the stomach. "What? What are you talking about?"

"Ted Puck was murdered the day his engagement announcement hit the paper, Abby. An announcement that you yourself admitted to seeing. And now two other exes—who broke up with you—reported attempts made on their lives just days after ending your relationship. If you do not have an ironclad alibi, Abby, for both dates, I will be back with an arrest warrant. Just because you didn't use your brother-in-law's gun doesn't mean you didn't get your hands on another one."

I had to sit down. This was crazy.

I took a deep breath. "Which former boyfriends?" I asked.

He sat down across from me and flipped a page in his ever-present notebook. "Riley Witherspoon and Tom Greer."

"You're telling me that someone tried to kill Riley and Tom? That's what you're telling me?"

"That's what I'm telling you," he said.

"So someone is going around trying to kill my ex-boy-friends," I said. "Am I on Mars? *Am* I on *Punk'd?* Is this one very long joke? A bad long joke?"

"Oh, it's no joke, Abby."

"I didn't kill anyone! Or try to kill anyone!"

He stared at me. "So clear yourself. By telling me where you were over a year ago, on December 22 at 7:15 p.m."

"December 22?" I repeated. "I have no idea."

"I'd find out if I were you," he said. "Do you have your calendar or appointment book? The twenty-second was a Saturday."

"Oh wait, I remember—that was the day after the holiday party at work. Tom e-mailed me like five minutes before the party to tell me he wasn't coming after all, that he'd met someone else. That day." I rolled my eyes. I'd spent almost three hundred dollars on a little red dress for a party I probably would have blown off, only to *be* blown off. "The twenty-second, the day after the holiday party, was Opal's engagement party. I remember because Opal originally wanted to have her party on the twenty-first, but she actually changed the date for me. Tom was supposed to come with me to Opal's."

"So you were at Opal's engagement party the night of the twenty-second?" he said, jotting something down. "What time to what time?"

"I got there at five-thirty to help set up," I said. "I didn't leave until after midnight."

"Who did you spend most of your time with at the party?" he asked. "I'll need witnesses to verify that you were there at various times."

"Opal can. Olivia, too. My stepmother. I talked to a guy for a while, a friend of Jackson's. He'd just been dumped, too, so we commiserated for a long time, actually. Honestly, I forget his name, but you can ask Jackson."

"I will," he said.

"So what exactly happened to Tom?" I asked.

"You might want to put on some coffee before we get gory at seven in the morning," he told me.

I gnawed my lip. "Gory? How gory?"

"How's that coffee coming?" he asked.

"This isn't Dunkin' Donuts."

He glanced up at me and smiled. That smile was his ticket out of jail. Too bad mine didn't have that effect on him.

I got up and headed into the kitchen, glad for the reprieve. I wasn't sure I wanted to know what had happened to Riley. Or Tom. Gory didn't sound good. It sounded as if they were eaten by grizzlies. Not that either was a hiker. Or camper.

Five minutes later I brought two steaming mugs of coffee into the living room. "First, can you tell *me* something, Detective? Why the crack-of-dawn visit?"

He took his mug and sipped it. "I wanted to catch you before work. It's easier to talk in the home versus the workplace."

I wrapped my hands around the hot mug. "So I'm ready for the gory details."

"Someone pushed Tom Greer in front of a speeding truck at 6:00 p.m. last December 22. He was waiting at a crowded intersection when he was shoved. Many broken bones."

That did sound gory. And painful. "Could it have been an accident?" I asked. "Tom was sort of accident prone. During our brief relationship he managed to break his nose by walking into a plate-glass window."

"Mr. Greer doesn't think so. He distinctly remembers being pushed. Hard. There was a huge crowd waiting to cross—it was right before Christmas, and he said he'd never seen so many people bustling with gifts—but he also said he knows the difference between jostling and being pushed."

"I didn't push Tom in front of a truck. And I have the alibi to prove it. At six that night I was already at Opal's. You can ask her and a whole bunch of other people who were there. Including the catering team. That's airtight, Ben."

"We'll see," he said. "Where were you one year ago on February 28 at 7:15 p.m.?"

"I need to look it up. I don't know offhand." I headed into my bedroom and grabbed my old day planner from my desk drawer. Good thing I didn't need this year's date book, because I couldn't find it. "On the night of February 28 I was at my stepmother's birthday party. It started at six-thirty." I wondered if I would be invited to this year's party.

"Riley was attacked by a pit bull that was let loose in his house," Ben said. "Two days after breaking up with you."

I take back the truck being gory. *This* was gory. "A pit bull! Is Riley all right?"

"He has a large hole in his leg," Ben said. "But other-wise he's fine."

"Wait a minute," I said. "This is insane. Two of my exes were attacked right after breaking up with me. What the hell is going on?"

"You tell me."

"'What the hell is going on?' means I don't know," I pointed out.

"Abby, if you come clean now—"

I bolted upright. "It wasn't me! I had nothing to do with any of this!"

"So it's all a coincidence," Ben said, those eyes intense on mine. "Ted being killed after his engagement an-nouncement hits the papers. Tom being pushed in front of a speeding truck. Riley being mauled by a pit bull. Days after breaking up with you."

I had to admit it didn't sound like a coincidence.

"According to Riley," Ben said, flipping a page in his notebook, "you told him he was the lowest of the low, the slimebucketiest of the slimebuckets."

Huh. I did say that. "He dumped me the day the *Maine Life* issue came out naming him one of the best CPAs in Portland. He used me to get listed. It's the only reason he went out with me in the first place. Every word he said, every kiss, every everything, was a big fat lie. He *is* the lowest of the low. He is the slimebucketiest."

"Sounds like motive to me," Ben said, jotting something down in his notebook.

"Wait a minute! That's not a motive. It's an explanation!"

Ben nodded. "Yes, that explains why you let a pit bull loose in his home."

"I didn't!"

"Riley said you were *very* upset when he broke up with you."

"I *was* upset. Because he used me and all but said so." *I'm just not feeling it, Abby,* he'd said. Mysteriously the very day I couldn't delete him from the Best CPA in Portland listing.

"Tom also said you were very angry with him when he broke up with you. In fact, I have a copy of the e-mail reply you sent to him." He unfolded a piece of paper from his notebook. "'Tom, I hope you and your new girlfriend both choke on a piece of moldy fruitcake.'"

Huh. I'd said that, too. "Okay, that was a little immature,"

I conceded. "But I was upset. He broke up with me five minutes before my company Christmas party. By e-mail!"

"And so you stalked him the next day and saw your opportunity for revenge. You pushed him in front of that truck."

"No, I didn't," I said. "I have an airtight alibi for both nights."

"You have an alibi, Abby. And going to parties isn't airtight. Your every moment can't possibly be accounted for."

"So why isn't Mary-Kate Darling a suspect?" I asked. "Her every moment in Crate and Barrel is officially not accounted for. In fact, thirty moments in prime time are unaccounted for!"

"You're forgetting that Mary-Kate Darling isn't a suspect," he said.

"She *could* be."

He stood up and put on his coat. "You should know, Abby, that you're no longer a person of interest in the murder investigation. You're our prime suspect."

I stood, too, but my legs trembled and I collapsed onto my scratchy kilim rug. Ben rushed over and helped me up, those dark eyes working, obviously trying to figure out if I was acting.

"I didn't kill Ted and I didn't *try* to kill Riley or Tom!" I said. "I couldn't hurt a fly!"

Silence. And then, "There's a gap between middle

school and college," he said. "Didn't you have any boy-friends in high school? I probably know them."

I shook my head. "Nope. I didn't date in high school."

He eyed me. "You didn't even go to the prom?"

The prom. When I realized that Ben was never going to notice me, let alone magically ask me to the junior prom, especially because his family moved out of state that spring, I said yes to Petey Strummer, who'd been asking me out, much like Roger, for a year. I guess I was his Ben Orr.

"I did go the junior prom. With Petey Strummer."

"Petey Strummer! Really." Was he trying not to laugh?

"Yeah, really," I said. "What's wrong with Petey Strummer?" Besides everything.

"Nothing," he said. "Nice guy. A little spatially challenged, if my memory serves me right."

Petey Strummer was famous for bumping into walls. Water fountains. Open lockers. I once asked him why he didn't notice the two cheerleaders blocking the middle of the hallway, as usual, and he said, "I was thinking about you. And how to change a trigonometric graph."

"Well, your memory isn't so great," I pointed out. Reaching. "You don't remember me."

How could you not remember someone who spent an entire year staring at your profile in English 11? Spanish 3? The cafeteria? The hallways? I bumped into a few open lockers myself while stealing glimpses of Ben Orr in the hallways.

"Touché," he said.

"I didn't kill Ted," I whispered. *So let's go back to the start. Ted isn't dead. I'm not a suspect. You were standing in the doorway of my cubicle because you disagreed that Island, a hot new restaurant, has the best lobster in Portland. You want to take me to your best lobster. You do remember me. You not only remember me, but you also had a secret crush on me. Ah, if only we'd known, you say. We could be celebrating our tenth anniversary as Best Couple in Maine.*

"Abby?" Ben asked. "You looked like you were a million miles away."

Like Mars.

"Penny for your thoughts, as they say."

I smiled. "A penny? I'd think a prime suspect's thoughts are worth a lot more than that."

"Touché again," he said. "Dollar for your thoughts?"

I sat down again and so did he. "I was just thinking about high school." I was about to ask him if he'd had a crush on anyone when I realized that he wasn't flirting with me. He was *investigating!*

I felt my cheeks burn. Stupid. Stupid. Stupid.

"Do I need a lawyer?" I asked.

"That's up to you," he said, standing again. "You're not under arrest. I'll be in touch," he added.

Just when I thought an imaginary boyfriend—as Ben Orr had been for two years of my teenage life—was the way to go in love, he had to go and destroy that by thinking I could kill someone. And *try* to kill two others.

That left Petey Strummer as the only guy who'd never caused me a moment's grief.

Coincidence. There *were* coincidences. Take Mark Twain. Born on the day Halley's comet made its appearance. Died on the day the comet made another appearance.

I racked my brain to figure out the connection between Mary-Kate Darling and Riley and Tom. That she killed Ted I could understand; perhaps she did catch him cheating on her, or maybe he ended their engagement. But the Riley and Tom factor threw a major monkey wrench into my theory.

It *was* possible that the Tom and Riley incidents were coincidental. Maybe someone simply bumped Tom, as he'd originally thought, on that crowded intersection. And maybe a pit bull just happened to make its way into Riley's house. It was sort of possible. Theirs could have been random incidents. But Ted's murder was no random incident. And that left Mary-Kate still viable as a suspect.

I picked up the phone. Ted had a cousin he'd been close to. I'd met him twice. Unless the guy believed I was the guilty one, maybe he'd talk to me. And maybe I'd get him to tell me a few things about the sobbing, flower-destroying fiancée.

"I still can't believe he's gone," Jonathan Alexander said, shaking four packets of sugar into his coffee. We were at Starbucks in the Old Port—coffees, a brownie for him and a giant chocolate chip cookie for me, on the little table between our club chairs.

Jonathan, Ted's cousin on his mother's side, was in his late thirties, married and the father of three—triplets. He looked a bit like Ted, except that he wasn't quite hand-some. And he had a paunch. And he wore a navy sweater with tiny red lobsters all over it. I couldn't imagine Ted in a sweater like that. But I could imagine Ted married with triplets. I'd imagined him married to me, father of our triplets. Well, twins, maybe.

The two occasions I'd met Jonathan were barbecues at Jonathan's house. One was a birthday party for the trip-lets, who were now six. Ted had splurged on a new swing set for the kids, which had been installed that morning in the backyard. The structure had come complete with a slide and ladders and a huge fort at top, where Ted had spent a good deal of time playing pirate with the kids. He'd been so involved in their play, their joy, their changing-every-five-seconds mood swings from full-out sobs to shrieks of joy, that I'd fallen fast in love with him that day.

I wished I could just remember the bad. But Ted had had a wonderful side, too.

"I can't believe he's gone, either," I said. "He was so much larger than life."

Jonathan nodded. "He came to my house for Thanks-giving every year. He didn't have anywhere else to go. His parents were gone, and he was an only child. I guess that's why he had so many girlfriends at once. Just in case one of them didn't work out, he'd have another in reserve."

Bingo. Now it was my turn to pull out my little notebook.

"So Mary-Kate wasn't his one and only?" I asked.

Jonathan bit into his brownie. "Actually, she was. Before her, I meant."

Oh. Meaning me.

He froze, a chunk of brownie wedged in his cheek. "Uh, I hope I didn't hurt your feelings by telling you that, Abby. I figured it was all 'been there, done that' kind of stuff."

That was a good way to put it. But even though I'd "been there," I was still "doing that." My inability to judge Henry Fiddler as a jerk proved that.

"So I guess I should tell you that the police asked me about you," Jonathan said. "They asked me about all Ted's girlfriends, actually. I said you were the nicest."

"Thanks," I said. "I appreciate that. Especially because as his last ex-girlfriend, suspicion is falling on me for no real reason."

"They asked what I thought of you," he said. "And I told them I'd be shocked to find out that you killed Ted."

Amazing. A total stranger, someone I'd met twice for a few hours months and months ago, had no doubt of my innocence. But everyone I dealt with on a daily basis had no doubt I was a cold-blooded killer.

I sipped my latte. "Just out of curiosity, Jonathan—what makes you so sure I didn't have anything to do with Ted's death?"

"Because when my sons pushed my daughter off the fort, you ran over to her and sat her on your lap and dried her tears and braided her hair and taught her how to make a daisy chain," he said. "I don't think killers do that."

Why did I doubt Ben would agree?

"And when she blew her nose all over your hand, you didn't get grossed out and push her off you," he added.

"It was pretty gross," I said.

He laughed. "Yup, but it demonstrates self-control, if you ask me. And empathy. You're hardly a psychopath."

"So you told the police that I wasn't the only woman Ted was seeing during our relationship?"

"I told them he was dating a couple of other women, but that they only went out a couple of times. It wasn't a relationship like you and Ted had."

Hmm. Knowing Ben, he must have paid both women a visit and eliminated them as suspects. Maybe they were out of the country the night Ted was killed. Or maybe they were good liars.

"What was your take on Mary-Kate?" I asked.

"She was Mary-Kate," he said. "Nose in the air. Polite enough, but I wouldn't say *nice*."

Interesting. "So is she from a very wealthy family?" I asked.

"I don't know," he said. "She said she was from Barmouth, and you know how that can go. Multimillion-dollar mansions on the water or tiny capes on side streets."

"Wait a minute. Are you sure she said she was from

Barmouth?" I was from Barmouth. Ben was from Barmouth. How could neither of us know her or her family? There were no Darlings in Barmouth, and I'd certainly remember someone with that name at my school.

He nodded. "Positive. I remember her saying she was vice president of her class."

Mary-Kate didn't look like a vice president. Not that smart girls couldn't grow up to become trampy slutty bitches.

To quote *Alice's Adventures in Wonderland,* things were getting curiouser and curiouser.

"So why do you think Mary-Kate was his one and only? I mean, if he had a bunch of girlfriends in the hopper at once, why would a not-so-nice one be his one and only? What was so special about her?"

He shrugged. "Beats me. She was very pretty, but no prettier than you or any of Ted's girlfriends. He did say—" He blushed, then waved his hands. "Eh, forget it."

"No, you can tell me," I said.

He leaned forward. "She was kinky. She'd do anything. Threesomes. Swinging. Sex clubs. Anything. Ted was in heaven. I sure hope he is now."

That seemed to deserve a moment of silence, so I sipped my coffee and picked at my cookie. Kinky, huh? That was the way to Ted's heart? Disappointing.

"Did you meet any of Ted's other girlfriends?" I asked. "The ones he dated while he was seeing me?"

"I met both of them once, randomly. I ran into Ted

with Ariella at the lighthouse park. They were having a picnic. She had a really loud, weird laugh. You know, like the Janice laugh from *Friends*."

I smiled. A staffer at *Maine Life,* the production manager, had a laugh like that. Sort of sounded like a bloated seal.

"How did you know they were dating?" I asked. "Maybe they were coworkers having lunch, or third cousins?"

"His head was in her lap, and she was leaning down to kiss him," he said. "He had a finger dipped inside her bikini top. I had to shield all my kids' eyes. Not easy with six eyes."

Oh. "And the other one?"

"Twinkle. Not her real name. Apparently had a thing for gold and diamonds, so everyone called her that. I ran into them at the mall. Ted introduced her as his girlfriend. I just assumed you guys had broken up."

"So there was the *Friends*-laugh girlfriend, the jewelry girlfriend, the not-so-nice girlfriend-slash-fiancée, and me. What was I?"

He smiled. "You were the sweetheart. That's how Ted described you, anyway."

Funny how the sweetheart was the one suspected of his murder. Irony, anyone?

Unbelievable. While I was busily in love with Ted, spending my free time writing "Abby Puck" on napkins, he was choosing which girlfriend he was in the mood for that night.

And then he dumped us all for the kinky girlfriend. Maybe Ariella or Twinkle didn't like that. Maybe Ariella or Twinkle *snapped*. Or maybe Ted had started seeing them again. Maybe he'd been cheating on Mary-Kate. And maybe she'd found out about it.

Arg. There was no way Ben would have let this kind of information slip through the cracks. He must have checked out Ariella and Twinkle and determined they'd had nothing to do with Ted's murder. Unless, of course, they were excellent liars, like all psychopaths were.

The good news for me was that I now had three suspects.

"Jonathan, would you happen to know Ariella's and Twinkle's last names?" I asked.

"Sorry," he said. "I don't even know Twinkle's real *first* name."

Okay, so that was bad news for me. But I was sure there was a way to ferret out the info. Maybe from Miss Darling herself.

I raced home to check my yearbooks for anyone named Mary-Kate. Not my year. There was a Mary-Katherine Mulch a grade ahead. And she was vice president of the class. But unless Mary-Katherine Mulch had been an *Extreme Makeover* recipient, she and Mary-Kate Darling were not one and the same. Mary-Katherine Mulch had wildly curly light blond hair that stuck out in odd directions. She also had some nose. And light blue eyes, the kind that looked sort of demonic rather than angelic. She reminded me of Carrie from the movie based on the Stephen King novel. I tried not to imagine mean girls throwing tampons at Mary-Katherine Mulch.

I grabbed my white pages and looked up Mulches in Barmouth. None. I called information for Mulches in Barmouth. None. In the surrounding towns. None.

"I have no Mulches in the county," the operator said.

"Are there unlisted Mulches?"

"I'm not at liberty to say" was her response.

Was that the latest catchphrase?

My head hurt. I was going to have to talk to Mary-Kate Darling myself. *If* she'd talk to me.

Chapter 8

When I arrived at the offices of *Maine Life* magazine the next morning, Marcella was not pointing, giggling or full of snark. Instead, she greeted me with a gushing hello and held out an open bakery box.

"Rugelach?" she asked. "There are three kinds—chocolate, raspberry and apricot. Take one of each. I know how much you *love* rugelach."

Okay. What was this all about? Marcella French never shared.

"Um, thanks," I said, plucking a chocolate one. And a raspberry one.

She shot another megawatt smile at me. "I love your boots."

Okay, something was definitely up. Marcella French hadn't complimented me once in the two years she'd been working for the magazine.

On my way to my cubicle, my coworkers either took one look at me and darted into their cubicles or they also gushed hellos and were full of compliments. Hmm. When my father died three years ago, I came back to work after four days' bereavement leave to business as usual and a condolence card on my desk, signed by everyone. My ex-boyfriend died, and everyone was falling over themselves. Something was definitely up.

I peered into Shelley's cubicle, but she hadn't arrived yet. Uh-oh. The photograph of Baxter was missing from its usual spot next to her *Maine Life* pencil holder. Which meant Baxter was in the doghouse or possibly permanently in the outhouse. If Shelley didn't show up in the next ten minutes, I'd call her. She and Baxter had broken up briefly at least five times in the past year, but they always got back together. Still, she'd never taken the picture of him off her desk.

My message indicator was blinking like crazy on both voice mail and e-mail. I had twenty-seven voice mail messages and thirty-six new e-mails.

The first four voice mails were from Henry Fiddler.

"Abby, this is Henry Fiddler. I'd like to apologize for my behavior last Sunday. I was under the influence of cough medicine and not myself."

Cough medicine! Delete.

"Abby, it's Henry Fiddler again. I think you should know that I've filed an order of protection against you. That means you cannot come within fifty feet of me or I can have you arrested. I

want to make sure you know that I will call the police if you violate the order."

Delete!

"Abby, it's Henry. I hope you'll understand why I felt the need to do that. I do have elderly parents to take care of, and if something happened to me, they'd be destitute."

Oh, brother. Double delete.

"Abby, me again. I forgot to add that it's not that I think you're guilty. Bye now!"

I hit Delete and slumped over my desk.

"Abby?"

I glanced up to find Marcella standing in my doorway with the box of rugelach.

"Why don't you take the whole box," she said. "You're so thin, you can afford to gobble them all up. I love your shirt. New?"

Ah. Now it made sense. Ben had questioned everyone I know, everyone I've ever known, in connection with my list of romantic involvements. He'd probably checked my alibis from every conceivable angle. *Abby says she was at her half sister Opal's engagement party, but perhaps you saw her walking down the street, following an attractive young man and looking around for trucks?*

Or maybe you saw her a couple of months later at the pound while you were adopting a cat or dog? Did she happen to be looking at pit bulls?

"If you want me to file your finished reader mail letters,

just let me know," Marcella added, leaning over as far as she could to set down the box of rugelach on my desk without having to get too close to the murderer. *You won't kill me for laughing at you the other day and making your life here a living nightmare, will you? If you spare me, I'll talk you up to Finch!*

"Thanks, Marcella," I said, opening the box and taking a moment to choose a particularly delicious-looking apricot one. Hey, if being a murder suspect was going to get me presents and compliments, fine with me. "I do *love* rugelach."

She flashed her smile again and flitted away.

I ignored the blinking red light on the voice-mail register on my telephone and checked my e-mail.

Hi, Abby! Remember me, Laura Corry from Barmouth Elementary? I just wanted you to know I am so sorry for how I treated you in the fifth grade. I was jealous of how good you were at fractions. Anyway, I've been meaning to e-mail an apology for like twenty years. I'm moving to Alaska, so I can't stop by. Best, Laura

Laura Corry tormented me at recess by sticking sucked-on lollipops in my hair while whispering a menacing "Tell and you're dead meat, beanpole."

So Ben was going back that far? Maybe he'd paid a visit to Raymond Phipps to ask if he'd seen me skulking around his house. This was so embarrassing! Did everyone really know that I was a suspect in a murder case?

Put it all out of your head. Focus on your real life. The life that makes sense. Answer some reader mail. You're now two days behind. I took the first letter from the stack in my in-box.

Dear Best Of Editor,
I'm getting married in eight months and would like you to go through your last Best of Bridal column and send me a list of the very best in all the categories. I already have my gown, so you can skip that.
Yours,
Darlene Carl, Cape Elizabeth

I was surprised the letter wasn't from Princess Opal.

I reached into my file drawer for a form response. "Dear Reader, Our volume of reader mail precludes me from personally answering every letter. Please check our next issue to see if your query has been covered...."

The phone rang.

"Hello?"

"Abby, it's Oliver Grunwald, your brother-in-law."

"I recognize your voice," I said. "How's Os—"

"Just great," he interrupted. "Look, I wanted to remind you that you *are* next on our list of godmothers for Oscar. You weren't *not* chosen because we don't trust you with our baby—I mean, of course we trust you."

Of course you do. That was why you had me drive all the way up to your house to sit me down in your formal living room to tell me that given my history of inappropriate boyfriends, I couldn't be counted on to marry a man of quality, and therefore, you and Olivia were choosing a more mature person as godmother. He was sure I understood.

"So I'm next on your list?" I asked.

"That's right. Next."

"Meaning, if something happens to the person you *did* choose, I'll be godmother."

Silence.

"Well, yes, I suppose," he said.

"Aren't you worried I'll kill the person you've chosen so that *I'll* get to be godmother?" I asked while rolling my eyes heavenward. "Who is it, anyway?"

He hung up on me.

Shelley was bringing me another cup of tea (not because she thought me guilty but because she thought I needed soothing) when Ben called ten minutes later.

"Oliver Grunwald has filled out an order of protection against you. You're not to go within fifty feet of him or Oscar Grunwald."

"Wait a minute! What? That's crazy! I can't go near my own nephew? Does Olivia know about this?"

Ben said he had another call and would be in touch. *Click.*

Phone receiver in hand, I dialed Olivia's number. This was ridiculous! She'd set Oliver straight, I was sure.

"Hello?"

"Olivia, it's Abby."

Silence.

"Olivia?"

"Abby, I really can't talk right now. I'll be in touch, okay?"

"From fifty-one feet?" I asked.

"I'll call soon," she said, and hung up.

I stared at the receiver in my hand, tears stinging the backs of my eyes. Oliver was one thing; he'd always been an arrogant jerk. But Olivia?

I heard a discreet cough and whirled around.

"I wasn't eavesdropping," Marcella said, tucking her thin brown hair behind her ears, which she always did when she was nervous. "I really wasn't. I didn't hear anything."

"Did you need me for something?" I asked.

Nervous smile. "Mr. Finch would like to see you in his office."

"I'll be right there," I said, and she darted off in her ridiculously high heels.

"Am I being fired?" I whispered to Shelley. "Could you get fired for being a murder suspect? You probably could."

Your discrimination lawsuit has been thrown out, Miss Foote. If your boss believes you might kill the entire staff, he may fire you.

"Don't worry," Shelley said. "Maybe he's just going to give you the rest of the week off until this crazy circus dies down. Come on, Abs, he's known you for three years. There's no way he thinks you could have killed anyone."

"My brother-in-law has known me for four years and thinks I not only killed one person but tried to kill two more."

She squeezed my hand. "Tell me everything Finch says."

I stood up. "Lunch today?"

"You're a sweetie," she said. Shelley and Baxter had lunch together every day except Fridays, when he had a staff meeting, and now that they'd broken up, she would probably be feeling very weird come noontime. She'd arrived a half hour late today, a little red eyed from crying. She and Baxter had broken up two days ago because she wouldn't move in without a ring, and he wouldn't offer a ring without a trial run. "But stop worrying about me. I'll be fine. Baxter and I will be back together by next week. Maybe. If he coughs up a diamond." She sighed. "I'd even take a cubic zirconia." Her eyes teared up again. "But forget my stupid love life," she said, dabbing under her eyes. "Just go see what Finch wants. And report back. Then we'll deal with your dumb brother-in-law. I'm sure if you talk to your sister, she'll get her husband to undo the order of protection."

I squeezed her hand. I might be a murder suspect, but at least I had friends.

I headed down to Finch's corner office. Cutting

through the kitchenette, I almost knocked into our contracts manager.

"I am so, so, so, so sorry!" he said. "I do hope you're all right."

This was the same man who had literally barked at me last week for taking the last of the awful office coffee. *I assume you'll be making a new pot!*

"Did you want a fresh cup of coffee?" he asked. "I'd be happy to make some. My turn!"

Yeah, right.

I ignored him and continued on to Finch's office.

I knocked and walked in. "You wanted to see me?"

"Ah, there you are!" he said in his proudest, most fatherly tone. "Yes, indeedy, I did. Why don't you have a seat? Would you like Marcella to bring you a cup of coffee? A scone from the bakery downstairs?"

"Yes, actually, I would," I said. I might as well milk this for all it was worth—at Marcella's expense.

He buzzed her with my order. "Abby," he said, turning back to me, "I have good news. You're being promoted to associate editor."

My heart leaped. I'd only been after this promotion for the past year. Working overtime, asking directly. I'd gotten the "just keep doing what you're doing" speech.

"You've done fine work here for the past three years," Finch said. "You've been a real go-getter, and you're being rewarded for your hard work and dedication to the *Maine Life* magazine organization. Of course, you'll receive a *ten* percent raise—that's a bit more than our usual promotion raises, but you deserve it!"

Hey, wait a minute. Was I promoted? Or was Finch just protecting himself and his staff from a murderer? The last time I'd asked for more meaningful reporting assignments, Finch had sent me to "hang around" outside Stephen King's mansion in Bangor in February without informing me that the famous author and Maine resident wisely wintered in Florida.

My promotion was more protection for Finch and his staff. I had no doubt. Still, a promotion was a promotion. "Thanks, Gray. I couldn't be happier. Will I be assigned a particular area of the magazine to cover?"

"Well, I'd actually like you to build the Best Of column into a real feature," he said. "And I'd like to start off your increased coverage by sending you on an all-expenses-paid trip to a wonderful locale to do your research. Leave in the morning. Spend the entire weekend."

Oh, please tell me I'm going to Camden, I thought. I loved Camden. Or maybe Augusta, the capital. Moosehead Lake? I'd go anywhere to get away from Portland this weekend. Away from Ben and his questions. Away from my family, who clearly thought I was capable of murder.

Don't leave town…

"Where am I headed?" I asked. Wherever it was, I'd just clear it with Ben. He could investigate me without me, couldn't he? I had a cell phone. And a laptop with e-mail. He could e-mail me questions like *I'll ask you again—did you try to kill Riley Witherspoon by letting a pit bull loose in his house?* And I could type back a simple *I did not.*

He smiled. "Moose City! Pack your bags ASAP, since it's a long drive. Marcella's booked you a lovely room at an inn for a few days."

I frowned. A few days in Moose City—practically the farthest north you could go and still be in the United States. The Moose part applied, as Moose City was eighty percent moose, twenty percent people. It was the city part that was misleading. Not too many people needed to know where you could get the best manicure or the best custard in Moose City.

Fishy. Very fishy.

"Um, Mr. Gray, I think I might have to clear this with Detective Orr," I said. "I was told not to leave town. In case he needs my help in solving Ted Puck's murder."

"Oh, don't you worry your head about that," he said. "I've already cleared it with the police."

Chapter 9

A five-hour drive gave me a lot of time to think. Namely of why. Why, why, why was someone after my ex-boyfriends? If I looked at it that way, Mary-Kate Darling looked a lot less guilty and more like someone pissed off at the world for taking her fiancé.

Fact A: Tom Greer broke up with me via e-mail. The next day he was pushed in front of a truck.

Fact B: Riley Witherspoon broke up with me via telephone. Two days later a pit bull snacked on his leg.

Fact C: Ted Puck broke up with me— Hey, wait a minute. Ted hadn't broken up with me; he'd cheated on me and had gotten caught. He'd said he was going to "tell me anyway," but would he have? If he'd strung along me and Twinkle and Ariella, maybe he would have strung along me, them and Mary-Kate. Maybe he'd figured kinky wouldn't last past a month.

Interesting. Ted hadn't broken up with me. Not the way Riley and Tom had. What Ted had done was pull a Charlie Heath—he'd gone the passive-aggressive route and let his actions engineer the breakup for him.

And Charlie Heath was (a) still alive and (b) apparently not the victim of foul play, or I would have heard about it.

But I'd been crazy about Ted and Charlie and only in serious like with Riley and Tom. Why wait six months, till Ted was engaged, to go after him? Hopefully Charlie wasn't planning on proposing to anyone.

I practically stopped short, which wasn't a problem because there was no one behind me and hadn't been for thirty miles. I pulled over to think. Would the killer go after Charlie if he got engaged? Was Henry Fiddler saved because he'd pulled a Charlie/Ted and let his actions do the dumping? Actually, I had to amend that. Henry hadn't broken up with me so much as he'd ditched me and taken off so he wouldn't have to go to the bris. I hadn't called him to tell him he was a wussy superjerk and that we were *through;* he hadn't called me to tell me that since I probably hated his guts anyway, we might as well call it quits. We just both assumed correctly.

I rolled my eyes at myself and pulled back onto the road. As if the killer was thinking this hard? Analyzing my breakups down to the boring details? Doubtful.

Which led me back to who. And why. If I could figure out the why, maybe it would lead me to the who. Or maybe if I figured out the who, I could just ask him or her the why and call it a day.

I would have liked to call it a day right now. Welcome To Moose City greeted me via a green sign on the side of the road. There was nothing *but* road. And trees. I wouldn't mind seeing a moose. Not in front of my car, of course.

Ah. There—up ahead was another sign. Moose City Center. I turned off the highway and followed a curve for a mile and came upon a village square, which looked very quaint. *Moose City Boulevard, make left,* said Marcella's directions to my bed-and-breakfast, which was called Fowler's Inn. Marcella had chosen well (*of course* she had). The inn was a gorgeous antique farmhouse in the middle of the village, which was as quaint as New England villages came. There was a clapboard general store and several eateries, which catered to skiers and snowmobilers. (Moose City was well-known for its miles of trails, both beginner and advanced.)

I pulled into the parking area next to the big red barn and lugged my suitcase up the porch steps. I was so looking forward to my cozy room, my heavy-down-comforter-covered king-size bed, a hot bubble bath and a good night's sleep—not that I expected *that*.

A jangling bell overhead announced my arrival, and I was immediately welcomed to the inn and Moose City by the proprietors, a fiftyish couple who introduced themselves as the Fowlers, Ed and Mary-Jane. Ed took my suitcase, and they led me to a good-sized room with wide plank floors, quilts on the walls, a thick down comforter on the bed and a private bathroom with radiant-heat floors. No need for the Winnie the Pooh slippers. On the bedside table was a plate of chocolate chip cookies and a mug, with a selection of teas and a note: "Hot water available in common room at all times."

I unpacked and sifted through the stack of brochures next to the cookies. Marcella had been instructed not to tell the Fowlers that I was there on business as Best Of editor. Otherwise, the small town of Moose City would roll out the red carpet when they saw me coming, and that would skew the results. I'd done some research online before I left and I had a few places on my to-visit list, but I figured I'd find most of the establishments to visit by walking through the village. There were at least three restaurants, each of which served breakfast, lunch and dinner. I could easily hit them all between today and Sunday morning. There were also two coffee bars, a few shops that sold mostly ski gear, two bakeries, three hair salons, three bookstores, four antique stores and two fortune-tellers.

Ha! I could have my fortune told complements of *Maine Life* magazine. The one that said my future didn't involve prison would be declared Best.

I was about to hit the common room with my brochures and a tea bag when there was a knock at my door.

"Abby, it's Benjamin Orr."

Oh, for God's sake. He had to be kidding.

I opened the door, and there was Ben's gorgeous face. "You trailed me to Moose City? You really do think I'm guilty, don't you?"

"I'm just doing my job, Abby. I was wondering if you'd like to have dinner with me, since I'm here and you're here and you need to find the best steak in Moose City."

Charming. I had to remember that.

"Actually, for my first meal I was planning to hunt down the best *moose* steak in Moose City," I said. "You do like moose, don't you?"

That famous unreadable expression failed him for just a moment, then he broke into a smile. "You're good. I'll have to remember that."

We thought alike.

The plan was to meet in the common room in half an hour. The moment the door closed between us, I tore through the closet and chest of drawers. I'd once read in a women's magazine that a seasoned traveler always packed for every occasion, even if she was headed to snow country in the middle—or should I say *top*—of nowhere. I'd brought mostly warm-weather clothes—heavy jeans and heavy sweaters—but also my black wrap dress and my knee-high boots, one pair of good black pants, one skirt (flippy and red) and one slightly low-cut cashmere-esque black sweater.

I was deciding between my white everyday bra and my black push-up when a little something called reality grabbed me by the shoulders. I stared at myself in the mirror.

This was *not* a date.

★ ★ ★

I opted for the *Maine Life* magazine dress code: a combination of business casual meets dress-down Friday. Black boot-cut pants and the slightly low-cut black sweater. I was glad I didn't go the appropriate-for-Moose City route; Ben was wearing nice pants, dark gray, and a gray sweater. I smelled just a hint of aftershave.

"You look nice," he said, standing up.

This is not a date. This is not a date. This is not a date. "You, too," I said.

"Ready?" he asked.

The Fowlers came out of the dining room and burst into smiles at the sight of us.

"Well, isn't that nice!" Mary-Jane said, her hand over her heart. She leaned forward and whispered, "Separate rooms. You don't see a lot of that nowadays."

Ed nodded and smiled his appreciation, as well. "You two enjoy yourselves," he said, holding open the door. "It's a cold one."

It was. The moment we stepped outside, a blast of cold air sneaked inside my down coat. A temperature gauge attached to a tree in front of the inn read twenty-one degrees. Ben and I pulled on our gloves and zipped up our coats to the chin.

"So I guess you didn't inform our kind hosts that you're a big-city detective and I'm a murder suspect," I said.

"There's no need. None of your exes live around here. I checked."

"You're very thorough," I said.

"I have to be."

"So I assume you checked out whether or not Ted was dating anyone else when he was dating me?"

"I did."

"And?"

"And—" He stopped walking. "Are you sure you want to know? You might not like what you hear, Abby."

"Oh, I love hearing that I'm a suspect for murder—and attempted murder."

"Gotcha," he said, and resumed walking. "He was dating two other women. He went out with both only a few times and ended the relationship, one by phone, the other in person, a couple of weeks before he met Mary-Kate."

"Why didn't he end things with me?" I wondered aloud.

"Maybe he wasn't sure he wanted to," Ben said.

"Then he wouldn't have cheated on me at my party. He wanted out. He wanted to get caught."

Ben nodded. "Sounds like it."

"I hate dating."

He smiled. "Everyone does."

"Including you?" I asked.

He pointed at a tree a few feet in front of us. "Is that white pine?" He studied the bark intently.

"You could just say no comment, you know."

"No comment," he said, shooting me a smile.

I raised an eyebrow at him. "Oh, I see. This is a one-sided question-and-answer session."

"That's right."

At least he was reminding me—often—that this definitely was not a date.

This is not a date. This is not a date. This is not a date.

Benjamin Orr is not a guy. He's a cop. A detective who trailed you five hours away!

"So about Twinkle and Ariella," I said as we crossed the street. "I assume they had airtight alibis."

"Abby, I can't discuss the case with you."

"Well, if you're here and not there, then I assume they did have airtight alibis."

"I'll tell you what they didn't have," he said. "They didn't have two other ex-boyfriends who were the victims of attempted murder."

There wasn't much I could say to that.

Actually, there was! "Unless I'm being framed!"

"Framed backward?" he asked. "Push one ex in front of a truck that may or may not kill him. Send a pit bull to attack another ex, who may or may not end up dead. Yet shoot, at point-blank range, Ted Puck, who broke up with you six months ago, seemingly because he got engaged to another woman. It doesn't add up to a frame job, Abby."

"It also doesn't add up to me," I said. "I mean, I know it looks like I had something to do with it all, as they were all my former boyfriends. But I had nothing to do with any of it!"

"We're investigating all leads, Abby. That is what I can tell you."

"But I'm your biggest. I have to be if I've moved up from person of interest to prime suspect. If my family and co-workers are scared to death of me. You've apparently spoken to everyone I ever walked past. Did you really have to talk to the girl who tormented me in elementary school? Did you know she e-mailed me an apology, lest I track her down and make her pay for calling me beanpole?"

He eyed me. "You filled out nicely."

I sucked in a breath. That was flirting. That was pure, one hundred percent flirting!

"Just a statement of fact," he said. "No one could call you a beanpole now. At the Portland police station, body type is crucial in ID'ing perps and/or victims."

Oh. So maybe he wasn't flirting.

Whatever he was or wasn't doing, I was about to tell him, again, that he was wasting his time—that I didn't kill or try to kill anyone—but for just the moment I wanted to fantasize that Benjamin Orr was mine. That we were a couple away for a long weekend. That a dream I'd had at sixteen had come true. That he *was* flirting.

"Tonight's restaurant is the Moose City Tavern," I told Ben as we continued down Moose City Boulevard. "It's just a few doors away. Here it is," I said, peering in the front door. "Hey, it's pretty crowded."

The hostess led us to a candlelit table by a window. Too romantic.

Within minutes we had menus, had ordered and our soup and salads were served.

"This is not the best Caesar salad in Moose City," I whispered to Ben. "They forgot the grating of Parmesan cheese. And the chef was stingy with the croutons."

"The clam chowder's delicious," he said, holding up a spoonful to me.

He surprised me. I leaned forward and took it with my mouth, aware that he was watching me.

"Mmm. You're right. That is good. Thick and flavorful. One more spoonful to be sure I can declare it the best?"

He smiled and fed me again.

"Yes, that is definitely in the running for best," I said, taking my own mini notebook out of my purse and jotting down some thoughts on the soup. "You're not the only one with a notebook, you know."

Our entrées arrived. For Ben, the filet mignon. For me, swordfish.

"Not bad," Ben said. He forked a piece for me and held it up.

"Mmm again," I said. "That's actually delicious."

"I wouldn't call it the best, though," he said. "And I know steak."

I smiled. "You'll be my judge, then." I glanced up at him, my appetite gone. In a way, he *was* my judge.

"I'd love a bite of the swordfish," he said.

I forked a piece for him and he took it with his mouth. I couldn't take my eyes off his lips.

"Really good," he said. "So tell me, Abby Foote, if you were the answer to a Best Of, what would it be?"

I glanced at him. "I have no idea."

"Sure you do. Best cook? Best practical joker?"

"I'm not a practical joker," I said, realizing that he was slyly investigating me.

"You have a sarcastic streak, though," he said. "Unless what you said to your brother-in-law wasn't meant to be sarcastic."

"It was," I said.

"Were you upset that you weren't named god-mother?" he asked.

I shrugged. "I can understand why they wouldn't name a single person godmother."

"But were you upset?" he repeated.

"A little, I guess. I might have been more upset if they'd named Opal godmother. But they chose Oliver's married sister."

"Do you want children?" he asked.

Did he really want to know? Or was he fishing for my feelings on marriage and motherhood to determine if my jealous desperation for a husband and baby led me to kill the guy who chose someone else to marry and procreate with?

Repeat mantra: *This is not a date.* Of course he was fishing.

"I really am your prime suspect, aren't I?" I said, poking at my rice, my appetite gone.

"That's a good segue into why I did follow you here, Abby. Yes, it's to keep close tabs on you, but there is a possibility that someone else killed Ted and tried to kill Riley and Tom. And you're the only person who can help me figure out who that person is."

I perked up. "I'd be very happy to help you. But how?"

"If it's not you, Abby, it's someone you know. Well."

"Someone I know?" I repeated. "Why would someone I know—*well*—kill Ted or try to hurt Riley or Tom?"

"Because they hurt you," he said.

"I don't know about that theory, Ben. I racked my brain during the five-hour drive up here trying to figure out why someone would be going after my exes. And who. But first of all, no one I know is capable of it. Second of all, no one would—" I stopped. "Forget it."

He paused, forkful of steak midway to his mouth. "No one would what?"

I took a deep breath. "I can't imagine who in my life would murder my ex-boyfriends on my behalf."

"Why?" he asked. "Don't your friends and family love you?"

"I guess," I said. "But..."

He paused again. "Not enough to kill for you?"

Okay, how weird was this conversation. I shrugged.

"Well, that leaves you, right?" he said. "But if it wasn't you, give my theory some thought. Think about where you were those nights that Ted was killed. When Tom was pushed in front of that truck. When a vicious pit bull was let loose in Riley's house. Think about where your family and friends were. And who might have slipped away from the engagement party and Veronica's birthday party."

"I don't want to," I said. "This is crazy. My friends and family aren't lunatics!"

"Someone is a cold-blooded murderer, Abby. And it all points to you or someone who cares about you in a warped way."

I pushed my plate aside and gulped my Diet Coke. "I don't know what to say. I can't help you."

"I'm just asking you to think about it, Abby," he said. "Just think."

"I'd rather think about Mary-Kate Darling and her connection to Mary-Katherine Mulch," I said.

"What?"

I explained what Ted's cousin had told me about Mary-Kate being from Barmouth and about my investigation.

"Your investigation of a yearbook?" he said, smiling. "Abby. Please, don't waste your time. She had no motive. And her opportunity, based on what the salesclerk said about when she left and when he noticed she returned, was slight."

"So you spoke to the salesclerk?" I asked, feeling hopeful for the first time.

"I speak to everyone, Abby. I'm a detective."

"So she *could* be a suspect? I just really, really don't want to be the only one."

He laughed, and I smiled. He had great teeth. Long and white and sparkly.

"I really need you to think about friends and family, Abby. Give it some thought tonight, okay?"

"Okay," I said, glum again.

I didn't give it a single thought. Because it was ludicrous. Yeah, I could just see Opal shooting Ted because he (a) broke up with me six months ago and (b) got engaged to someone else.

Because it was late and Ben and I were both exhausted, we headed back to the inn for a cup of tea and those cookies. We settled in the common room and had it to ourselves. He looked so out of place among the overstuffed floral blue love seats and chintzy pillows.

I sat in the big recliner adjacent to his love seat and waited for the tea to steep.

"Did you give it some thought on the walk home?" he asked. "You were so quiet, I figured you had."

I shook my head. "I'll tell you what I did give some thought to. To the disconnect between the Riley/Tom attempted murders and the murder of Ted. Riley and Tom were attacked in the days immediately following our breakup. Ted was killed six months later. And only seemingly because of his engagement announcement. Why go after Riley and Tom right away, but not Ted?"

"Maybe the killer tried and failed," Ben said, handing me two packets of Sweet'n Low and a nondairy creamer. "Maybe he or she went the push-him-in-front-of-a-truck route, but nothing worked. So then the engagement announcement comes out, and the killer gets furious and decides to make sure Ted is killed. By shooting him."

"You sure do a lot of surmising," I said. "Nothing is concrete."

"Nope," he agreed. "It's not like we can ask Ted if he had any close calls last July when you first broke up. Nothing was reported, though." He eyed me. "We're thorough, Abby."

"I'll say."

He smiled and sipped his tea.

"But don't you think that's strange?" I said. "Not that you're thorough—I mean, about Ted. Why would the killer wait six months to go for the kill? Why not keep trying immediately after he broke up with me, like the Riley and Tom attempts?"

Ben glanced at me. "Maybe because you loved him."

"Huh?"

"You loved him, he broke your heart," Ben said. "If he'd been murdered right after breaking your heart, you'd only be more heartbroken. Devastated. The killer waited until you didn't love him. Until you started dating again."

"That's pretty weird," I said. "That makes it sound like the killer cares about me."

He nodded. "Which is why I want you to think about people in your life, Abby."

"Ben, I could sit here and say name after name of my friends and family. Not one is a killer."

"Don't you think it's interesting that the killer went after Riley and Tom right away? They dared to hurt you, and someone you know wanted to make them pay for it. Right away. It's not like you'd be devastated by their deaths—you weren't in love with either of them, and the killer knew that."

"What I'd like to know is how *you* know that."

He glanced up at me. "Police work."

"So people in my life, my friends and family, just sat down and told you everything you ever wanted to know about me?"

He nodded.

"Unbelievable. Flash a badge and people just talk?"

"Basically," he said.

"So if it *is* someone I know, then you already made contact with the killer. It's someone in that little notebook of yours."

"If *you're* not the killer, then yes, that's right."

"No, that's *scary.*" I'd had enough. I didn't want to think about this. I didn't want to talk about it. "Can we change the subject?"

"To?" he asked.

I shrugged.

"Why don't we just have our tea and see if there's anything good on TV," he said.

"Now you're talking," I said, biting into a cookie. Yum. Homemade.

We watched a reality-TV show with half-naked celebrities, and I must have fallen asleep because the next thing I knew, he was scooping me up in his arms. Strong arms. My head was resting on his collarbone. He smelled like Ivory soap. I could so easily just start kissing his neck. Well, his sweater.

I kept my eyes closed. He carried me to my room, fished inside my purse for the key (I'd have to discuss that with him tomorrow) and brought me to my bed. He laid me down, then took off my boots, which required pulling up my pants legs to unzip the knee-high zipper.

We were alone in my room in Moose City. I could pull him down on top of me and drive him crazy with lust (*if, if, if* he was remotely physically attracted to me). If he went for it, it would mean he knew I wasn't guilty. If he didn't, then he was either a good cop or he believed I was a cold-blooded murderer—or had friends who were.

Eyes closed, I reached up and felt for his hand and tugged. He held my hand for just a moment, then gently released it and pulled the blanket over me.

"Night, Abby," he whispered before closing the door behind him.

Okay, so maybe he was just a good cop.

Chapter 10

I must have drifted off right in the middle of my fantasy about Ben, because the sun was now streaming into my room through the curtains. I glanced at the clock on the bedside table—7:00 a.m. I stretched in the comfy bed—without a doubt the most comfy in Moose City (that I'd managed to sleep at all was a testament to that)—wondering what Ben was doing. He was right beyond the wall, maybe naked in bed. Or naked in the shower.

I wanted to see his face so badly that I popped out of bed, despite how tired I was. After a fast shower, a little too long with a blow-dryer and "natural" makeup and the most flattering of my superwarm clothes, I knocked on Ben's door. It was just after eight.

"Looking for me?" he called.

I whirled around. He was sitting in the common room, reading *The Moose City Marveler,* a muffin and coffee on the side table next to him. He wore jeans and a dark green Shetland sweater, a hint of white T-shirt peeking out.

"I don't need to try another to know this is the best," he said. "Corn."

"You should have saved your appetite," I said, leaning against the wall. "Breakfast is on Finch. He likes all his Best Of columns to include scrambled eggs and bacon and coffee. I was planning to test out that greasy spoon across the street from where we ate dinner last night. Greasy spoons make the best breakfast."

"I agree," he said. "And I'm ravenous, actually," he added, staring at me.

My mouth went dry. Is he flirting? Am I reading into everything he says and does because I am so attracted to him that I might burst into a million pieces if I don't have him soon?

Ha. Like I would. Maybe I would burst into a million pieces just as I was being arrested. That would work just fine.

He grabbed his coat. "I'm ready if you are."

"You know, I could probably complain to the authorities that I'm being harassed," I pointed out, pulling on my gloves.

"I could trail you surreptitiously, if you prefer," he said. He stood up and walked toward me. He was so tall. So...*hot*—even hotter than he'd been in high school.

Senior year, Jolie had been nuts over a tortured-poet type who walked around with the anarchy symbol in white spray paint on his black leather jacket. She'd been crazy about him for four years, but he mooned over tortured-artist type girls, and Jolie was the epitome of perky—a cheerleader with a perpetual smile. Anyway, a few years ago we ran into the guy at the mall. He was practically bald, except around the ears, had a beer belly and was wearing the same leather jacket. Jolie had been so disappointed that her fantasy was ruined forever. She'd held all other guys up to how she felt about James Cole, who'd never looked once at her.

With Ben, on the other hand, the reality was even better than the fantasy. Except about the suspecting me of murder part, of course. He'd taken complete control of my heart without saying a single word to me, something you could only get away with in high school. And now that he was saying many words to me, they were mostly very nice. He was as attractive inside as he was outside.

Demetria's Diner was bustling with the snowboarding crowd. We had to wait ten minutes for a table, which was a good sign, since there were several other places to eat breakfast. My stomach started rumbling just as a waitress curled her finger at us and pointed at a booth in the back.

Ben ordered a Swiss cheese omelet and French toast. I went for the scrambled eggs and bacon. As we awaited our order, I took out my brochures.

"Hey, look at this—not one but two fortune-tellers here in Moose City. I'd love to get my fortune told."

"Can I listen in?" he asked as the waitress delivered more plates than we had room for.

"So you put stock in five-dollar palm readers?" I asked him once she left and promised to come back with more coffee.

"I put stock in listening" was his answer.

"I get to listen to your reading, too, then," I said. "That's the deal."

He laughed. "Fine with me."

We dug in to our breakfast, declaring the eggs scrumptious, the home fries even better and the Swiss cheese omelet needing better Swiss. The coffee was so-so. I made my notes, and then we were off to Allegra's House of Fortune, which, from the little picture on the brochure, was a storefront at the other end of the village.

It was actually the store*back* of Allegra's Antiques, a small shop full of items I wanted. Like an old cherry secretary desk. A floor lamp that looked as if it had come from a twenties-era bordello. A very old snow globe of a long-ago Moose City. I turned it over and gave it a little shake, and it snowed over Moose City. A glance at the price tag on the bottom told me it was mine—just five bucks. And there was a gorgeous baby-blue cradle that Olivia would love. I turned over the price tag. Seventy dollars. With the tiny raise that went with my pseudo-promotion, I *could* buy it. Whether I could give it to her was another story. I had no idea if she'd let me near her.

"Can I help you?" asked a woman.

"We're interested in having our fortunes told," I said, holding up the brochure. "I'd also like to buy that snow globe," I added, pointing. "And the blue cradle."

Once I was all paid up at the cash register, the woman eyed me and Ben for a long moment. Then she clapped twice. "Sarah, come take over the store for a little while." A young woman appeared from behind the cash register. "Follow me," she said to us.

She led us through a doorway with a small sign: Allegra's House Of Fortune. The room was all fortune-teller. Billowy white material was draped from the ceilings. Red velvet cushions lined a bench in front of a small square table draped with black lace.

"That will be fifteen dollars each," she said, her hand out.

I paid her, and she gestured toward the bench. "Please, sit. Unless you would like separate fortunes. I'll be back in a moment."

She returned in a getup, which didn't have the same effect once you'd already seen her in a fleece sweatshirt. Her short dark hair was now covered by a bright red turban. She wore a long multicolored robe. Each finger had a large-stoned ring. And her lipstick was as bright as her turban.

"I am Madame Allegra," she said. "Welcome to the House of Fortune." She sat down across from us. "I will read you first," she said to me. She closed her eyes and held out her hands. I reached over, and she held my hands very gently, then squeezed. She took an exaggerated breath, then rolled her head on her shoulders the way we had to do during stretch time in high school gym class. She let go of my hands and opened her eyes. "You are conflicted," she said. "Someone is judging you."

I turned to Ben, eyes wide. This woman was good! "Is this person right to judge me?" I asked.

"That is not for me to say" was her nonanswer. She opened her eyes wide. "You are in danger. I cannot be sure if this danger is physical or emotional. You must proceed in all aspects of your life with caution." Then she turned to Ben. She closed her eyes and reached out her hands, which he took. She said nothing for a few moments, then squeezed his hands, and slowly opened her eyes. She stared at him. "Someone close to you passed," she said. "This person wants you to know he or she is at peace. I cannot tell if it is a male or female."

I glanced at Ben; he held her gaze, but I couldn't read him. As usual.

"Ah, you are not at peace," she told him. "You do not need to be Madame Allegra to see that."

"Thanks for your time," Ben said, standing up.

Madame Allegra stood, too. "I have more to say, if you are interested."

I was interested. But Ben shook his head and ushered me out the back door.

"Ben, I—"

"What's next on your list?" he asked.

"Wasn't that uncanny?" I said. "The first thing she said was dead-on—that someone is judging me. So I assume the next thing was also—that I'm in danger."

"Of course you're in danger," he said. "You're a suspect in a homicide. That in itself is dangerous."

"Did someone close to you die?" I asked, holding my breath.

He pulled on his black leather gloves. "What's next on your agenda?"

I stared at him, wondering if he'd ever answer a question. Maybe not such a personal one. "I was just thinking that if it was true, then I'd know what she told me was true," I said.

But I knew it was. Someone close to him *had* died. And it was enough to cut short the half hour with Madame Allegra.

"I mean, if my life is in danger," I added, "I should take steps to protect myself."

"Why do you think I'm here, Abby," he said. Statement. Not a question.

Huh. I stopped walking and stared at him. "I thought you were here to investigate me. Follow me. See if I leave clues. See if I say anything incriminating. See if I kill anyone."

He nodded. "All that—*and* to protect you, too. Because if it's not you, Abby, then it *is* someone you know. Or someone who knows you."

"I am looking directly into your eyes and telling you it's not me."

He smiled. "That doesn't work on cops."

"Yeah, I guess it wouldn't," I said. "Shall we continue on to Pammy Grunt, palm reader?"

"Pammy Grunt?" he repeated, smiling. "That doesn't sound very fortune-tellery."

I laughed. "She's probably even more on the money than Madame Allegra."

She wasn't. Pammy Grunt looked all of nineteen. Her "shop" was one of the small round tables at the end of a delicious-smelling bakery owned by her parents. With the exchange of five dollars apiece—she was much cheaper than Madame Allegra—we sat down across from her. No change of dress. No jewelry.

"Okay, so can you give me something of yours?" Pammy asked. "I need to obtain your aura, then I'll read your palm."

I was about to hand her my new snow globe, then realized it wouldn't really have my aura, and I didn't want my reading mixed with a bunch of strangers who'd previously owned it. I handed her one of my gloves. She closed her eyes and squeezed the glove, then brought it up to her nose and inhaled. Good thing I hadn't dropped it in the dog poop I'd sidestepped down the street. She took my hand and stared at it, then released it so fast I knocked my knuckles on the table.

"Someone on the other side is trying to connect," she told me.

"Is it my mother?" Ben interrupted. "Julia Johnson?"

Pammy closed her eyes, then opened them slowly. "Yes! She said her name was Julia and that she loves you very much. There was no pain."

Ben smiled. "I'm so glad to hear that. Well, we got our money's worth," he said, standing up. "Coming, dear?"

Huh? I followed him out. "Now can I ask questions?"

He rolled his eyes. "My mother is alive and well and named Gertrude."

"So she's not the best fortune-teller in Moose City," I said.

"No, she's definitely not. The other one isn't too shabby, though. Perhaps I should go ask Madame Allegra if you left anyone off your boyfriend list. If you did, there could potentially be another victim out there."

Aha. So someone close to him *had* died if he was putting stock in what Madame Allegra had said to me. I wanted to know who. I wanted to know everything about him. I wanted to hug him, feel those arms around me.

"Three victims are enough, thanks," I said.

"Could you have left off anyone? Even a one-night stand? A date who never called again? Anyone who hurt you, no matter how insignificant the relationship or lack thereof?"

"Nope," I said. "No one. Shall we move on to the best movie-theater popcorn in Moose City, even though there's only one theater? Couldn't you go for a movie? A little removal from reality for a couple of hours?"

He stared at me. "Abby, I know this is hard. But remember, if you didn't kill Ted, it's very likely that someone you know did. So I need to know if there could be anyone else that you might have forgotten to include. That someone could be a witness."

"You mean a victim," I said.

"A victim who's now a witness," he corrected.

I glanced up Moose City Boulevard, at the beautiful, white powdery snow on the rooftops, on the bare branches of the trees. What I wouldn't give for that movie, to sit next to Ben and laugh at a romantic comedy for a couple of hours, to share popcorn, to feel for just a little while that I was away for a romantic weekend with the guy of my dreams.

"Abby?" he asked. "There is someone, isn't there? Someone who hurt you?"

I took a deep breath. "There is one guy who broke my heart, unintentionally. I didn't put him on the list because we never dated. Not once. I was more secretly enamored."

He pulled out his little spiral notebook. "What's his name?"

"Benjamin Orr."

He glanced up and snapped the notebook closed. "Ah. I didn't know."

"If you hadn't moved away at the end of junior year, I might have just thrown myself at you just so you'd know I was alive," I said like an idiot. But that had been my big plan.

"Do you know why my family moved?" he asked as we continued walking.

I shrugged. "Your dad got a job in Massachusetts?"

He shook his head and gestured at Moose City Coffee and Cake, and I nodded. We headed in and sat down at a love seat by the window. Ben went up to the counter to order two coffees. At the condiments table, I noticed he added just the right of amount of milk and two Sweet'n Low. Just the way I liked it. He really did watch everything I did.

He sat down next to me and sipped his coffee. "I had a kid brother. He was killed by gunfire meant for one drug dealer from another. Low-level dealers. A turf war. My brother was caught in the crossfire. He was eleven years old. And a great kid."

I had to bite my lip not to burst into tears. "Oh, God, Ben, I'm so sorry."

He glanced down at his coffee. "I try not to talk about it or about him at all because it blindsides me. If I'm thinking about Joey, I can't think at all."

I wanted to touch him so badly, to just take his hand, but I couldn't. "So that's why the captain of everything isn't a neurosurgeon or an investment banker. You became a cop because of your brother. Joey."

He nodded. "Actually, I wanted to become a rocket scientist. Really. For NASA. My parents tried to convince me to at least go for FBI, but I wanted to be a cop on the streets of Portland. I wanted to be where I could potentially save another kid from crossfire."

"Was your brother's killer found?" I asked.

He nodded. "He's still in prison. He'll be there for a long time."

We sat there for a while in silence, and then Ben said, "I wish I'd known you in high school. I didn't have a lot of friends back then, despite being captain of everything, as you called it. I kept to myself then, like now. I would have liked to have you as a friend."

I smiled and reached across the table to squeeze his hand. He squeezed back.

We spent the afternoon in various shops and businesses. Best Hat Shop in Moose City was Hatfield's Hats, wall-to-wall hats of every kind imaginable. I bought a cowboy hat, something I've always wanted. Ben bought a Boston Red Sox cap, even though he said had four already. Best Place To Kiss was a tiny snow-covered garden in the park, where someone had actually carved a heart-shaped bench out of wood. We came upon two teenagers making out and were so charmed we didn't even realize we were staring until the guy called out, "Pervs!"

We laughed and continued on down Moose City Boulevard, stopping in here, trying on there, sipping hot chocolate. Teens on the street, selling hot chocolate out of thermoses to raise money for their school team's uniforms, had the best hot chocolate, hands down. It was Swiss Miss with mini marshmallows, but it was heaven.

In just one full day I'd amassed a list of fifteen Best Ofs. Which meant there was really no reason to stay past tomorrow morning. But I didn't want to go home. I wanted to stay here forever. With Ben.

We were in Moose City's Moose Memorabilia, a tiny
store packed with everything moose, from books on
moose to moose heads to moose-stamped pencil holders
to mugs with every kind of moose imaginable. I was mar-
veling over yet another snow globe, two moose head-to-
head, when Ben took my other hand and held it. I sucked
in my breath and put down the snow globe.

"Abby," he said. "I want you know something. It's important that I tell you this. I should have said it much earlier."

*Tell me. Tell me. Tell me. You love me, too. You're crazy about
me. You can't wait for this all to blow over so that we can make
mad passionate love on that heart-shaped bench in the Best Place
To Kiss in Moose City.*

He led me to the back of the store and looked into my
eyes. "Abby, if you confess now, I can probably work out
something with the prosecutor."

I gasped. I am not a gasper, but I stood there and gasped
not once, but twice. My puffy down coat, which I'd taken
off in the warm store, just dropped out of my hands, as
did my mini tote bag. I felt as if I would fall over at any
moment, too.

I am an idiot. I am an idiot. I am an idiot. Tears pricked
the backs of my eyes. "Ben, much as I'd like to help you
out. I can't confess to something I *didn't do.*"

And then I ran.

I was halfway back to the inn and out of breath when
I heard him call, "Abby, wait, please."

I turned around. He jogged toward me, carrying my coat and bag.

"Abby, it's sixteen degrees," he said. "I think you need this." He held up my coat and helped me into it. He stood so close to me, never taking those dark, dark eyes off me as he zipped up the long, puffy jacket.

Take it back, I wanted to scream. *Take it all back so I can just fling myself into your arms and you can make this whole nightmare go away.*

"I didn't mean to offend you," he said.

"I know," I snapped. "You're just doing your job."

He stopped and put his hand on my arm. "Abby, there's nothing truer than that."

"No, there is," I said. "I didn't kill Ted. There's nothing truer than *that.*"

And then I ran inside and locked the door to my room behind me.

I ignored his knocks. I'd watched enough *Law & Order* to know that I didn't *have* to talk to him. Every twenty minutes he'd knock and say, "Abby? Let's talk."

At his fourth attempt, I surprised him by opening the door, dressed and ready to go, my notebook and brochures at the ready. "There is nothing to talk about, Ben. You are wasting your time in such a monumental way. You could be back in Portland going after a killer."

Two heads popped out of the common room and stared at us. Ben gestured to my room, and we went inside.

I sat on my bed. He leaned against the door.

"It's not a waste of my time, Abby. As I've said, if it wasn't you, it's very likely someone who cares about you and has a very warped way of showing it. I'm going to need you to work on a list of possibles when we get back to Portland."

I took a deep breath. "No one I know is capable of murder, Ben. That's what it comes down to."

"Do you know how many times I've been surprised by people?" he asked.

"People you know? Your closest friends? Your relatives?"

He walked over to the bed and sat down next to me. "A few months after my brother died, my mother had a complete breakdown. She left her husband, me, her entire life, and moved to a commune. She's still there. Then again, maybe that's not so surprising. I have no idea what it's like to lose a child."

"I'm so sorry, Ben," I said. "You know what it's like to lose a brother."

"I guess you know something about a parent just up and leaving, too."

Now, there was something that wasn't surprising. I had no doubt that by now Ben knew every part of every major facet of my life. "I was two days old when my father left." I shook my head. "I can't even begin to imagine how my mother felt, how she coped."

He glanced at me. "She had you."

"Oh, I'm sure a two-day-old was a big comfort," I

said. "Trust me, I see how hard Olivia works. Totally hormonal, not a second to herself, nervous wreck about caring for a newborn."

"No, I mean, that's what your mother said. I asked her how she coped. And she said, 'I had Abby. I had Abby, and that was like having the world.'"

"She really said that?" I asked, my heart flipping. "That's really, really nice." And definitely surprising. My mother was loving, but my father's betrayal had changed her—or so people who'd known her before and after had said—and she'd moved down to Florida the second I graduated from high school. She was remarried now and had her own life.

Ben nodded. "She really said that. See, even close relatives are capable of surprising you."

"I guess so," I said.

"So what's next on our agenda?" he asked. "Dinner? Do we have time for Best Place To Make Snow Angels in Moose City?"

I smiled. "Let's go."

We made our snow angels. Twice our hands and feet bumped together. The second time I didn't move my foot right away. He glanced at me with those unreadable dark, dark eyes, and then sat, holding out a hand to pull me up.

"So why don't you take the next couple of hours to yourself," he said. "I need to catch up on some phone calls anyway."

Either he trusted me or he wanted me to think he trusted me.

Regardless, my butt was freezing and I had to get up.

We headed back inside to change out of our wet clothes. The moment walls and doors were between us, I missed him.

Two hours later he knocked on the door. He looked gorgeous, as always.

"Wow," he said, eyeing me up and down. "You look incredible."

I smiled. Beaming inside, of course. "Well, I figured since it was our last night here, and it would be back to reality tomorrow, reality I don't particularly want to face, I'd get all dressed up for Moose City's finest restaurant."

At the last minute I'd changed out of my flippy skirt and sweater and gone for the black wrap dress and knee-high boots. There was a hint of cleavage. Curves. If he found me at all sexy before, he'd find me very sexy now. If I did nothing for him, then the dress would be my Magic 8 Ball and reveal all.

So far, so good.

When I picked up my coat from my bed, he took it and held it open for me. Again he was so close I would barely have to move to kiss those lips.

"Ready?" he asked.

"Definitely," I said.

We hurried to Carelli's, one of Moose City's few expensive restaurants. It was Italian, and Finch was an

Italian food freak and always liked The Best Place To Get an Old-Fashioned Bowl of Spaghetti and Sauce in his on-location columns. Carelli's didn't have spaghetti as an entrée; this was more a bizarre vegetables-and-vertical-food type establishment.

A perfect white candle flickered between us, casting shadows on Ben's face. I had the urge to reach across the table for his hand, but luckily the waiter stopped by to recite the specials and take our drinks order.

"Wine?" Ben asked.

I smiled, and he ordered the house red.

Please let this be a good sign, I said heavenward. Instead of, say, a tactic to get me to drink up and spill my guts on a snow-covered street corner. Not that there were guts to spill. Except for being madly in love with him.

Oh, hell. There it was. I was madly in love with the cop who thought me guilty of murder. Later I could tell Opal that it wasn't my fault, since there hadn't been a first date.

Do not drink more than three sips, I ordered myself. Or you will make a total buffoon of yourself.

Of course, I'd had the third sip before our salads arrived. Not the best salads in Moose City. Nor the best pasta. Ben had ordered some crazy chicken dish with layers of vegetables. He ate three bites.

"Let's get out of here and hit Fry Hut," he said, smiling. We'd passed Fry Hut four times on our route today, and there was always a long line. It was a take-out joint that served only thin-cut French fries. There were five kinds of ketchup.

We bundled up and walked the four blocks to Fry Hut, where there was a crowd of teenagers waiting. The little storefront smelled so good. It took almost twenty minutes, but we each had our white bag of fries, salted and ketchuped. We walked back to the inn, popping fries into our mouths. Best fries in Maine. Possibly the world.

"This was a very good idea," I said. "Finch appreciates good fries."

"Me, too," he said.

"Me, too."

And then we were back at the inn.

He glanced at me. "Well, I've got hours of paperwork to catch up on, so…"

So I guess this is it.

"What time are you planning to leave tomorrow?" I asked.

"Whatever time you're leaving," he said.

"You're going to be behind me the entire way, aren't you?"

He nodded. "I was behind you coming up, too. Didn't you know that?"

I should have.

"Well, good night," he said. "See you in the morning."

Don't go. Don't go. Don't go. Let's make more snow angels. Let's drink tea! I'd even talk about the case, if it meant keeping him next to me.

But he smiled and disappeared behind his door.

Chapter 11

I pulled into a restaurant to use the bathroom. So did Ben. I stopped for gas. So did Ben. I sped up to see if a cop would go past the speed limit. (The answer was yes.) I went annoyingly slowly for a stretch, just to see if he'd get frustrated and pass me.

Nope.

Every time I looked in my rearview mirror, there he was. Except once, three hours in, when I thought I'd lost him, only to find he was right beside me. In that moment, when I looked in the mirror and expected to see his car, his face barely visible behind the windshield, and seen a bright red Jeep Cherokee instead, my heart had sunk.

Foolish, foolish girl.

Finally I pulled into my parking space near my building, Ben idling a few feet away. I waved, and he waved back, and I went inside. When I looked out the window, he was peering up at me. And then he drove away.

Marcella was her new gushing self when I arrived at work on Monday morning. *How was the bed-and-breakfast? I hope to your satisfaction. We all missed you!*

Uh-huh.

The little red light on the phone on my desk was blinking. No doubt there were hundreds of messages. When I got home from Moose City on Sunday afternoon, my answering machine was so full that it had stopped recording. Two messages were from Olivia. "Oliver's just being overly cautious. He'll come to his senses. I'll see to it." Several were blasts from the past, all the same. "Abby! Been so long! Just calling to say hi and let you know I've been thinking about you!"

Uh-huh.

"Hey!"

I looked up, and there was a face I was happy to see: Shelley's.

"Any news from Baxter?"

"Well, we're talking. Not making any headway, but at least we're talking. How was the trip?"

"It was good to get away," I said.

She smiled. "I'll bet." Her phone rang and her head popped down.

I had my own phone to attend to. Fifty-four voice mails. I usually had no more than ten.

Out of morbid curiosity, I checked my e-mail. Seventy-three.

I listened to my voice mail first. Three were from former boyfriends who were now shaking in their shoes. Marco Cantinelli, famous for deflowering the most girls in Chillsworth Hall, just so happened to be thinking of me this weekend and "wanted to say hello! Hope you're doing great! Wish we could get together, but I'm heading to Tibet to soul-search. Take care, now!"

Jonathan Alterman, pig latin king, was living in New York City. "You don't get down here much, do you?" he asked, his voice at a slightly higher pitch. "If you do, of course, I'd love to see you, but give me advance notice, okay, like a few weeks, so I can plan." Yeah, plan to go to Tibet to soul-search.

And then Slade! Unbelievable. Slade, whom I dated for just a few weeks when I was twenty-two, was the typical tortured-artist type who wore black turtlenecks, even in summer, and decided to speak only ten words a day to conserve world energy. Oh, but was he cute! "Abby, Slade. Look, if you have any interest in killing me, could you wait until Saturday? I have a gallery showing on Friday night and would like to live for it. Thanks." Click.

The first honest one. For that, I would let him live.

And *quelle surprise,* Charlie Heath, who hoped my aunt Annette's ankle had healed properly. "I was such a fool for letting you get away. I was crazy about you. But I was so young and stupid…"

I think he was forgetting that was two years ago and he was thirty then.

I pressed number seven for delete so many times, my pointer finger started to go numb.

"Abby?"

Ugh. I knew that voice. Henry. I swiveled around in my chair, trying to perfect my man-killer smile, something Uma Thurmanesque. He was carrying a bouquet of roses in one hand and my four-foot-tall fuzzy monkey in the other. I supposed the honey cake had turned to mold.

As he stepped into my cubicle, I realized he was limping.

"Skiing accident?" I asked.

His face was frozen into a polite smile. "That's exactly what I told the police," he whispered.

Oh, good Lord! "But what *really* happened, Henry?"

Actually, nothing should have happened. If I followed Ben's logic, Henry was safe until he found someone to marry him. Since I had actually liked him quite a lot before he ditched me in L.L. Bean, the killer shouldn't go after him, in order to spare me additional heartache. If the killer did know me well, that was.

So did I believe the killer was someone I knew? Someone who cared about me, albeit in a very sick and twisted way?

What if the killer knew that the moment Henry took to the highway because of a little ceremonial snipping, I'd been so turned off by his wussiness that I wouldn't be the least bit devastated by something a little bit awful happening to him?

Not death. Not even pain. Just a little public humiliation of his own.

Had I talked about Henry to anyone? Opal. Olivia. Various relatives at the bris. But then the telephone version of events had made its way around the party, so the only people who really knew what had happened—and how I felt—were my sisters. Opal wouldn't let me be a brunette in her wedding; she wouldn't kill for me. And Olivia wouldn't even let me see my nephew because she thought I *could* be guilty of murder. So I felt very certain that I could cross my sisters off Ben's list.

Henry was standing here alive and well. So the killer clearly wasn't going after him.

"I took a bad curve skiing the intermediate slope," he said.

"No one came crashing down from behind you?" I asked. "Wearing a ski mask?"

He peered at me. "Why, were you there? Wearing a ski mask?"

I rolled my eyes. "No, Henry, I was not."

He thrust the roses at me. "Uh, look, the thing is, I guess I didn't realize how much you liked me. If I knew, I never would have— Why don't we try again? If you have any more brises to go to, you can count on me to attend. I really miss you."

Henry was a worse actor than I was. His good leg was

trembling, and that polite smile was still plastered on his face. Which I no longer found cute, by the way.

I leaned toward him and beckoned him closer with my finger. He took one step. Then another. He was in such a state of panic that I almost laughed. "Henry," I whispered, "do you really want to make it easier for me to kill you by having me around as your girlfriend?"

His lower lip trembled and the blood drained from his face. He dropped the monkey and ran.

I put the roses in a vase and set them out on the conference-room table. By the time I got back to my cubicle, Ben had left a message. Henry had called to tattle on me.

By noon I'd finished my Best of Moose City column, e-mailed it to Finch for approval and answered all last week's reader letters, dropping off my responses in Roger's box for copyediting. Now I could once again focus on who was trying to do me a warped favor.

Or, or, or: was someone framing me? But why? Could someone else have had Ted Puck, Riley Witherspoon and Tom Greer in common? How could I find out? And what was up with Mary-Kate Darling and her connection to Mary-Katherine Mulch? If there was one.

Ugh. I could see why Ben focused on the someone-who-knew-and-loved-me-to-death theory. It actually made sense.

I heard Roger's trademark whistle, which most of my coworkers found annoying. I turned around, and there he was, hunched slightly so as not to hit his head at the top of the frame of my cubicle's doorway.

"You must have a lot on your mind," he said, placing copy in my in-box. "These reader-letter responses were full of grammatical errors. Usually you're a much better speller, too."

How's this: G-O A-W-A-Y.

"Thanks for cleaning up my copy as always," I said, offering a smile. "Appreciate it."

"I know you do," he said. "Unlike some people around here," he added, gesturing his head to the left, where the features editor's cubicle was.

I smiled. Roger was okay, if a little—just slightly—creepy.

Creepy.

If you didn't kill Ted, someone you know did…

Did Ted have any enemies? Just you, Roger…

"Um, Roger, I'd better get back to finishing up my first feature column or Finch'll demote me," I said.

"Don't get too big for your old friends," he said, shooting me a smile.

The minute he was gone, I grabbed some letterhead and wrote People I Know Who Could Possibly But I'm Sure Did Not Kill Ted, Push Tom in Front of a Speeding Truck and Let a Pit Bull Loose in Riley's House.

I couldn't even write down Roger's name. He was harmless. A big, lumbering, geeky, copyediting harmless guy who had a harmless crush on me.

Which meant I had to do a little digging on our Mary-

Katherine Mulch and our Mary-Kate Darling. She was the only person I wanted on that list. Of course, I'd have to cross out the last two incidents and chalk those up to coincidence.

I picked up the phone and called Ben.

"Orr here" came that voice I heard in my sleep.

"Ben, it's Abby. I need to know something."

"Shoot," he said. I waited for him to make a joke, but he didn't.

"As a cop, what's your *official* take on coincidence?"

"I've seen my share. I'm also very leery of it."

"Good enough," I said. "Thanks." Leery was all well and good. But he'd seen his share. Which meant that there *was* such a thing as coincidence. Which meant Riley and Tom could be totally coincidental. Which meant Mary-Kate Darling was *guilty!*

I slumped over my desk. I didn't even know if Mary-Kate Darling *deserved* to be guilty. Yeah, she was wildly inappropriate at parties. And she'd known I was Ted's girlfriend when she arrived with him at the party. He'd introduced me to her—his cousin, Mary—as his girl-friend, the birthday girl, Abby Foote. So she'd known. Yes, she deserved to be guilty.

"Anything else you want to share?" Ben asked. "Are you working on your list of people in your life who might have had something to do with the murder?"

"I absolutely am," I said.

"Perhaps I could come by tonight to go over it with you?" he asked. "Around seven?"

Yes! "Okay," I said. I am dying to see you. Not dying to make that list, though.

The moment I put down the phone, it rang again. "Uh, Abby, it's Opal."

"What's wrong?"

Silence. "I really don't know how to tell you this, so I'm just going to tell you, okay?"

Oh, hell. "What?"

"My mom is kinda freaked about the whole murder investigation, and she and Oliver were talking this weekend while you were away, and they sort of both decided that they don't feel comfortable with you seeing any family member, including me, unsupervised."

"What?"

"She's just freaked," Opal said. "But to tell you the truth, Jackson sort of agrees with them."

"I didn't kill Ted!" I yelled.

"I'm sure you didn't, Abs. But, um, if you want to come to the wedding events I've got planned, you need to bring Detective Orr."

"Opal, he's not my boyfriend!"

"We know," she said. "Oh, and Abs, if you're offended, like, at all, about having to wear a blond wig for my wedding, that's totally okay. Okay?"

"I'm not offended, Opal."

I heard her sigh of relief and the sound of a hand closing over the mouthpiece and a garbled *"She said she's not offended!"*

"Look, for what it's worth, Abby, I'm really sorry, okay?"

There was that phrase again. It was worth *nothing*.

I much preferred the sucking-up to this.

Jolie didn't require a police escort to meet me for lunch. She took one look at my face and hopped off her stool at the burrito place and hugged me.

"Abby, in a week, two weeks, this will totally go away. They'll find the killer and everyone will be begging your forgiveness."

"They'd better. On both counts." I ordered a chicken burrito that I probably wouldn't have an appetite for. "Jolie, do you remember a girl named Mary-Katherine Mulch from high school? She was a grade ahead of us?"

She shook her head. "Doesn't sound familiar."

I explained about the connection between Mary-Katherine and Mary-Kate.

"I know!" she said as our burritos were served. "Go pay a visit to Petey Strummer! You can kill two birds with one stone. Find out where *he* was the night Ted was killed and find out if he remembers Mary-Katherine."

My appetite returned and I inhaled my burrito. Not the best in Portland.

Petey Strummer, who now called himself Peter, lived and worked in South Portland, just a five-minute drive away. On the phone he said he thought it was hilarious that I was a notorious murder suspect, given how *un*femme fatale I'd been in high school.

"But I thought you had a huge crush on me," I pointed out. "Doesn't that make me a femme fatale by default?"

He laughed and said he'd meet me at five-thirty. That gave me at least an hour before I'd have to leave to meet Ben at my place.

No wonder Ben hadn't noticed me in high school. Petey Strummer had barely noticed me! I wondered why he had such a huge crush on me, then. He could very well be the first guy in the world to go for personality.

We met at his favorite pizzeria, which I'd voted Best Of two years ago. Petey, whom I couldn't think of as Peter, even though he now had a beard, sat in a booth munching on a garlic knot from a basket full of them.

"Help yourself," he said as I sat down. "Wow, you look exactly the same. But even better."

I smiled. "You, too, Petey. Peter, I mean."

"I ordered us a large pepperoni," he said.

"Perfect. So Peter, do you remember someone from high school named Mary-Katherine Mulch?"

He popped another garlic knot into his mouth. "Mary-Katherine Mulch. Wow, she hasn't crossed my mind in ten years."

"So you knew her?"

"She was a grade ahead of us, but we had some clubs together. Band, Greek and Latin, fencing. Chess. She lived at the end of my block."

Yes! "So when you visit your parents, do you ever run into her?"

"The first few years, yeah," he said. "But after college, no. I don't think I ever saw her again. But then again, I doubt I'd have recognized her. According to my mom, she had head-to-toe plastic surgery."

I almost jumped out of my chair. "Head to toe, huh? That's something."

"She was a real candidate for it," he said. "Buggy eyes, hook nose, no chin, the works. My mom said she was made into a real knockout."

The counter guy called out, "Large pepperoni," and Peter headed up to get our pizza. I went to the condiments table to load up on plates, utensils and napkins.

Head-to-toe plastic surgery. Which meant Mary-Katherine Mulch had become Mary-Kate Darling.

Henry served me a slice and took one for himself. "I remember my mom said that she wanted the doctors to make a human Barbie doll. A brilliant Barbie."

How smart could she be if she'd gotten herself engaged to a total jerk?

"What was she like?" I asked. "Nice, mean, shy, weird?"

"She always seemed like the wheels were turning, you know? Like if you asked her a simple question, she'd think about it from three different ways, then answer. Which was good for the debate club, but annoying in just regular conversation."

Interesting. So she was a plotter.

"Do you remember Ben Orr?" I asked as though I didn't really care.

He took a second slice and slurped off a pepperoni. "Ben Orr. Yeah, nice guy. Captain of everything, right? Left before his senior year."

"That's the one," I said. "What did you think of him?"

He shrugged. "He was one of those guy gods who ruled the school, so I hated his guts by default. But he was actually really nice. He was in two of my classes. A couple of times some jerk-off friends of his were picking on me, and he gave them the ax-under-the-chin gesture. They never bothered me again."

"Did he have a girlfriend?"

He shrugged. "Wouldn't know. He didn't have the one girl in school I was in love with, so that made him okay with me. And he could have had any girl he wanted."

I laughed. "Maybe he didn't have that girl because he wasn't interested in her."

"Not interested in you?" he asked, shaking his head. "C'mon. Please. What guy wouldn't be crazy about you?"

"I thought I wasn't a femme fatale."

"I like clean-cut," he explained.

I laughed. "Thanks, Peter." I started on a second slice, but I was full after a bite. My Moose City foodathon would last me a week. "So, do you have a girlfriend now?" I asked, noting that he wasn't wearing a wedding ring.

He looked nervous. "Uh, yeah. I have a *very serious* girlfriend. *Very serious.*" He peered at me. "You're not mad, are you?"

Ben had got to Petey Strummer, too? Who hadn't he talked to? My kindergarten teacher? No, he'd probably talked to her, as well. To see if I seemed pathological as a five-year-old.

"Peter, I thought you said that the idea of me as a murderer was hilarious."

"I just wanted to stay on your good side," he said. "I was sort of afraid not to meet you."

"I didn't do what I'm suspected of," I said. "I'm trying to figure out who did."

He looked relieved. "I wouldn't have pegged you for a cold-blooded killer, but you never can tell," he said.

That was true. You never could tell. Which meant that if everyone I ever knew thought I could be a killer, the killer could be someone no one would ever suspect, especially me. Which had been Ben's point, I supposed.

Chapter 12

"Ben, you will not believe what I found out about Mary-Kate Darling!" I said the moment he came in. He took off his coat, and for a moment I was dumbstruck by how incredibly *hot* he was. He wore a dark blue sweater with a hint of white T-shirt peeking out. Faded jeans. He looked like Ben instead of Detective Orr.

"Abby, I told you. I'm not interested in Mary-Kate. I'm interested in you."

If only that were true.

I went into the kitchen and got us two bottles of Diet Coke. "What if I told you that Mary-Kate Darling was once a very unattractive girl named Mary-Katherine Mulch?"

"So being unattractive makes someone a killer?" he asked, taking a bottle.

"She had an extreme makeover!" I said. "Head to toe. Don't you find that interesting?"

"Not really. And as a matter of fact, I'm well aware of Mary-Kate Darling's history."

Oh. "But—"

Arg! Why was he always seven steps ahead of me?

"Abby, having plastic surgery doesn't correlate in any way shape or form to the word *murder*."

"I just think there's something suspicious about her," I said. "Hiding that she grew up in Barmouth. Hiding that she used to be a completely different person."

"So looking different makes you different?" he asked. "When you don your blond wig for Opal's wedding, are you still Abby Foote? Or are you suddenly someone who's capable of murder?"

"You're very frustrating," I said.

He laughed. "So are you."

I sat down on my sofa, out of ways to pique his interest in investigating Mary-Kate. Though perhaps he already had, if he knew about her past. "Maybe someone *is* trying to frame me," I said. "Someone I *don't* know."

He sat, too, flipping open the mini notebook. "If someone is trying to frame you for the murder of Ted, they would have been less subtle. There was nothing at the scene to connect you to the murder at all. There might have been a forged note from you in his pocket to meet him at the pier or something like that. But there wasn't."

Oh, again.

"And that would make the Riley and Tom incidents

coincidental. And I don't think they are. The timing, the viciousness, the connection of the three men as boyfriends of yours who broke up with you, tells me that either you or someone in your life is the perpetrator."

"I prefer being called a perpetrator to a murderer," I said.

"And I prefer that you stop making sarcastic remarks to people like Henry Fiddler," he said. "'Oh, she was just kidding,' isn't going to cut it with my captain, Abby. So please refrain from statements that will make my job harder. Okay?"

I hadn't thought of that. "Okay. So, following your theory, the killer won't go after Henry because I liked him a lot, right?"

"There's a big difference between love and like. Did you love Henry?"

"No," I said. "But I liked him. I was excited about our relationship. I was finally moving on after Ted."

"And that was common knowledge among your friends and family?" he asked.

I nodded. "Is he in trouble?"

"Maybe. Let's just say I won't remove his protection. He claims he felt like someone was following him all last week and this weekend. He said he felt eyes on him on the slopes, which is why he crashed."

"Aha!" I said. "You know full well where I was Friday night, and it wasn't following around Henry Fiddler!"

"Well aware," he said, flipping another page. "Let's

move on to the list. Start from the beginning. You talk, I'll write. Something you'll say will lead to a memory or a segue or something I'll write will lead me to remember something someone said when I initially interviewed them in connection with you, or it'll lead to my having more questions."

"Okay," I said, settling back on the sofa. I curled my legs under me and took a sip of my Diet Coke. Here goes nothing.

"Let's start with your stepmother," he said, pen at the ready. "Veronica Foote."

Margaret Hamilton's green face immediately came to mind, but with Veronica's namesake blond pageboy, down to the slight wave that made her still sexy at fifty-four. The tall, thin, big-breasted body helped, too.

"Don't think, Abby," Ben said. "*Talk*. Talk everything that comes to your mind."

"I was just thinking about how sexy Veronica is for a fiftysomething. How even though she's not mean—well, not really mean—she's always reminded me of the Wicked Witch of the West because she has the same shape face, like a triangle."

"So would a not really mean Wicked Witch of the West try to rid the world of ex-boyfriends who hurt or humiliated you?"

"I think we can cross her off the list, Ben," I said. "Veronica tolerated me fine my entire life. I was invited to her and my father's anniversary dinner every year, whether to remind me that he had a new family and lived with them or to make me feel included, I don't know. My birthday cards from my father came signed in her handwriting, my gifts were clearly picked out by her. Opal and Olivia were always at my parties, at important events in my life. She did the right thing by me in that kind of regard, but she didn't exactly adore me or hug me or make me feel like part of her family. I was separate, the daughter of her husband's first wife. So no, I don't think she feels this deep burning need to avenge my pain."

He stared at me. "But maybe she feels guilty. Maybe she's always felt guilty for stealing your father from your mother, stealing your father from you, and so she acted out. Your father died, what, three years ago, right? Perhaps she snapped. Perhaps the coldness you described manifested itself in some kind of vengeance against men who leave."

"Is this what detectives do at work? Come up with this kind of crap?"

He smiled. "It's not crap, Abby. It's *possibilities.* You sort through all the maybes and you find answers."

I leaned my head all the way back on the sofa cushions and stared up at the ceiling.

He flipped a page in his notebook. "How did Veronica feel when your father died?"

Good. A question that wasn't about me. I sat up. "She was devastated. She sobbed through the funeral. She cried for weeks afterward. Even I seemed to be a comforting presence for her. Anyone connected to my dad made her feel better."

"So it's conceivable that she developed a new kind of love for you, Abby. And it's possible that she turned her devastation about your father's loss into something very dark."

I rolled my eyes and shook my head. "I'd eat a bucket of crawling beetles if Veronica Foote had anything to do with Ted's murder. Ben, you know when someone cares about you. Veronica doesn't care about me."

The moment the words were out, I froze. I'd never out-and-out said that before, never wanted to believe it, never wanted to feel it. But it was true and it felt damned good to not only acknowledge the truth but accept it.

"It's strange that it doesn't sting," I said. "It used to kill me. Feeling like an outsider in my father's house, with my father's family. But it doesn't sting anymore."

He nodded. "Good. That means you've got it together."

"Aha!" I said, sitting upright. "Murderers don't have it together."

"Ever read a biography of Ted Bundy?" he asked. "Cool as a cucumber. How many women did he kill?"

I scowled at him. "Who are you, your partner, Fargo? I thought he was the Bad Cop in Good Cop, Bad Cop."

"Touché," he said, shooting me a smile. "You know, Abby, sometimes I'm so hard on you because I want to see what provocation does to you. I've got to say—you handle it well. You've often surprised me."

We eyed each other for a moment. I had nothing to say to that. I didn't want to surprise him; I wanted him to just know that I couldn't have done what he believed me capable of. If I could surprise him, I could be capable of what he believed me capable of.

Great. Now I was thinking in circles.

"All right. Let's move on to your half sisters," he said, flipping yet another page. "Olivia."

"I won't go there," I said. "This is ridiculous. Olivia and Opal, murderers. That's truly the most insane thing I've ever heard."

"Abby, we're just talking possibilities. Look, your loyalty to your family and friends is commendable. But it won't be if you're arrested for a murder and possibly attempted murders that you didn't commit."

"Olivia didn't kill Ted. Trust me, she wouldn't have had time. Ted was murdered the night of the bris, when Oscar was eight days old. All Olivia does is breast-feed, change diapers and rock the baby to sleep. Plus clean and cook and do the gazillion other things lazy entitlement-king Oliver doesn't do."

"For someone who sounds so frazzled, she certainly looks very pulled together," Ben said. "Makeup, jewelry. Nice clothes. I've interviewed Olivia twice in the past week, Abby. She dressed up for the occasion. Or she always wears skirts and heels to care for a week-old baby."

"She does," I said. "That's Olivia. That's Veronica. That's Opal. They're not jeans people."

"My point is that if she has time to dress up, if she has the *wherewithal* to dress up, she has the time that you say she doesn't."

I shook my head. "She makes time because she cares, Ben. It takes just as long to put on a pretty sweater as it does a ratty one. I'm a ratty-sweater person. I don't even own nice sweaters. She owns only nice sweaters."

"I like your sweater," he said, eyeing my black wool V-neck. "That's not ratty."

Why did he do this? Why did he stop me cold, mid-thought? Was this good police work? Rattle the suspect?

"I got it at a thrift shop for seven bucks," I said. "*Maine Life* doesn't pay their assistant editors or associate editors too well."

He nodded, glanced at my sweater again—my chest?—and then flipped another page. "Would you say Olivia was or is suffering from postpartum depression?"

I stood up. "That's it," I said. "I'm not answering that. I'm not answering anything anymore. Arrest me, Ben. I've had it."

He stood, too, and flung the notebook on my coffee table. "Abby, I'm sorry. I didn't mean to offend you. I'm just trying to establish potential state of mind—"

"Well, you did offend me. If you want to establish Olivia's state of mind, go talk to her yourself. I won't talk about my sisters behind their backs. They mean too much to me. I spent years trying to get closer to them, and we're finally just now getting there, after the death of my dad, and I'm not going to talk crap about them." I pointed to the door. "Just go, Ben. Either arrest me or leave."

He stared at me for a moment. "Abby, I'm not going to arrest you. And I don't want to leave. I want to help you."

I flopped down on the couch and stared up at the ceiling.

"What about Opal?" he asked. "I won't ask specifics. Just tell me what you want."

"Opal's not that giving, trust me," I said. "Being a bridesmaid in her wedding is contingent upon being blond for the night."

"Was she Daddy's Little Girl growing up?"

I rolled my eyes. Mostly because I've always hated that expression. Maybe because I wasn't Daddy's Little Girl. Ever.

"I suppose," I said. "She was the baby and so, so pretty, with those huge blue saucer eyes and her light blond hair. And she was the ultimate girlie girl as a kid. Not a tomboy bone in her body."

"Was Olivia also Daddy's Little Girl?" he asked.

"Not to the extreme that Opal was, but yes. She was his star princess, with her Princess Di looks and maturity and great grades."

"And you were?" he asked, staring at me.

"I was just me," I said. "It made me independent."

Once, when we were young kids and Veronica had invited me to my father's birthday party at their house, Opal had had a tantrum. She'd seen me coming in wearing my stiff party dress and shiny black shoes, a big wrapped gift in my arms, and she'd screamed at me, *"Go away! He's our father now. Not yours anymore!"* I'd been frozen to the spot. Tears had fallen down my cheeks, but my dad had gone to Opal. "Of course I'm still Abby's father," he'd comforted Opal, scooping her up in his arms. "I'll always be Abby's dad. But that doesn't make me any less your dad."

I waited for him to tell me the same, that being Olivia and Opal's father didn't make him any less my dad, but he didn't. And it did.

Once, I made the mistake of opening up to a boyfriend about my family (Tom Greer, who was a therapist), and he said, "I think the reason you're holding on to this relationship and why you stayed too long in other bad relationships is because you don't have a family. So you try to make your boyfriend your family, but we're not your family. We're just a *short-term* boyfriend."

We'd been in bed—his—which meant me huffily pulling on my clothes and demanding he drive me home that minute, even though it was snowing and two in the morning. The next day he broke up with me via e-mail on the night of my company holiday party.

"Abby, think out loud," Ben said, tapping his pen against my knee.

"Nothing relevant," I said. But from the way he looked at me, I knew he didn't believe me. He'd gotten me where he wanted me. Thinking. Remembering. Wondering.

"Let's move on to your friends," he said. "Jolie Olensky and Rebecca Rhode."

"Oh, because talking about them behind their backs is okay with me."

"So let me turn the questions around," he said, sitting back down. Guess he wasn't leaving. Guess I was actually answering questions I'd just said I wouldn't answer. As I mentioned, I knew from watching *Law & Order* (all versions) that you could demand a police officer leave your property. Not that this $850-a-month rental was technically my property. "Tell me why Jolie or Rebecca could not possibly have killed on your behalf, in the name of friendship."

"Because Jolie marches for the abolition of the death penalty," I said. "She doesn't believe in two wrongs making a right. That's how she puts it."

He scribbled in his notebook. "And Rebecca?"

I smiled. "Rebecca marches for handgun control. She'd never touch a gun."

"The coworkers at *Maine Life* you're close to—Shelley Gould?"

"Until last week, Shelley Gould was lip-locked to her boyfriend for the sixteen hours she's not at work," I told him. "As for Roger Hunker, I have no idea what wouldn't make him a killer except that he's exceptionally nice."

"Roger Hunker, the one who has a crush on you? Would you describe him as a close friend? He's not on my list of your friends that I created from talking to your family and friends. He's on the who-has-a-crush-on-Abby list."

I raised an eyebrow. "He's the only one on that list, right?"

He nodded.

He shook his head, those dark, dark eyes smoldering with desire. "Actually, Abby, there's someone else on that list. No— actually, that's not really accurate," he said, pulling me into his arms. "I don't have a crush on you. I full-out love you, baby...."

Ha. Now I was delusional!

"So it's conceivable to you that Roger Hunker killed Ted and tried to kill Riley and Tom?"

I gnawed my lip. "It's only conceivable because I don't know him well. There is something just a tiny bit creepy about him."

"At least I have one person on the list now." He stood up. "One more thing. Did you save someone's life and forget? Did you ever do anything really nice for anyone with a history of mental instability?"

"I thought you said Ted Bundy was cool as a cucumber," I reminded him. "I've done a lot of nice stuff for people."

He nodded, grabbed his coat and headed for the door. "Thanks for your help, Abby."

"Are you being sarcastic?" I asked. "Sometimes I think I know you and then most of the time I realize I don't know you well enough to know anything."

He shook his head. "No sarcasm. Not my style."

Didn't think so.

"Ben," I said as he reached for the doorknob, "why didn't you ask me about my mom?"

"Because I'm not the cold cop you think I am," he said. "And besides, it was bingo night at her condo development. She won two rounds between the hours of six and eight the night Ted was murdered."

I smiled. "Good for her." I'd called my mom to let her know—in very sketchy fashion—what was going on up here so that she wouldn't be surprised if she was paid a visit by the Portland Police Department for a little chat about her only child...but not enough to worry her. "And thanks," I said.

He gave me his usual closed-mouth smile, then opened the door. "Abby, if you do think of anything, anything at all, no matter how seemingly insignificant, you'll call?"

"I will."

"In any case, I'll see you on Saturday for your brides-maid-dress fitting."

What? "What?" I repeated aloud this time. *What brides-maid-dress fitting?* I almost asked. I'd forgotten all about it. Aside from my good reason—I'm a murder suspect—I'd had such little contact with my family that there weren't the usual daily reminders of Opal's wedding.

"Veronica requested your visits with your sisters and their family be supervised."

"So you're going to hang out for two hours at Best Bridal?" I said, shaking my head. "You'll be, what, sitting on a little stool in the fitting room just in case I try to strangle someone with a veil?"

"Yup." And with that, I got another closed-mouth smile and a closed door.

I missed him. Crazy. For four days Detective Benjamin Orr had not called, stopped by, trailed me anywhere or asked a single question.

Because someone on his list was looking suspicious? Roger with his how-dare-you-spurn-the-woman-I-would-kill-*badumpa!*-to have? *I'm sorry, Roger, but if someone has to be on Ben's list, it's going to have to be you. I can't spare any of my friends or family.*

Had he spent the week trailing Roger from home to work, from work to home? Roger had one other passion besides grammar and me: Sci Fri Friday on TV. *Battlestar Galactica. Stargate Atlantis.* In between work and his Friday-night date with his television, he didn't go out much. If Ben had been trailing Roger, Ben must have been bored out of his mind.

I'd spent the week working on The Best of South Portland, which left me exhausted. Maine was not known for its shopping, with the exception of the superb outlet haven known as Freeport Village, where there was every-thing from a Patagonia outlet to a Ralph Lauren outlet. But South Portland was one giant outdoor mall that you needed a car to traverse. Every store imaginable was packed into South Portland, and every chain restaurant. My column had Best Place To Buy Bridesmaid Shoes (Francesca's Fancy Shoes), Best Fast Food (was there any fry like a McDonald's French fry?), Best Place To Buy a Bed, Best Place To Find a Date for the Weekend. (Startini's Singles Lounge, which was a dance club just for singles. Couples weren't even allowed to enter.)

"I can't believe you're single," a none-too-cute guy had said the moment I'd walked in. His eyes had raked me from my thighs to my chest and back again. "I like that you didn't try to babe yourself up like all the other chicks. You're, like, natural."

I'd talk to you, really I would (not!), but if I do, you're going to end up dead when you dump me in a few months, so see ya! Ah, he had no idea how close he'd come to death.

I glanced at the clock on my living-room wall. Uh-oh. Only had an hour before I had to be at Best Bridal, where Ben would be meeting me. I wondered if I was allowed to actually enter the premises without my armed escort.

I typed the final line to Best Place To Change Your Baby's Diaper (shockingly, the women's *and* men's restrooms in Hummingbird's Super Supermarket, which not only had three changing stations, but came stocked with wipes and diapers in two sizes; there was also a rocking chair, albeit slightly ratty, for breast-feeding—a mom was doing just that when I arrived).

I checked my e-mail. Hello and miss you and hope you're holding up okay from Jolie and Rebecca. And yesterday's: Abby, please bring/wear the following to your bridesmaid-dress fitting, Bra and underwear and hose that you'll be wearing at wedding. If unsure what type of support garments would best suit, I can help you. Please bring your wedding shoes. Do not wear jewelry. Thank you. All best, Veronica

Oh, she cared, too! Deeply!

Jewelry wasn't a problem. I didn't have any. Well, I had some cute earrings and fake diamond studs and a ring I'd bought on a trip to Paris five years ago that for some reason fit me there but was too small the moment I got home. And I had a beautiful gold heart locket necklace on a delicate gold chain that I loved but never wore. My father had given it to me for my eighteenth birthday. I liked having it in my jewelry box, but I couldn't bear to wear it. Because I didn't believe the heart meant anything or because it made me too emotional, I wasn't sure.

I headed into my bedroom and opened my undies drawer. I had an array of sexy bras and tummy-control underwear and panty hose in every possible shade of nude. Why, I didn't know, since I rarely wore panty hose. I had no idea what kind of dress Opal had in mind, but I had a feeling it would be pink and probably velvet, since she loved both. Or maybe red in honor of Valentine's Day, since her wedding was so close to it.

Hey, I just realized I'd have a date for the wedding, since I wouldn't be permitted to go alone. Ben would probably have to escort me down the aisle.

I shook my head, grabbed my pink push-up bra, which did wonderful things for my chest, and my tummy-control/no-panty lines undies and my shimmery nude stockings and stuffed them into my tote bag.

I glanced at myself in the freestanding full-length mirror in the corner. I stood on tippy-toe. I'd always wished I were tall, like Opal and Olivia, who took after their mother. I took after my mother, who was also five foot three and small boned. I reached for the wedding shoes; they were plain *peau de soie* pumps with a pointy pinching toe and a three-inch heel. I slipped into them and they hurt immediately. But they did great things to my legs.

What do you see when you look at me, Ben? I wondered. Did he even notice me—as a woman? Or was he not the least bit attracted to me? Like ten years ago?

Why he was so annoyingly unreadable was a better question.

Chapter 13

Ben was waiting in the vestibule of Best Bridal when I arrived. He looked so male amid all that lacy floaty gauze separating the store's entrance from the bridal shop. He waved at me through the glass door.

It struck me that someone passing by would think that I was a bride-to-be waving a hello to my groom-to-be, waiting for me at my wedding-dress fitting. That was a *pictures* do *lie* photograph I'd love to have.

"Long time, no see," I said.

He smiled.

"Ah, you must be our missing bridesmaid" came the voice of a tall, thin woman with a tape measure around her neck. "Welcome to Best Bridal. I'm Helena, proprietor." She turned to Ben. "Sir, you may have a seat in our gentlemen's lounge." Ben and I both surveyed the salon for the gentlemen's lounge. Ah. There were two very girlie chaise longues in a heavy brocade, next to which were two magazine racks. I could see a *Field & Stream*. I wondered if Ben was the fishing type. What *did* he do with his free time? Not that he seemed to have any.

"If you hear any bloodcurdling screams, run in," I whispered. "Though it might be Opal if a bridesmaid gained an ounce."

He said nothing and sat down. Sarcastic and catty didn't seem to work on him.

"Come with me, dear," said Helena. She led me into a large room with racks of dresses against the walls. The very blond bridal party was hard at work, sliding into dresses, writing numbers on little slips of paper, holding up gowns against their bodies and peering into the floor-to-ceiling mirrors.

"Abby!" Veronica said when she noticed me. Her voice was ridiculously unnatural. "How nice to see you! Every-one, Abby's here."

Everyone stopped and stared. I wanted to believe that they were staring because as a brunette, I was so out of place among the eight blondes, including Helena. But I knew better.

"Is that nice young man here?" Veronica whispered. "The police officer?"

"He's in the gentlemen's lounge," I said.

Olivia came over and kissed me on the cheek. "Let's talk after, okay?" she whispered in my ear. "Oliver's just being a jackass, as usual."

My shoulders unslumped for the first time since I'd arrived. "I'm relieved to hear you say that, Olivia. For a while there, I thought you thought the worst."

She shook her head. "I'm sorry. Between being up all night taking care of Oscar and my crazy hormones and all this stress, I just spontaneously combusted, I guess. I'm sorry I didn't reach out more."

I smiled. "I totally understand, Olivia. As long as you know I could never do what I'm suspected of doing."

"Not a chance," she said. "I grew up with you. I probably know you better than anyone does."

I nodded. "You probably do. Except maybe Ben."

"So, Abs," Opal said, "I'm thinking pink velvet. No bows." She took a dress off its hanger and held it up to me. "This would look awesome on you. On everyone. How amazing is it that all of my bridesmaids are size six? Okay, so we'll each model a different gown that we all agree on and then we'll vote on our very favorite."

There were fifteen pink velvet gowns on the try-on rack. The reason we were picking dresses five weeks before the wedding? Because Veronica was worried someone would gain or lose before the big day, throwing off the entire "look" of the bridal party.

"Abby, you first," Opal said. "Shimmy into your support stuff and then slink into this."

I took the pretty pale pink gown into the fitting room with my bag.

"Do you think it's safe that she has her bag in there?" I heard Veronica whisper.

"Mom," Olivia snapped.

"How's it going, hon?" Opal called through the curtains.

"Just putting on the hose," I said. Which were totally unnecessary given the ankle length of the gown. I took off my everyday white bra and put on my pink push-up. Sexy! Then I slipped into the gown. The lining felt so silky against my skin. I put on the shoes and glanced at myself. The bra did its amazing things to my chest. I had just a hint of cleavage but could be easily called stacked. I felt very I'd Like To Thank The Academy. "Okay, here I come."

"Wow," Opal said. "We might not even have to try on any of the others. That's gorgeous!"

She really must have thought so, because even Opal wouldn't suck up at the expense of her wedding.

I looked in the full-length mirror. The dress really was gorgeous. Simple and elegant, but movie-star.

"We need a man's opinion. Go show the good detective!" Opal said.

Well, I had wondered if he ever saw me as a woman. If he hadn't, even in my black wrap dress, he would now.

"Wait! Your wig," Veronica said, taking the long blond tresses off a mannequin. "It's no use making a decision on the dress unless she's wearing the wig." She scooped up my hair in a net, then settled the wig on my head, fussing with the placement. She stood back. "Terrific. We were right to go dark blond, given your brown eyes."

"You really should consider coloring your hair," one of the other bridesmaids said.

Oh, yeah, that wouldn't make me seem even more suspicious.

"Go show the detective," Opal said.

Here goes nothing, I thought, heading out into the gentlemen's lounge. He sat on the girlie chaise, reading his little notebook. I coughed discreetly, and he glanced up, then did a double take.

"Abby?" he said, standing up.

"They want a man's opinion of the dress."

Those dark, dark eyes traveled down the length of me, then back up. I saw him swallow. He did! He swallowed! He did see me as a woman! I had to play dress-up for it, but I was a woman!

Veronica came out, hands on her lack of hips. "So, what does our gentleman think?"

"Stunning," he said, then sat back down.

"Good enough for me," she said, taking my hand and pulling me back into the fitting room. "The gentleman says *stunning*."

"Eight size sixes," Opal announced triumphantly to Helena. "We're done here, gals."

As the chattering blond bunch exited the try-on area, Ben stood. All eyes swung to him.

"For the record," I announced, before I could change my mind, "I didn't kill Ted. And I didn't try to kill my other two ex-boyfriends."

Dead silence. One gasp. (Helena apparently had no idea such a controversial bridesmaid was in her shop).

"You don't need to tell us that," Olivia said, taking both my hands.

"Because you *all* know it?" I asked, looking from Opal to Veronica.

"Of course we know it," Olivia said. "We *all* know it, right?" she added, glancing around with that *right, people!* look she had.

"Of course!" Opal said quickly.

"It's crazy!" two other bridesmaids said in unison.

Veronica remained tight-lipped.

I squeezed Olivia's hand and Opal's. "You have no idea how much that means to me." I had no idea if they—even Olivia—meant it, but it made me happy to hear it.

They both hugged me. "You know who else would know it," Olivia said, staring at her mother. "Dad."

Veronica smiled her tight smile. "Of course."

Of course your warm and fuzzy daddy wouldn't think his little girl was a coldhearted, cold-blooded murderer, but I know better!

There were more hugs and kisses, and then everyone left. Olivia was going home to Oliver and Oscar. Veronica and Opal were heading across town to another bridal shop for Opal's third wedding-gown fitting. And the other bridesmaids were standing outside the shop, staring in at me through the glass door. They glanced away like startled deer, then hurried away.

"Sorry," Ben said, putting on his heavy leather jacket. "I can't even imagine what this feels like."

"Are you sorry enough to tell everyone you made a mistake? That you've been investigating Mary-Kate Darling and *she's* your new suspect? That you've gotten to know me so well you know I didn't do it?"

"No," he said.

Sigh. "So are we in agreement that no one you saw today is a killer?" I asked.

He shook his head.

It was time to pay Mary-Katherine Mulch a visit.

Mary-Kate was hostess of a trendy, expensive restaurant in the Old Port section of Portland, a fun, hip area of cobblestone streets, one-of-a-kind boutiques, more coffee lounges than you'd think possible and restaurants and bars. If Mary-Kate was a killer, she couldn't very well kill me in a restaurant. So I decided to confront her there and see what happened.

Small tape recorder in my pocket, I headed in. It was between lunch and dinner, so I figured she'd have a few minutes to spare.

"Table for—" she began in a fake lovely-to-see-you-in-our-restaurant voice until her brain registered who I was. "What do you want?"

"I had no idea you worked here!" I said. "What a co-incidence! And it's uncanny—I was just talking to someone about you."

Her brown eyes narrowed. "Who was that?"

"Petey Strummer," I said. "You remember him, from Barmouth High."

"Of cour—" she began, then shut her mouth. "Barmouth High? You must have me confused with someone else. I grew up in Kansas."

"Kansas! Really," I said. "What town?"

A million bucks she said something obvious like Kansas City. Or some town that didn't exist.

"Topeka," she said.

That's what I got for betting a million. But it proved nothing. She was class valedictorian, after all. Of course she knew her capitals.

"That's interesting, Mary-Katherine," I said.

The eyes narrowed into slits.

"Did you go on *Extreme Makeover?*" I asked.

She glanced around wildly and pulled me over to the waiting area. "Keep your voice down."

"So it is true. You are Mary-Katherine Mulch."

"I'm not going to bother lying," she said. "Clearly you've been lurking into my life for some reason. The trail isn't difficult."

Holy cannoli. Lightbulb. I flashed back to her angrily destroying the roses and throwing them at the spot where Ted had been killed. I'd been right. That hadn't been the act of someone mad at the world. That had been the act of someone mad at the dead. At Ted. "He found out about the plastic surgery and was freaked out by it."

She stared at me.

"He told me," I lied. "He said he needed someone to talk to about it."

Please, let that be a good bluff.

A gurgling sob escaped her, and then she burst into tears. "I never expected his reaction. I mean, yes, I expected him to be freaked out by it. But I didn't expect what he said."

Bingo. *Okay, now please continue. Please, please, please.*

She sniffled. "I never in a million years expected him to break up with me because of it." She broke down in sobs and I handed her a tissue from her station.

"When did he break up with you?" I asked.

More sniffles. "The day before the engagement announcement was coming out. The day before his murder." She covered her face with her hands. Another sniffle, and then, "Do you want to know what that bastard said?"

That bastard?

I nodded. Waited.

"He said, 'Everyone always says how beautiful our kids are going to be. But now there's a good chance that they'll look like you used to!'" She sniffled. "He said he was freaked out and needed to think. So he left and came back in a couple of hours and said he didn't think he'd be able to get it out of his mind, put it behind him, that it was too weird."

Whoa. What kind of guy had I been in love with? Had I even known Ted Puck?

"And then he told me the engagement was off, that we weren't necessarily breaking up until he had a chance to digest, but he wanted to take a giant break. I asked him not to tell anyone, to just go on like everything was fine, and he agreed to do that until he had a chance to think things over."

"And then what happened?" I asked.

"I didn't see him for the rest of the day. And we always spent Saturdays together. And then the next day, Sunday, the day our engagement announcement came out, I went to his apartment with the paper to show it to him, and he said he didn't even want to see it, he wasn't ready to think about any of it and he didn't know how he felt."

"Wow, just because you used to look different?" I asked. "That sounds kind of extreme. I mean, this is you now."

"He said he wouldn't be able to get the image of the photograph I showed him out of his head."

"What a jerk," I said, and she nodded.

"Then what happened?" I asked.

"Then he was killed," she said, breaking down in sobs again. "God, it feels so good to tell someone this. I haven't been able to tell anyone except my mom, and she never liked Ted to begin with."

"Mary-Kate, did you kill him?"

She flew up and wiped under her eyes. "No! I didn't. *You* did."

"No, I didn't."

"Then who?" she asked. "Everyone thinks it was you."

"I think it was you."

"Well, it wasn't."

"Well, it wasn't me, either," I said. "Maybe your mom was so offended that *she* killed him," I suggested.

She shook her head. "First of all, that's ludicrous. Second of all, I didn't tell her about the breakup until after he was killed."

"I'm sorry about what happened," I said.

She glanced at me. "I'm sorry about what happened at your party."

Yeah, because if it hadn't, Ted would still be my boy-friend and wouldn't have ended up breaking your heart.

"Why did you do it?" I asked. "I don't mean what happened at my party. I mean, the plastic surgery. Couldn't you just have gotten contacts and had Japanese hair-straightening treatments?"

"I didn't do much more than that kind of stuff," she said. "I got a nose job, chin implants, an eyelid restructuring, colored contacts, the Japanese straightening, color, I lost forty pounds. It's not like I went *crazy* with plastic surgery."

That sounded like crazy to me.

She narrowed her eyes at me. "Do you know that when I used to walk down the halls of Barmouth High, boys would bark? That I never had a date? Not one in all of high school. I had only one female friend, and she moved away my junior year. How you look means everything. You're so naturally pretty, you wouldn't have any idea what it feels like to be ugly. Really ugly."

I sat there for a moment, just taking in what she was saying. "Do you still feel like Mary-Katherine Mulch? Or do you only feel like Mary-Kate Darling? I mean, does how you feel match what's in the mirror?"

She perked up. "Absolutely. I'm fucking gorgeous."

Maybe she and Ted *had* deserved each other. "Mary-Kate, I'm curious about something. Why did you go to Crate and Barrel to register for wedding gifts the day after he broke up with you? I mean, wasn't that painful?"

She let out a deep breath. "Because I thought there might be hope that he'd come back and tell me he was sorry, that of course we were still engaged." She shook her head. "I knew he wasn't coming back. Ted is—was— so superficial. The idea that he could have an ugly kid— or God forbid, *kids*—who took after me was all he needed to know. So I guess the real reason I registered was because that day our announcement came out, I was allowed to believe it was true like everyone else who read the paper that day. And I wanted it to be true. So off I went with my clipping to show everyone and to register."

"I can understand that," I said.

She glanced up; a harried-looking chef was waving her over. "I've got to go," she said, and walked away without looking back.

I thought about waiting for her to return to her post so that I could tell her what I was going to do in two minutes—which was run to the Portland Police Department to tell Ben about this little development—but I didn't want to give her a chance to work on her alibi for that missing half hour.

Ben wasn't in, of course. I left a message for him to call me as soon as possible, then went home, trying to imagine how tough high school—middle school—must have been for Mary-Kate. Mary-Katherine. I spent my sophomore and junior years in a Ben Orr hazy dream, so boys' lack of interest didn't really matter much to me. Yeah, Petey had a major crush on me, but no one else asked me to the Spring Fling or the Winter Carnival or the junior prom. I didn't even go to my senior prom. What it all came down to, I thought, was self-esteem. The lack thereof was something Mary-Katherine Mulch and I shared in high school.

Ben called an hour later, and I told him the entire story.

"Thank you for the information" was all he said.

"Is she a suspect, too, now?" I asked.

"You know I can't discuss the case, Abby" was the second thing he said. "Goodbye" and "I'll be in touch" were the third and fourth.

Chapter 14

Mary-Kate's alibi turned out to be airtight. Not only did the clerk recall the timing of her trip to the store, but he had sales records of two items she bought that were unrelated to the registry. The missing half hour was spent at Starbucks with a friend who confirmed it; there was also a credit card receipt in Mary-Kate's name verifying when she arrived.

There was no way she could have killed Ted.

Which left me. In fact, Mary-Kate paid back my tattling by informing Ben that she believed, deep in her heart, that I killed Ted.

All rightie, then. It was time to figure out who killed Ted. Who *tried* to kill Riley and Tom. And I had to at least open my mind to the possibility that it was someone I knew. Or someone who also had Ted, Riley and Tom in common. But who?

I needed to start with Riley and Tom. If they thought I was guilty, I wasn't sure they'd talk to me. But I could find out.

To: RileyW@bbb.erb; TomGreer@whipple.erb
From: Abby.Foote@MaineLifeMag.erb
Re: Police Investigation
Hi, Riley and Tom,
First, I want to tell you both how sorry I am about your accidents. Detective Orr informed me that he interviewed each of you separately and then together, in the hopes of sparking a comment that might lead him to the perpetrator, so I hope you don't mind that I'm e-mailing you together. Second, I want you both to know that I did not have anything to do with what happened to you. Both of you. Yes, I was hurt when things ended between us, but I would never even think of causing anyone physical harm. I also had nothing to do with the murder of Ted Puck, but as you know, I am under investigation as the potentially spurned ex-girlfriend. Your accidents, right after our breakups, add to the suspicion.

Ugh. This didn't sound natural at all!

Just type. You're not writing an article for *Maine Life*. You're trying to sound professional. At a distance. Policey.

Would you each consider meeting with me, at your convenience, to further discuss the incidents? My hope is that you might say something, remember something that might spark a memory for me, leading me to aid Detective Orr and Detective Fargo in their search for the killer and the perpetrator of the crimes against you.

Did I sign it *Best*, like everyone at *Maine Life?* Or *Sincerely?* Or just *Abby?*

I typed Sincerely, Abby and hit Send before I could change my mind.

And then I waited. No pings of new mail. Five minutes. Ten. Twenty. Half an hour. I went to get coffee. I drank two cups. No new mail. I made a new pot of coffee. Made a list of potential column ideas and e-mailed it to Finch. I cleaned my desk drawers.

Ping.

Riley. He'd CC'd Ben. I will meet with you to answer your questions if a detective is present.

I typed back a thank-you and asked where and when. He wanted to meet at his house, where the dog attacked. I tried not to imagine a pit bull racing toward me, looking angry. Riley was the lowest of the low, a total user, but at most I'd wished him a few lost clients, maybe a big mistake on the calculator.

Tom took his sweet time replying, but his response was the same as Riley's. Tom also wanted to meet at the scene of the crime, which wasn't far from my apartment.

Well, it looked as if Ben and I would be spending a lot more time together.

As Ben and I approached Riley Witherspoon's tiny bungalow on Portland's Back Cove, I tried to imagine someone leading a pit bull to the door. The perpetrator would have had to be walking Pitty on a leash in a completely normal manner, since he or she hadn't aroused any suspicion. And I didn't know anyone who owned a pit bull.

"What a crazy plan," I said to Ben as he rang the bell. "How would the killer know the door would be open?"

"Apparently Riley never locked the door—common around his neighborhood."

"I'll bet he does now," I said.

"I'll bet," he repeated as footsteps approached the door.

And there was Riley Witherspoon, looking as good as always. His sandy-blond hair was boyishly rumpled, and his I'm-supposedly-an-angel blue eyes were the color of the sky on a perfect summer day. People were always surprised when they found out he was an accountant and not, say, a Ralph Lauren model.

"Detective Orr, nice to see you again," Riley said. His eyes slid to me. "Abby," he said without a smile.

"Riley, I know I told you this when I e-mailed you, but I want to say in person that I'm very sorry about what happened to you," I said. "And I also want to repeat that I had absolutely nothing to do with it."

He ignored me and held open the door, then led the

way to the living room. I'd been here just a few times. Riley had wined and dined me in this room on our second date. He made Mexican, my favorite, and very strong margaritas, and we were naked in his bedroom before he could even serve dessert. Riley was so handsome and charming, and I'd fallen for the lot of it. He was the first and only guy who dated me because he wanted something from me—besides sex, of course. I looked at him now and I wanted to throw the bowl of peanuts on the table in his face.

Riley gestured for us to sit down, and Ben got straight to work.

"Mr. Witherspoon, Abby feels that discussing the events of the night in question may lead you to remember something that might trigger something for her. If someone she knows is trying to harm her former boyfriends, she may be able to aid in the investigation. Maybe you saw something that night—someone running, or someone watching you that day. Maybe something stuck in your mind—"

"So you have proof that Abby *didn't* kill that guy?" Riley asked. "That she didn't sic that dog on me?"

"We don't know," Ben said. "It's entirely possible that she did. It's also entirely possible that she didn't, that she's being framed or that someone she knows is trying to get back at her ex-boyfriends for breaking up with her."

Riley stared at me, then turned to Ben. "Who'd do that?"

I was getting tired of being spoken about in the third person as though I weren't sitting right there. "I don't know," I said. "As Ben—Detective Orr said, I'm hoping you might remember something, anything, about that night, or the days before, anything that might register as out of the ordinary."

He shrugged. "Nothing. I was home alone, watching a video I'd rented, when I heard the front door open. I turned around and the pit bull was just there and suddenly on me."

"Riley, I realize that we didn't date long, but do you really, truly think I would sic a pit bull on you?"

He eyed me and nodded. "You were so angry when I broke up with you. I believe your exact words were 'You're a low-down dirty dog.' Stress the word *dog*. I think it's quite meaningful."

Yeah, me, too, jerkface.

"So you didn't see anyone running away?" I asked.

"You mean when the dog had its jaws clamped around my leg?" he asked. He jumped up, hobbling on one leg. "I don't know why I agreed to this meeting. It all makes sense. You served your purpose for me, I dumped you, you got all hell-hath-no-fury, sicced the pit bull on me and then you killed your new boyfriend when he dumped you. You're sick!"

I refrained from eye rolling. "Actually, Ted Puck was murdered six months after our relationship ended," I said.

"Yeah, when he got engaged to that hot babe," Riley said. "You were thrown over for another chick and you snapped."

"You should really think about becoming a prosecutor, Riley," I said. "You'd be great at it."

"Mr. Witherspoon," Ben said. "Just to make sure I have this straight. Did you date Abby so that she'd list you as one of the best accountants in Maine?"

Riley froze, then sat down slowly and pasted on his I'm-an-angel smile—an injured angel. "Uh, that's not against the law, right?"

Ben shook his head.

"It should be," I threw in.

Riley slid his snake gaze to me, then said to Ben, "Yeah, I did. She was a means to an end, nothing more. We were at Boo's for happy hour, and the owner, who's a friend of mine, pointed out Abby and said she'd named Boo's Best Happy Hour in Portland in her capacity as Best of Maine editor for *Maine Life*. She interviewed him for a little sidebar and everything. I wanted that kind of publicity for my business, so I figured I'd talk my way into giving her my business card, maybe set up lunch or something. But I could tell she liked me, so I figured I'd go the faster route."

"The faster route?" Ben asked.

Riley smiled a good-ole-boy smile. "You know—the old fuck and chuck."

It took every ounce of my willpower, which wasn't strong to begin with, not to jump up and do something. Like pummel him to the ground—not that I could. And I supposed that wouldn't do much for my current situation. Yet despite my beet-red face—from anger and mortification—and my deep desire to run out the door, I still noticed that Ben *flinched*. He stared at Riley for a second, and I knew Ben hated his guts and thought he was gutter slime.

He cares about me, I realized. Ben Orr, detective, cares about me. He wants to punch Slimo in the face!

But he controlled himself, of course. Ben was Mr. Control, Mr. Unreadable. That momentary look of hate, of *How dare you have the thought, let alone say it—and right in front of Abby*—was replaced by Ben's standard cop detachment look. He stood and handed Riley his card. "Mr. Witherspoon, if you do think of anything else—someone you might have noticed around your block that day, anything—please get in touch."

Riley glared at me. "Oh, I will."

"Nice to see you again, Riley," I said. "I have a new accountant this year. I'm sure you understand."

Ben escorted me to the door. As we got into his car, I realized that the pit bull might be the key to finding the killer. "We could check all the pounds in the area! Find out who adopted a pit bull in the days before the attack on Riley. We could call breeders, too. Whoever or wherever people get pit bulls!"

"What do you think Detective Fargo has been doing all this time?" he said.

"He's been checking every dog shelter for weeks?"

"That and every other lead," Ben said.

"I sure am lucky it wasn't the other way around," I said. "I mean, you out canvassing for leads and witnesses, and

Fargo constantly at my door. I don't think I'd want to share a moose steak dinner with Frank Fargo."

Ben smiled. "Fargo's all right. A little rough around the edges, maybe. But that can be quite useful for a cop."

"So the dog shelters were a dead end?"

He nodded. "No one connected to you adopted or bought a pit bull in the last five years, let alone five days before the attack. The perpetrator might have gotten the dog under an assumed name, though."

I leaned back against the seat. This was so frustrating. Everything was leading to a wall. And the less it looked as if someone else killed Ted and tried to kill Riley and Tom, the more it would look as if *I* did it.

As Ben drove away, he said, "You can't tell me that Riley Witherspoon was a nice guy while you were dating."

There were so many things Ben could have said. From *You're looking guiltier and guiltier* to *Where'd you get the pit bull, anyway?* But he'd said the perfect thing.

And so I kissed him. I just leaned over and pressed a quick kiss on his cheek.

And for the second time in ten minutes, he flinched.

I was still glad I'd done it, though. "Sorry," I said. "I'm just glad you said that. About Riley being a jerk."

"Those weren't my words," he said. "Exact words are important in my business."

I smiled. "The weird thing is, he was a nice guy. Well, maybe *nice* isn't the right word. He was slick. Witty and charming, but always looking elsewhere. He'd say, "'Abby, you look so nice tonight,' while glancing around the room."

"So why did you go out with him twice?" he asked.

"You sound like Opal. She says that everything you need to know about a guy you learn on your first date. Riley never took his eyes off a Pamela Anderson look-alike on our first date. I should have known he wasn't really interested in me."

"So why did you say yes to a second date?"

I slumped in my seat. "Well, in my defense, I guess I like to have faith in people. Give people the benefit of the doubt. Yeah, he ogled a Playboy Bunny all night, but what guy wouldn't?"

"I wouldn't," he said. "Not if I was on a date."

I glanced at him. Of course he wouldn't. I already knew that.

"Okay, I know it's stupid, but I was a little starstruck by him. He looks like a model. And he was so charming—"

"You were charmed by him ogling some babe all night?"

The beet-red was back. "I guess I really don't pay enough attention on the first date. Opal thinks that'll solve my problems with relationships. What kind of first date are you?"

He smiled. "It's been so long that I don't even know."

Interesting. Very interesting. And he'd actually said something personal! That would make, what, the third personal thing I'd gotten out of him. Not bad. "Is that because you're in a long-term relationship and can't remember back that far?"

Please answer. Please answer. Please answer.

He shook his head. "More like I don't have time for a relationship. My last girlfriend hated my hours, which sometimes run into nights, holidays, special events. It's been at least a year since I've even been out with a woman."

"Does this count?" I asked.

He laughed. "No, this definitely doesn't count."

But I was beginning to think that it did.

Ugh. Tom Greer. Smug was a good word to describe him. And therapisty, if that was a word. He had a bad habit of speaking to most people as though they were in kindergarten. When I first met him, in a supermarket, of all places, I'd thought he was smart and funny.

"The way you're squeezing that roll of toilet paper says a lot about you," Tom had said. "You're clearly trying to find out if it's soft because it's the generic brand and not Charmin. So you're obviously thrifty."

Toilet paper in hand, I'd said, "Just think, if we start dating and people ask how we met, we'll have to tell them we met over toilet paper. And the store brand, at that."

It was crazy how people met. I met the linebacker, Charlie Heath, when he stepped on my foot on Crescent Beach.

Opal would shake her head that I even gave Tom Greer

my phone number after an opening like that over toilet paper. But our first date was magical. So was our second and third. I even liked his therapisty tone (he was a great listener) until he just up and dumped me for another woman. Whom he probably met over paper towels.

Ben and I parked on Exchange Street and walked up to the corner where Tom had been pushed in front of the speeding truck. I spotted him right away. He was leaning against the side of a building, one foot up against the wall behind him. He wore a tweed cap.

When he saw us approach, he stood up straight and walked toward us. "Detective Orr, Abby," he said. "Hard as it is to relive the moment, I'm ready to show you again where I was the victim of attempted murder."

He was a little too into it. Maybe Tom had engineered the whole thing. He'd had a thing against Ted Puck. Maybe Ted was a client (he'd been deeply in need of therapy, after all), or there was a gambling ring or something sinister, and Tom killed Ted, then said he'd been pushed in front of a speeding truck to cast extra suspicion on me!

Yeah, but what about Riley? That hole in his leg didn't get there by itself. And since I'd seen him naked, I could attest to the fact that it hadn't been there the week before we broke up.

Eh, so maybe Tom didn't kill Ted and lie about being pushed in front of a truck. Unless he paid Riley to lie. Riley didn't have an ethical bone in his body. Clearly!

Possible. Highly unlikely scenario, but possible. And

wasn't Ben's motto *could?* Tom *could* have done all that. I'd share my little theory with Ben afterward.

"Tom, thank you so much for meeting with us," I said. "Good thing it's a warm day."

"I'm not here to chat about the weather, Abby," he snapped.

Keep it nice, I ordered myself. "Can you show us exactly where you were standing when you were pushed?"

"I'm surprised you didn't say 'allegedly pushed,'" Tom said.

Oh, brother. "I'll take your word that you were pushed. And I can give you my word that I didn't do it. I'm here because Detective Orr thinks it's possible that someone I know may have pushed you in some kind of sick retaliation. So, if you could show us where…"

He stood at the curb, in the center of the crosswalk zone. "I was right here."

"Can you talk us through the moments right before and after you were pushed?" I said. "Maybe something you say will trigger something for me."

"How do I know you won't make something up?" he asked. "She could do that," he directed to Ben. "I could say a tall blonde was right behind me, and Abby could play it up and say she knows a tall blonde and send you on a wild-goose chase when she's the perp."

Suddenly everyone was a master of cop lingo. "Tom, I can assure you that I'm not interested in sending the police on wild-goose chases. I can't shake this one, no matter what I say or do. So don't worry. I want to find the person who did this as much as you do. My life depends on it."

He stared at me. "I guess it does."

I waited for him to continue.

"Okay, well," Tom said. "I was standing right here, waiting for the light to change. It was mid to late December, an entire year ago, so it's not like I remember it like it was yesterday. And there was the matter of that concussion."

"I understand," I said. "So just say anything and every-thing you remember."

"There were a lot of people waiting for the light to change, coming at the intersection from all angles. It was prime holiday shopping time. I was standing at the edge of the curb, and I didn't even see the truck coming. Someone shoved me just when a truck was speeding past."

Now it was my turn to flinch. That must have hurt. Badly.

"Can you remember anything about the people around you?" I asked. "Maybe you noticed the guy standing next to you? Maybe he was unusually tall or had a weird hat or maybe you noticed a woman who had long brown hair?"

"Abby, in my line of work, we call that leading the witness," Ben said.

"I was just giving examples," I said. Of Roger. And Mary-Kate Darling.

"You know, come to think of it, there was a really tall guy next to me," Tom said. "Like around six foot four. If he hadn't been so tall, he wouldn't have registered. No one else did."

"Can you describe this tall guy?" I asked, hoping he wouldn't say on the doofy side, with thinning brown hair. I didn't want Roger to be the one.

"I just remember that he was tall," Tom said. "He wore a hat, like a ski hat, I think. Or maybe that was a different guy. I don't know. After I was hit by the truck, I can't remember who I met in the hospital versus who I saw on the street. Anyway, it was an entire year ago."

Roger wore a ski hat. A gray ski hat.

"Tom, do you have any recollection at all about the color of the ski hat?" I asked.

He shrugged. "Like I said, I can't even be sure the tall guy was wearing a ski hat."

Keep him talking, I told myself. *He'll say something else. He'll remember something.* "When you were pushed, did it feel like a man was pushing you or a female?"

He shrugged. "Really can't say. It was just a push. Hard enough for me to fall forward and get hit."

"Well, Tom, thanks for your help," I said. I liked leading the investigation. "We're doing everything we can to find the person who pushed you."

Ben eyed me. "I'll be in touch," he said to Tom. "If

you think of anything else, please give me a call," he added, handing over his card.

"Will do," Tom said. "Oh, and Abby, I hope you're working on your issues."

"What issues are those?" I asked.

"You clearly have some deep-seated issues with rejection that began when your father abandoned you and your mother for the perfect blond family. I can recommend a good therapist—"

"Have a nice day," I interrupted.

I saw Tom shake his head at Ben. What a pompous jerk.

"They're *your* exes," Ben said as we walked away.

"Well, I guess you've got a point there," I said, batting him on the arm. "So it doesn't look great for Roger Hunker, my coworker at *Maine Life*. He's very tall and wears a ski cap. Shelley and I make fun of it all the time, but he wears it every day."

"You'd think someone who'd committed a crime in a ski cap wouldn't show up wearing said ski cap to work every day," Ben said. "Especially when his above-average height was enough of an identifier."

"That's another very good point, Detective," I said.

He smiled.

"I assume you've cleared Roger already?"

"I can't discuss the case with you, Abby. But I can tell you that we're working on all leads."

So why did all those leads lead to me? How could that possibly be good police work?

I told him about my theory—that *Tom* was the killer, that he'd lied about being pushed and had paid off Riley.

"Now you're thinking like a cop," he said. "I'm impressed. That's exactly how it works. You take all angles and you look at and into everything."

"So what do you think?"

"Well, after you take the angle, you discount what you can immediately so you don't waste your time. For example, Tom Greer's hospital records discount the 'he made up the whole thing' theory."

"Oh."

He smiled, those dark, dark eyes on mine. "But it was good detective work."

God, I love you, I wanted to whisper. But I opted to think of new theories.

"Maybe he flung himself in front of the truck," I said. I hadn't gotten to why, but with a few hours, I was sure I could.

"Actually, Fargo already checked that out. The angle he was hit suggested that he was pushed from behind, just slightly to the right."

"Wow, you can pinpoint all that?"

He nodded.

"And with all the evidence you can collect, all this forensic-science stuff, you still think I could possibly be guilty?"

He nodded again. "Key word is *could,* Abby."

Didn't I know it.

Chapter 15

For the past work week (it was now Friday) I'd watched Roger very closely. Mostly because he came to work every day wearing that ski cap. Then again, Ben had to be right about that. Wouldn't he have tossed it in a Dumpster if he was the pusher? Gotten rid of identifying objects? Wouldn't he have started stooping to disguise himself?

Thing was, how many six-foot-four guys did you run across in the Old Port? You noticed them because they were so, so tall. And I couldn't recall noticing any in the past few months.

I stood in the doorway to the kitchenette, ostensibly waiting for the awful coffee to perk, but really to observe Roger. He was cutting a huge sandwich. Tuna fish. Lettuce shreds and tomato bits were oozing out the sides. He opened a big bag of potato chips and poured some onto his plate, then grabbed a sticky from the magnetic pad on the fridge and wrote "Help yourself. RH."

Did someone that generous with potato chips go around pushing people, even jerks, in front of speeding trucks? Did they take advantage of pit bulls and sic them on destestable accountants?

Maybe they did if they had a huge crush on you and saw how hurt you were the night of the *Maine Life* company Christmas party the December before last. I'd taken a big breather from dating after the Charlie Heath incident. After the "he didn't want you to be next" moment of truth. And how I let myself be charmed by Tom's toilet-paper opener I'll never know, but I had been charmed. There was something in his tone, his delivery, his eyes, that said: *I am a good guy. A nice guy at heart. I might dump you one day, but I'd do it nicely.*

And as I said, our first date was magical. We had so much to say, so much to laugh about. There were so many *me, too*'s. And that kiss—oh, that kiss! I almost fainted on the street in front of my apartment building. He'd made me swoon. He hadn't been wearing that tweed cap when we were dating.

And then a month later, when I was drawing *Tom "heart" Abby* in giant red hearts on sticky notes in my cubicle, Tom was busy meeting someone else. If I'd known, I wouldn't have gotten tickets to an incredibly expensive concert (his favorite band was in town for one night only and I got us floor seats). I wouldn't have bought a three-hundred-dollar dress. Or new shoes. Or a new tiny beaded purse. Or a new sexy bra and thong. And I especially wouldn't have agreed to do a few semi-kinky things in bed that I was a little *eh* on (let's just say they involved toys). Anyway, the night of the holiday party I was waiting in my cubicle, all dressed up with somewhere to go, but my date was ten minutes late. Then twenty.

"Baxter, why are you answering your phone at five-thirty!" I'd heard Shelley saying in her cubicle. "You should have been here fifteen minutes ago!" Silence. And then, "You have got to be kidding me, Baxter! Everyone is dying to finally meet you!" Silence. "Fine. I'm not upset! Yeah, you'd better make it up to me. Okay." Giggle. Another giggle. "Okay. Bye, sweetie."

"We can be each other's dates," I'd called over our cubicle wall. "I've been stood up."

Her head popped over. "Oh, Shelley! You look so beautiful!" I said. And she did. She usually didn't wear makeup, but for the party she'd gone all out, which, for her, was still natural looking but sparkly. She also had on dangling earrings—something else she never wore. And from the straps of her dress, which was all I could see at the moment, I knew she was wearing red.

She scowled. "I hate his stupid job. This is how it's going to be for the rest of my life if we get married." Baxter was an intern at Maine Medical Center. "He's not even a doctor yet!"

Ping. New e-mail.

I hit Open Mail.

Abby, I'm really sorry, but I'm not going to be able to make it tonight. I've met someone else and she invited me to her company party and it's tonight, so... I would have called, but I didn't know what to say and thought as an editor, you'd appreciate the written word. It would also give you something to save, since I know you like mementos. Fondly, Tom

So his Dear Jane letter was supposed to be my memento of the relationship? *Jerk!* And he'd clearly thought of what to say, so why not say it on the phone? Somehow a phone breakup was better than an e-mail breakup. At least he hadn't text messaged me. That would have been really bad. "U R DMPD."

"I give up," I said.

"Uh-oh, what's the matter?" Shelley asked.

"I just got dumped via e-mail," I said. "Do you believe that?"

Shelley came around the wall, read his kiss-off, shook her head and sat in my guest chair. "I'm sorry. You okay?"

I thought I was. So why were tears welling? "I really liked the stupid jerk," I said, feeling my fifteen-dollar mascara, specially bought for the occasion, running down my cheeks.

"What a jerk to do it by e-mail," Shelley said. "A decent human being doesn't do that."

"What doesn't a decent human being do?" came Roger's voice. He ducked down to enter the cubicle.

Shelley explained. "But the good news is that Abby and I can be each other's dates, since Baxter can't make it, either."

"I'll be your dates," Roger said, looking from me to Shelley.

Shelley and I almost burst out laughing. But we controlled ourselves. Roger was nice. He really was. But he sounded exactly like Snuffleupagus from *Sesame Street,* and it was hard to take him seriously as a guy.

"Let me fix my raccoon eyes and I'll be ready," I'd said, grateful that if I had to date jerks, I did have good friends.

"Ewww! Someone's lunch stinks!" came Marcella's shrill voice, startling me out of my memories of last year. "Gross!" She appeared in the other doorway, pinching her nose. "Roger, what are you killing in here? A fish? Are you gutting it or something? That stinks."

"It's called a tuna fish sandwich," he snapped.

"Well, spray some Lysol. God!" she added before flitting away, waving the air in front of her nose.

Roger slammed his fist down on the bag of potato chips. "Bitch," I heard him mutter.

Interesting. Roger had a little temper.

"We don't usually investigate people for smashing potato chips and being tall," Ben said. "However, the fact that he's had a long-standing crush on you and that Tom recalls seeing a very tall guy *is* meaningful. But we're already working behind the scenes, Abby. We're already on top of this potential lead."

"Why didn't you say that yesterday?" I asked.

"I told you—I can't discuss the case with you."

"You discuss me with everyone else," I pointed out.

"You're our prime suspect."

Oh. Again.

At least I now knew that there was someone besides me on Ben's list. Even if that someone was clearly a long shot by what Ben was saying. Or not saying.

We were in a coffee lounge in my neighborhood. I'd called Ben the minute I saw Roger leaving the office with his smelly sandwich in tow. I told Ben I'd follow Roger, see if he was headed to, say, Henry Fiddler's place of work to slip some cyanide into his coffee mug or something, but Ben said, "No. Under no circumstances are you to follow him. Got that?"

"I got it," I said. That didn't mean I had to listen.

And so I followed Roger—at a good distance, since he'd once complimented my perfume, and if he truly did have some twisted love for me, he might sniff it a mile away and turn around. He didn't seem to be going anywhere, though. He was just walking, looking in windows. He popped into a coffee lounge and came out a minute later with a small cup of coffee, then headed back in the direction of *Maine Life* magazine.

I called Ben. "Well, he didn't do anything suspicious."

"Not a half hour ago I specifically told you *not* to trail

him!" he yelled. "Abby, you're the one who put him on the suspect list. That means you think he's capable of pushing someone in front of a truck. Setting a pit bull loose in someone's house. Pointing a gun at someone and pulling the trigger. Get it?"

"Now I've got it," I said, gnawing my lip.

"This is serious business, Abby. You've got to be very careful. If it's true that the killer is someone you know, then that person is around you all the time. A killer is in your midst."

I shivered and wrapped my scarf more tightly around my neck. He was absolutely right.

"Well, can I talk to Henry Fiddler?" I asked. "He's not a suspect. I just want to ask him what I asked Riley and Tom. If he's noticed anyone following him, if he's had any accidents lately that might not be accidents."

"Beat you to it," Ben said. "Nothing."

"Maybe the killer's new thing *is* to wait until my exes get engaged and then go after them," I pointed out. "It's just that Henry should be warned against falling in love."

"We all should be," Ben said. "I've got to go. I'll be in touch. No trailing, Abby. Promise me right now."

We all should be. We all should be. We all should be.

Do. Not. Read. Anything. Into. That. Ben was famous for his throwaway comments. Even if "exact words are important in my business."

Arg.

"Abby? I didn't hear you say the word *promise*."

"I promise," I told him. *For right now.* Later or tomorrow was another story.

I followed Roger as he left work. He was as boring as the rest of us. Not that I should generalize. He was as boring as I was. He stopped off at the grocery store and came out with one bag. A loaf of white bread stuck out. Then he stopped and picked up his dry cleaning—a pair of pants encased in plastic that he slung over his shoulder. He peered into the window of a video store, stared up at what was playing at the movie theater, then walked past his apartment building. Maybe he had a hot date? Maybe he was buying groceries for his ill mother? Not that I knew if he had an ill mother.

He crossed the street and headed toward the water. And stopped across the street from my building. The back of my building. Where my bedroom windows were.

He stood there, staring up. I turned and ran.

Ben lived close by, also in a condo on the water, like Riley. I'd called him from the street, and he told me to come over. "We'll talk about your listening problem when you get here," he added before hanging up.

I knocked. He opened the door, and I just stared at him. He was barefoot. In worn jeans. And a black T-shirt.

"I'm afraid to go home," I said. "He's probably still there, staring up at my windows! I wonder if he does this every night."

"I'd first like to discuss why you followed him when I asked you not to," he said, gesturing for me to come inside. "You don't follow someone you suspect."

"You do," I said.

"Did I mention I carry a gun?"

Oh, again.

"Okay. I hear you. No following people," I said. "But you have to admit that I've done good work. If I hadn't followed Roger, I wouldn't have known that he stares moonily up at my bedroom windows. That puts him at the top of the list. Not that there's anyone below him."

"Do. Not. Trail anyone," Ben said, staring at me, his expression all too readable. "Are we clear on that?"

"So clear," I said.

"Good. Can I get you something to drink? Coffee?"

"I was thinking I'd better get to Olivia's. I don't want to get there too late and wake Oscar."

"You can't stay with Olivia," Ben said. "Are you forgetting your brother-in-law's little order of protection?"

Oh. "Opal, then," I said.

He shook his head. "Veronica filed an order, too."

Why wasn't I surprised. "Jolie or Rebecca," I said. "They live in tiny apartments, but I can sack out on one of their sofas."

"Unless one of them is the killer," he said. "Then you're alone in a killer's apartment. A tiny apartment. With nowhere to run."

"Ben, the killer isn't after me," I pointed out.

"You think murderers are logical people?" he asked. "You'll stay here."

"Here? With you?" Yes! *Thank you,* fates of the universe!

"I'll take the couch," he said. "You can have the bedroom."

"Aren't you afraid I'll rifle through your papers when you're sleeping?" I asked, glancing around. His apartment was modern, spare, masculine.

"I'm a very light sleeper. You tiptoe out of bed and I'll hear you. And anyway, I keep any files I take home from the station—and my notebook—locked in a safe."

"Smart guy," I said.

He winked at me. "Tomorrow I'll put a detail on Roger. I'll question him again as part of the routine investigation. Ask him about you. I'll let him know I'm talking to several friends of yours for information. I think it'll be fine for you to go to work tomorrow. Just don't drink anything he hands you, like a cup of coffee he got you on the way back from the kitchenette."

"You're discussing the case with me," I pointed out with a smile.

"I'm assuring you that we'll do everything in our power to keep you safe," he said without a smile.

I nodded. "So, am I interrupting anything?"

"Nope."

"I could cook," I said. "As a thank-you."

"Are you a good cook?" he asked.

"So-so," I said. "Depends on what you have."

What he had was pasta. And lots of it. While he sat at his dining-room table and flipped through his notebook, one bare foot up on a chair (he even had sexy feet), I opened cabinets and drawers. Rigatoni. Meat sauce flavored with garlic and mushrooms. Crusty bread. Even I couldn't ruin that.

And I didn't.

"This is delicious," Ben said after I forked a test piece into his mouth. He stood so close to me in the small kitchen. So close.

You are my boyfriend—no, my husband—and it's my turn to cook, so I made your favorite, rigatoni Bolognese and garlic bread, and here's a glass of wine…. Oh, you want to make mad, passionate love to me in front of the fireplace first? Sure thing!

Actually, Ben didn't seem to drink. Maybe he didn't drink on the job. And I wasn't dumb enough to think he wasn't on the job right now.

"What would you like to drink?" I asked him.

"Why don't you let me take care of that?" he said. "Sit. I'll set the table and serve."

The man of my every teenage fantasy was going to serve me? Be my guest. I sat.

He leaned over me to ladle pasta onto my plate. I could smell his delicious male soapy scent. "How's white wine?" he asked.

"Perfect," I said. A glass of wine, a little loosening up and we'll be lip-locked on his bed before second helpings.

He poured water for himself. So much for the kissing. "Don't you miss this?" I asked. "Sitting down to dinner with a woman. The possibilities…"

"Possibilities?" he said, forkful of pasta midway to his mouth.

"Sex."

"Ah, sex," he repeated, looking at me. "I'm pretty private, so…"

"So you're not going to answer that one."

"That's right."

And so we ate and made small talk and then Ben said he had a lot of work to do, so I took that as my cue to hit the bedroom. The moment the door closed with a "good-night," I stripped naked and slept more satisfyingly and more deeply than I had in years.

Last night, in my delight at sleeping in Ben's bed, I'd forgotten about the concept of The Morning. I had no toothbrush. No toiletries. No makeup. No nada.

I found him in the kitchen, adding grounds to the coffeemaker. There was a plate of muffins and fruit on the counter.

"Morning," I said. "You have a very comfortable bed. I had no idea what safe felt like until I slept in a police officer's bed."

He smiled. "Everyone says that."

Everyone? Like the countless women who'd slept in his bed until his moratorium on relationships?

He was staring at me. "I see why you have so many boyfriends," he said.

Was he being sarcastic?

He was still staring. He tucked an errant strand of hair behind my ear, and I almost jumped. "The way the light is streaming in from the windows and lighting you," he said. "You're like a painting."

Had he just said that? Even though I had bed head? Even though I was in yesterday's clothes?

I couldn't contain my ear-to-ear smile. "I don't think I've ever been complimented on my bed head."

He smiled back. "Help yourself to a muffin. Or two or three. And fruit."

I grabbed a corn muffin and a bunch of grapes and sat down at his table.

He did the same, except he chose what looked like blueberry, and sat down next to me. "I got a voice mail from your stepmother. You're invited to your father's birthday party. With chaperone," he added. "Can you explain this one to me? Not the chaperone part. The party part. For your father."

With all that was going on with the investigation and Ben, I'd almost forgotten that it was nearing my dad's birthday. "Family tradition," I explained. "Well, a relatively new family tradition. When my father died a month before his birthday, Veronica didn't cancel the party she'd planned. Just family at her house. It made everyone feel better to celebrate his life, so she kept up the tradition. We all still buy him Christmas presents, too."

He took that in and nodded. "I buy my brother presents, too. Little stuff I know he'd like. A baseball glove. A Mutant Ninja Turtle. Marbles."

I burst into tears.

"Abby?" he asked, his hand on my arm.

"I've never known anyone else who bought presents for someone who died."

He squeezed my hand, then let go.

"All I ever wanted was to be part of my father's family," I said. "And when my father died, I was so worried that they'd forget about me, but they didn't. We actually got closer. Well, my sisters and I. We made a pact to meet the first Saturday of every month, and even though we've only met a bunch of times in three years, the pact was *made*. And it meant something to me. And now…now I can't even see my new nephew. I don't even know if Olivia's pronouncement at the bridesmaid-dress fitting was bull or not."

"It'll all be over soon," he said.

"Are you saying that as the lead detective on the case?"

He nodded. "The killer will slip up, Abby."

"Are you including me in 'the killer'?"

He nodded again. "In any case, Abby, you'll get to see your nephew tonight."

"Tell me something, Ben. Are you there to protect my family from me or to slyly investigate them?" I asked.

"Which do you prefer?"

"None of the above."

He smiled.

"I hope you're getting paid overtime for this," I said.

Chapter 16

Jolie and Rebecca came shopping with me to buy my dad's gift, as they had for the past three years. Jolie's father had died when she was only ten. Rebecca's was alive and well and had raised her as a single parent when her mother died from cancer when Rebecca was only two. She also had a stepmonster. Rebecca's dad had remarried when Rebecca was thirteen. The worst possible age for a step-monster. They barely got along.

But both Jolie and Rebecca understood the strange ritual of buying a present for someone who was no longer alive and going to his birthday party. Jolie visited her father's grave in Florida—where he'd always wanted to be buried—on his birthday. Rebecca traveled to a different foreign country every year on her mother's birthday; her mom's dream had been to travel the world, and Rebecca was keeping something of a travel log for her.

Veronica's birthday celebrations gave her points with my friends, neither of whom liked her. Jolie had known Veronica since she was six, when we met and became best friends in Mrs. Gleeson's first-grade class.

"Why do you look so happy?" Jolie asked me as we walked around the men's department of L.L. Bean (I'd vowed never to shop there again, at least until the case was over, but it *was* my dad's favorite store).

"I look happy?" I asked, eyeing everything in my path. Nothing I saw was quite right. A sweater? What was the point? A wool throw with a giant moose? Again, the point?

"You do," Rebecca said, rubbing a cashmere sweater against her cheek. "You look *happy.*"

"Like you're in love," Jolie said. "You look the way you did that day I ran into you in the park with Ted."

I froze. I looked as if I was in love because I was.

"I sort of have a crush on someone inappropriate," I said.

They laughed. "What else is new?" Rebecca said, tugging on my hair. "Not that there's anything wrong with crushing on someone totally wrong for you. It's the American way. I've got a new crush on a guy at work— married—and it feels great. I'd never act on it, of course, but at least the crush itself gets my mind off jerkface."

"You'd better not do anything about the crush," Jolie said to Rebecca, her finger practically in Rebecca's face.

"I would never," Rebecca said. "It's just nice to have someone to fantasize about. Someone secret. Someone totally inappropriate and forbidden."

Like Ben.

"So who's your crush, Abs?" Jolie asked, holding up a huge fleece sweatshirt to her petite frame. "Some new cute guy at work?"

"He's cute, but he's not new," I said. "It's someone who sounds a lot like your guy, Rebecca. Only he's not married. It's Ben."

"Ben?" Jolie repeated. "Do we know a Ben?"

"Ben Orr," I said.

"Wait a minute," Rebecca said. "You mean the cop?"

I nodded.

"You have a crush on the cop who's investigating you for murder?" Rebecca asked.

"A big hopeless crush," I said.

"Totally hopeless?" Jolie asked.

I nodded again. "What Rebecca said."

"Yeah, but it's not like you did it," Jolie pointed out. "When he catches whoever did kill Ted, you and Ben will be free to move in together."

I laughed. "I'd be happy to start with an amazing kiss. Do you know long I've been waiting to kiss him? Let alone other things."

"Since sophomore year of high school," Jolie said. "That's a long time."

"He followed you to Moose City, and you slept at his apartment last night. He's coming with you to your dad's party. He's your boyfriend," Rebecca said.

"He's my *police escort*," I corrected. "A boyfriend doesn't tell you that if you confess now, he could talk to the prosecutor for you."

"Except in your case," Rebecca said, tugging on my hair.

Jolie smiled at me. "On a scale of one to ten, how in love are you?"

"Eleven," I said.

"Well, no matter what happens," Jolie said, "we're here for you. Okay?"

Thank God for good friends.

I'd gotten to know Ben so well I had no doubt what he'd say to that—so good that they'd kill for me?

There was that time in sixth grade when Jolie had punched a boy for telling the class that I'd kissed him with tongue, when it wasn't true. She nailed him in the stomach in the school yard. She also once told Opal off, something I'd never been able to do as a teenager. And she was the one who'd renamed Veronica *Demonica,* which comforted me when it was true and made me laugh when it wasn't. The day after my twenty-eighth birthday party, Jolie had called to check on me and told me she'd left a message on Ted's machine to let him know he was a "total slime-bucket bastard" and that karma would take care of him and his "cousin."

I glanced at Jolie, peering at the display of chocolate-shaped lobsters. If she'd killed Ted and tried to kill Riley and Tom because they'd dared hurt me, she would have gone after Rebecca's ex-boyfriend, too. And he was alive and well; I'd spotted him the other day in the window of a restaurant, all cozy with some woman. And Henry would be fish food.

As for Rebecca, we were good friends, but we weren't on the level of me and Jolie, friends forever. Jolie knew of every one of my boyfriends; Rebecca just the past few years' worth. Plus, I was one hundred percent sure that Rebecca would never touch a gun.

This whole line of thinking was insane. Jolie wasn't a killer. Rebecca wasn't a killer. No one I knew was capable of murder—probably not even Roger, despite being very tall and the owner of a ski cap and a long-standing crush on me.

I would know it in my bones, wouldn't I?

"Hey, Abby," Jolie said. "I have a great idea for a gift for your dad. Why don't you get him a fun picture frame, like this one with the moose on it, and put in a new photo of yourself looking the way you do today?"

"In love and happy," Rebecca said, nodding. "That's a great idea."

"In love and happy?" I repeated. "Try in love with someone who's investigating me for murder. Someone who thinks I'm capable of committing murder. How happy do you think I really am?"

"You're happy," Jolie said. "I know it. Look, like I said, Hot Ben will catch the killer soon, and then you'll be free to date."

I smiled. "Let's hope so." Thing was, I *was* happy. Despite everything. Because I *was* in love. Which led me back to my inability to fall for the right guy.

★ ★ ★

Just when I thought Ben couldn't be any more gorgeous, he turned up—on time, of course—in a charcoalgray sweater and nice gray pants and shiny black shoes. He looked less like a gun-toting officer of the law and more like a boyfriend dressing up for a family function with his girlfriend.

His girlfriend. I wanted that label.

"You look very nice," he said, those dark eyes on mine. "Red is your color."

At the last minute I'd gone for the red wrap dress and my knee-high black boots, which did nothing for making me look innocent. Every time I wore that outfit on a date (not that I was confusing a police chaperone to my late father's birthday party with a *date*), the guy went sort of nuts about getting it off me. It was clingy and sexy, but not too clingy and sexy. And it was well worth the small fortune it had cost on a shopping trip a few years ago with Opal, who'd insisted I buy it.

"Guys will be putty in your hands," she'd said, nodding at my reflection.

I tried to imagine Ben as putty. He was so damned in control of himself!

"You look very nice, too," I said. "Very uncop-like."

He laughed. "Good."

"Could you do me a favor?" I asked him. "Would you take a picture of me? It's for my dad's gift. I can print it out and pop it into the cute frame I bought."

"Sure," he said, taking my digital camera. He glanced around my apartment. "How about sitting on the sofa, next to the vase of tulips. That'll be a good shot."

I sat and waited for the "say cheese." He spent a few minutes getting the frame just right. "Okay, so move the vase just a smidgen toward you. Okay, now back just a bit. Okay, so sit back, slightly forward—no, straight up. Yes, that's just right. Okay, on three. One, two, three."

I had no doubt that my smile was huge and genuine and would tell the world that on the day the photograph was taken, I was, indeed, quite happy. And/or in love.

He handed me the camera and I ran to my bedroom to print out the photograph at my desk. "How is it?" he called out. "Need me to take another?"

I stared at the photograph of me in my red dress, the red tulips at my side, glad that I had the shot stored in my camera. I'd want another for myself. I looked as happy as Jolie said I did.

I looked as if I was in love with the photographer.

"What do you think?" I asked, joining him in the living room. I handed him the moose frame, which now contained the picture.

He looked at it for a long moment. "I'm good."

Yes, you are, I thought.

"I think your dad would love this," he said, handing it back to me.

I carefully tucked the frame into the tissue paper in the gift bag I'd bought. "Are you close with your dad?"

His expression changed for a just a second. "Reasonably."

"Were you always reasonably close?" I asked, reaching for my gloves and hat.

"Reasonably reasonably close," he said.

"Too personal?"

He glanced at me, then shook his head. "He did his own disappearing act when my brother died. In a different way than my mother, since he was physically there, which I'll appreciate for the rest of my life. He stuck around for me. My mother didn't. I'd just turned seventeen. Suffice it to say it was a very confusing time."

"So your dad just kind of retreated?" I asked.

"Yeah. That's a good word for it," he said, putting his hands into the pockets of his long black coat. "We moved to Massachusetts to be closer to my dad's mother, and if it hadn't been for her, I would have been totally lost. I'd wake up in the morning and come downstairs and my dad would already be gone to work, even though he was a lawyer and didn't have to be at work at seven, and I'd look in the fridge or the cabinets, and there'd be no groceries. There'd be a pile of cash on the counter instead, and a full coffeepot."

I walked toward him, my coat on my arm. "It sounds very lonely for a seventeen-year-old."

He took my coat and put it on me, and I thought, but I wasn't sure, that he lingered for just a moment behind me. "Well, like you once said, loneliness can breed a certain kind of independence. I turned out well."

"I did, too," I whispered. "I didn't turn out to be a cold-blooded murderer."

He looked at me but didn't say anything, just held open the door and then locked it behind us. And then we were off in his car, a small black SUV, a couple seemingly headed out on the town on a Saturday night. He didn't say much as we drove the twenty minutes north to Barmouth.

"Hometown," he said as he turned off the Barmouth exit. He seemed lost in his own thoughts, so I let the silence be, even though I was full of questions about how he felt about Barmouth and if it brought his memories rushing back and if he was okay. Then again, I doubted Benjamin Orr was ever lost in his own thoughts. He was always at the ready.

We pulled up in front of Veronica's huge white Colonial with its pretty red door and black shutters. I spotted Jackson's and Oliver's cars.

"Ready?" he asked.

"Not really," I said. "But I am looking forward to seeing my sisters and Oscar. Oscar is so cute and so tiny. And my only relative who's not judging me."

He smiled and came around the car to open my door for me. Nice gesture.

Veronica was already at the door before we walked up the path. "Abby! Lovely to see you," she said, hands on both my shoulders as she air-kissed me somewhere near my cheek. She smelled so strongly of perfume. "Detective

Orr," she said to Ben, taking his hand in both of hers as though he were an old family friend. "Thank you so much for agreeing to join us for this special occasion. Come in."

Something smelled delicious—it was fried chicken and corn on the cob and garlic mashed potatoes, my father's favorite meal.

"Opal's trying on some of my jewelry for the wedding," Veronica said. "And Olivia's changing Oscar, but they'll both be down in a moment. Help yourself to drinks," she added, gesturing at the bar.

Ben got us both club sodas, and we sat down with Veronica in her formal living room, which I was rarely allowed to enter as a kid.

"And of course you'll come with Abby to Opal and Jackson's wedding shower next week," Veronica said to Ben. "The wedding itself is in three weeks. You'll come to that, too, of course."

"If necessary," Ben said.

My heart leaped and sank simultaneously. *If necessary* meant if the killer wasn't caught and I was still the prime suspect. I wanted the killer caught. But I also wanted Ben to be my chaperone to everything. The grocery store. The dentist. Opal's wedding.

That would be that, I supposed, when the killer was caught. Ben would move on to some other case. He'd semi-romance some other suspect. There would be no reason for him to be in my life.

Opal and Jackson came downstairs and made nervous

small talk with me and Ben for a few minutes. Jackson asked Ben question after question about the "gnarliest shit" he'd seen, and Ben told a funny story that shouldn't have been funny but was because Ben was Ben and had charisma and charm and delivery.

"He is so cute," Olivia whispered to me at the bar. I hadn't even heard her come into the room. Oscar was wide awake in her arms, his tiny slate-blue eyes staring at me.

"Oscar or Ben?" I whispered back with a smile. "It's a toss-up who's cuter."

"Are you two dating?" she asked.

"I wish," I said. "Unfortunately Ben is very professional. Oh, and he thinks I'm probably guilty of killing Ted."

"How are you holding up?" she asked. "I can't even imagine what you're going through."

"I'm okay," I said. "I've got good friends. And…"

I was about to say "Ben," but that didn't make any sense.

"And family who loves you," Olivia finished for me. She nuzzled Oscar's head.

"And family who loves me," I repeated, trying not to sound numb. "Can I hold Oscar?"

I expected her to say, "Until Oliver comes downstairs," but she handed Oscar to me and said quite loudly, "Your auntie Abby loves you so much, Oscar Woscar!"

I laughed. "Oscar Woscar? You didn't just say that."

"You'll come up with the most sickening little rhymes when you have a baby," she said. "Trust me."

I want one of you, I said silently to Oscar. He or she would have Ben's amazing dark eyes and eyelashes. His strong nose. His gorgeous lips. His thick, shiny dark hair…

"Olivia, will you call Oliver down from the television?" Veronica asked. "It's time to sit down."

"Basketball," Olivia said, rolling her eyes.

"Is everything okay between you and Oliver?" I asked. "A baby must be a huge adjustment for a married couple."

"Marriage is a huge adjustment," she said. "A baby is hard work, but heaven-sent. Things are fine. I just have to keep after him for what I want. What I need. Like him to take my word for it that my sister is innocent."

That felt good. I squeezed her hand. "Thanks, Olivia. That means a lot to me."

She squeezed back and headed upstairs, and I went into the living room with Oscar.

Ben stood and oohed and aahed in guy fashion over Oscar, running a finger along his tiny blue cap. "Is it okay that I'm touching him? I know you're not supposed to touch a newborn."

"You only touched his hat," I said. "It's okay."

"He's beautiful," Ben said, unable to take his eyes off Oscar.

"You want kids someday, don't you?" I asked.

"Sure," he said.

My heart surged, and I envisioned our dark-haired, dark-eyed baby. I had no doubt I'd pass the long evenings coming up with potential baby names for our imaginary future child.

I burst into a smile as it occurred to me that I'd be adding another O into the O-crowded family. An Orr.

Orlando Orr. Othello Orr. Otis Orr.

A bell jangled. "Dinner!" Veronica called.

Olivia came down, Oliver trailing behind her. He eyed me, then stared at Oscar in my arms.

"Let's put Oscar in his infant seat," Oliver said, practically ripping the baby out of my arms.

Again, I missed his warm little body, so light. Oliver settled Oscar in his seat on top of the sidebar, shook Ben's hand and then we sat down. Platters and bowls of scrumptious food were passed around. Ben liked good old American fried chicken and corn and potatoes, I saw. And potato salad and green beans.

"Before we dig in," Veronica said. "I just wanted to say a happy birthday to George." She looked up toward the ceiling. "George, I know you're listening and watching. Happy birthday. We love you."

"Happy birthday, Daddy," Opal said. "I wish you could be at my wedding."

Olivia had had a hard time getting married without our dad. He'd died the year before, and there'd been no one to walk her down the aisle. There were uncles, but no one close enough. In the end, Veronica had walked her down.

"George, listen," Veronica said. "I know you're worried about Abby. But she's in Detective Orr's good hands, so what will be will be. Please, don't worry yourself sick." She turned to Ben. "The girls' father was always such a worrier."

In Detective Orr's good hands. I glanced at Ben. What did *that* mean?

"Well, if this all blows over," Oliver said, "let's just hope that Abby's taste in boyfriends improves."

"It's called *dating,* Oliver," Olivia said, adding another chicken wing to her plate. "I dated my share of toads, too."

Oliver was her prince? I almost laughed.

Oliver was staring at me. He threw his bread stick down on his plate, his expression one of disgust—his usual expression, actually. "Did you ever stop to think that maybe it's not them? That it *is* you?"

"Oliver!" Olivia snapped.

"No, no, Livvy," Veronica said. "I think Abby needs to hear this. I think it's time she faced the truth."

"What truth?" I asked, gritting my teeth.

"That you can't hang on to what doesn't exist, dear," Veronica said. "It's just like when you were a little girl and you wanted your daddy, but your daddy had a new family. You just couldn't accept it."

I glanced at Ben to see if his expression registered the "huh?" as mine must. "I'm not following your point, Veronica," I said.

"Your father left you and your mother for a new family," she continued. "And you were unable to deal with it. You've been perpetuating that scenario over and over again with each boyfriend, hoping one would stay. But they don't. They move on, too. You need to accept that relationships end."

Where the hell was this mumbo-jumbo coming from?

"So my relationship with my father should have ended before my first birthday?" I said.

"Well, no, of course not," Veronica said. "But you did need to accept that the relationship had changed. That your father had moved on."

"So how exactly did my relationship to my father change?" I asked. "He wasn't my father anymore?"

"Well, he was still your father," she said. "But he was now two other girls' father, and he lived with them and their mother, so of course things were going to be different for you."

For the first time in twenty-eight years I realized that it was Veronica who had the problem. I wasn't quite sure exactly what it was; perhaps she was simply pissed off that her husband, the father of her children, had another child out there. Perhaps this whole *your relationship had changed* crap was her own wishful thinking.

"You know what's interesting, Veronica?" I said. "That my dad worked so hard to make sure our relationship didn't change. The invitations to every family function, party, event. Your anniversary dinner, even! He went out of his way to include me. I guess you wished otherwise."

Her face turned red. "I just think," she said, "that you have a tendency to cling. Yes, that's the right word. *Cling.*

I think you clung to your boyfriends when the relationships were going nowhere, and when they broke up with
you, you eventually snapped. Just like you're clinging to
your relationship with your half sisters now that your
father is gone."

Everyone was staring at me. I stared back, waiting for
someone to say something, tell her off. Olivia seemed to
be in shock. Opal was admiring her diamond ring. And
Ben had his usual unreadable expression on.

"Is that what I'm doing?" I asked Olivia and Opal,
gazing from one to the other. "The pact I asked us to
make about getting together at least once a month. Is that
clinging? Our dad is gone, so there's no need for me to
be in your lives anymore? Or are we family? Which is it?
This would be a good time for me to know."

I caught Oliver nudging Olivia in the ribs.

"Of course we're family," she said, looking as if she
wanted to explode. "We're sisters."

I stood up. "You're saying this, at Oliver's nudging,
because he's afraid I'll pull out a gun and shoot you or
him. Is that right?"

"Yeah, that's right," Oliver said. "You're a suspect in
the murder of your ex-boyfriend, for God's sake. Two
of your other boyfriends were almost killed. We have
reason to be worried."

Was Olivia placating me to my face but agreeing with
everyone else behind my back? "Olivia, do you think I
killed Ted?"

She glanced at her husband, at her mother, then at me. "Not in a million years," she said.

Opal guffawed. "If you killed Ted, I'll eat Francesca."

Francesca was her miniature dog. Everyone stared at her.

"Well, clearly I don't think she did," Opal added.

"I'm just being cautious," Veronica said. "I'm thinking of my children and my grandchild."

If I ever did have a child, would Veronica be his or her stepgrandma? Or just plain Veronica? The step world got complicated.

"And I'm thinking of *my* wife and child. My child's family," Oliver said.

Too bad neither Oliver or Veronica was likely to be the killer. I could see Veronica and Oliver locked up in a jail cell, wearing orange jumpsuits. But based on Ben's reasoning, they'd actually have to care about me in order to kill for me.

"Veronica, do you remember what Olivia said at the bridesmaid-dress fitting?" I asked. "She said that my father would never in a million years believe I could have killed anyone. I'd think that would be good enough for you."

"Your father was a kindhearted romantic," she said.

"Like Abby," Ben said.

Now everyone stared at him.

"Detective Orr, why don't you give us your professional opinion," Oliver said. "You must know if Abby is guilty or not."

What I would give for him to stand up and say, *"There*

is no way in hell that Abby Foote killed anyone, tried to kill anyone or even thought of killing someone." But I knew exactly what would come out of his mouth.

"I'm sorry, but I can't discuss an ongoing investigation," he said as expected. Sometimes predictability was comforting.

"I'd like to leave," I said, standing up.

"That's probably best," Oliver said.

Olivia shook her head, but didn't say anything. Opal and Jackson were deep in conversation. And Veronica was dabbing at her lipstick with her napkin.

"Thank you for the delicious dinner, Veronica," Ben said.

"My pleasure. And thank you for enabling Abby to join in on her father's special day, Detective Orr."

Veronica was probably nuts. I had to keep that in mind.

I kissed Olivia and Opal goodbye, then gave Oscar a kiss on his forehead, Oliver hovering. Finally Ben and I were out the door.

I stopped on the porch and stared up at the twinkling stars. If my father was up there, listening and watching, I hoped he wasn't upset about what had just happened. *I'm okay, Dad,* I said. *Strange as it sounds. I've got Ben looking out for me. I'm okay.*

Ben opened the passenger door of his car for me. "That was tough," he said. "I wasn't expecting any of that."

"At least I know what she thinks of me," I said as I got in. "Not that I was disillusioned. Were you taking notes under the table?"

He squeezed my hand. "Nope. Just listening. Carefully."

"So what did you learn about my dear family?"

"Well, for starters, I think your stepmother's prickli-ness—that might be a good word for it—has a lot to do with insecurity," he said as he pulled out of the driveway.

"Insecurity?" I asked. "What does Veronica have to be insecure about? She's so attractive, her daughters love her and her husband worshipped her. She has a ton of money, a beautiful house—"

"I'm talking about the intangibles," Ben said. "Your father left his wife and newborn baby for another woman he got pregnant. Every day of your father and Veronica's marriage, she must have been waiting for him to leave her, as well."

I glanced at him. "The old karmic justice. I never looked at it that way."

"Maybe to her, you were always a reminder of what her husband could do," he said. "Leave."

Tears pricked the backs of my eyes and I blinked them back. "He never left her. That actually gave me a strange faith in men, in relationships. He left my mother and me, but he was loyal to Veronica for over twenty-seven years. Sometimes a relationship just isn't right for one of the people. So they leave."

He glanced at me. "That's a really good attitude, Abby. It took me a long time to realize that what you just said is true. It's why I'm able to talk to my mother at all now. She turned her back on me and my dad when we were grieving as hard as she was. But apparently it was what everything inside her *had* to do. I could let her be who she needed to be, or I could hate her guts. I chose to let her be."

I took a deep breath. "I guess that's how I handled my dad, too."

"I'll bet your sisters were also worried, subconsciously maybe, about your dad. If he'd up and leave them the way he left you."

"And then he up and left us all," I said.

"You know, it might take a while longer for you all to find your way together as a family. But it looks like you're trying. You're physically present, even if Veronica's a porcupine. If Olivia bows to her husband a little too much. If Opal is overly focused on her wedding. You all showed up tonight to celebrate your dad's birthday. That's something. It's a lot, actually."

I wanted to hug him so badly, but aside from the fact that he was driving, I didn't think I could just fling myself into his arms.

"Thanks, Ben. You've made me feel a lot better about everything. I was a shaky mess when we left, and now I feel okay again."

"Good."

"And I know my sisters are behind me," I said. "Even if they're under Veronica's and Oliver's thumbs. And I know my friends are behind me, too. That's why when you ask me to suggest that one of them would actually kill another human being, harm another human being, even if to avenge my broken heart, I can't."

He nodded. "You've got good people in your life, Abby."

"Except you think one of them is a killer."

"Or you," he said.

Nuh-uh, I thought. *You think I'm guilty about as much as Olivia and Opal do. I know it in my bones. In my heart.*

I placed my hand on his, which was resting on his thigh. "Thank you for being there tonight, Ben. I can't tell you how much your support means to me."

He glanced at me—no smile, no comment, no "You're welcome." I moved my hand back to my own thigh.

Was I completely nuts? Did he support me? Or was he doing his job—chaperoning me, as my stepmother had requested? Listening, slyly questioning, gathering evidence, witnesses. He hadn't been there tonight as my friend—or my boyfriend, for heaven's sake.

Why did I keep forgetting that?

Chapter 17

"Why don't I come in for a while?" Ben said as he pulled up to my apartment building. "To make sure no tall guys in ski caps are peering up at your window. I'd also like to check your locks and the entry points."

Well, I never said he didn't care.

"I'd appreciate that," I said. I also appreciated the fact that he'd solved the problem I'd been having for the past five minutes: how to get him inside my apartment.

I'd been working on my line for inviting him in. I'd thought about using the *I'm scared that Roger's lurking* approach, but I didn't want to lie to Ben; I wasn't scared of Roger. A little nervous about him, but not scared. I'd decided to go the coffee-and-dessert route, the so-do-you-think-Oliver-or-Veronica-could-be-guilty-even-though-that-makes-no-sense route. I did have an entire unopened box of Godiva chocolates, compliments of

Gray Finch for "all your hard work on the Moose City piece." When I was cleared, I had no doubt that Finch's "kindnesses" would be deducted from my paycheck.

A little coffee, a little chocolate, a little conversation. And then maybe I'd just *do it,* just jump his bones once and for all.

As he walked me to the door, glancing all around at the bare trees for lurkers, checking the locks and the vestibule door, I couldn't stop staring at his profile. At his perfect nose. His perfect chin. His perfect everything.

I love you, I love you, I love you, I said silently. Just like high school, except then I loved you with all my teenage heart for your face and your body and the way you walked down the halls. And now I love you because of you, because of who you are, and who I am when I'm with you.

I am going to make my move, I thought as I unlocked the door. But what if he *could* resist me? He hadn't even been aware I existed in high school, and we'd had two classes together. What if I made my play for him and he gave me the *Abby, I'm sorry, but I can't. I find you repulsive.* He wouldn't say that. Even if he thought so. He'd give me the *It's just not good police slash suspect interaction.*

Maybe once he was seated on the sofa, I would surprise him by sitting next to him. I'd let my red wrap dress do some of my work. And then I'd just lean over and kiss him. Slowly. Just press my lips to his and see what happened. The worst? He'd say he couldn't and pry me off him. The best? He'd rip off my dress and make love to me for hours, fulfilling every fantasy I'd ever had since age sixteen.

"You need a dead bolt," he said. "I'll arrange for a locksmith to install one in the morning. If it's all right with you, I'll stay here tonight. Your lock can be picked with a credit card, Abby. I'd feel better knowing you were safe."

I almost grinned. "I'd appreciate that, Detective."

He pointed at the floor. "There's something under your door."

I glanced down. A piece of paper was slipped underneath. I picked it up, expecting it to be yet another notice from the management company about recycling.

Typed on plain white paper was "Why are you such an idiot? The cop is just going to break your heart and dump you. And then I'll have to kill him, too."

I gasped and dropped the paper; it fluttered to the floor, and Ben picked it up and read it.

My legs started to tremble, and I rushed over to my couch and sat down. "What the hell?" Who was doing this?

He scanned the paper again and turned it over.

"Ben, I can't take this anymore," I said. "You have to find him. Her. Whoever."

"Wait right here," he said, heading outside. He returned a moment later with a plastic bag. For evidence. He dropped the note into it and sealed it. Then he closed the door and stared at me. "I have to ask, Abby. Did you write this yourself?"

I gasped. "What?"

"Did you write this?"

"This is ridiculous," I snapped. "Was it there when you picked me up tonight? Was I sitting by your side all night long? When would I have had time to slip out, drive home, slip this note under my door, drive back and act totally natural?"

"You could have slipped it under when we first approached the door," he said. "You could have done it when we left. I just need to ask you, Abby, that's all."

"You have to be kidding me," I said. "This is all on some list of questions you must ask when you find a note like that, right? Standard police procedure?"

"I'm waiting for an answer."

I stared at him, the pressure in my chest making me unable to speak. "After everything we've been through together, do you *really* think I'm a murderer? That I killed Ted? That I tried to kill Riley and Tom? That I'm going after Henry the second he gets engaged?"

"You *could* be, Abby. We've been through this time and again."

"I *could* be? What the hell does that mean, anyway? You've been saying that since the first time you questioned me. Anyone *could* be the murderer. Roger could be. You yourself said that someone I know could be. I mean, come on, Ben. Haven't you gotten to know me well enough by now to know I'm not the one?"

Wait a minute! I didn't say that last part right! I am the

one—for you. Can't you see that? Our chemistry? How we connect? What we've shared? But can't you see I'm not your "perp"?

"Abby, you're our prime suspect," he said. "That hasn't changed just because I've gotten to know you."

"But how could it not?" I asked. "How could you think me capable of killing someone?"

"As I've said, you *could* be capable, and that's all I need to know. Motive. Opportunity. Evidence."

"What's your evidence? That two of my other exes were on the killer's hit list? That's your evidence? That makes me guilty?"

"It makes you *look* guilty. That's why you're not under arrest. Because you only look guilty, Abby. Someone you know might have done it. A stranger with a fixation on you might have done it. A total stranger with no connection to you might have done it. The boyfriend connection could be completely coincidental. I don't think so, but it could be. Or *you* could have done it. All of it. You're lovely and funny and charming and sweet, but so are many psychopaths."

The world *psychopath* canceled out all the compliments. I couldn't even remember the adjectives. Psychopath. Psychopath. Psychopath.

"I know my rights, Detective Orr," I said. "I have the right to ask you to leave. So please do so. I'll hire my own locksmith."

He stood there staring at me, those dark, dark eyes

working, trying to figure something out, but *what* I couldn't tell. How to get me to trust him again? How to get me back on his side so that I'd eventually confess to my "best friend"? Had he been trying all along to make me fall for him? Was that why his partner was so scarce? No "bad" cop to scare me silent. Just Hot Ben whom sucker Abby used to love as a teenager.

Why are you such an idiot? The cop is just going to break your heart....

Well, whoever did write the note—and newsflash, Ben, it wasn't me—had gotten that part right. So maybe it *was* someone who knew me. I was an idiot when it came to love. Had been since kindergarten.

I actually did feel dumped by him. How ridiculous was that? Our relationship that never even existed (hey, just like high school!) was over.

And then I'll have to kill him, too.

I shivered. I couldn't tell anyone what was going on. I'd have to keep my mouth shut—about the note, about my heart being smashed to smithereens. At least that would keep Ben alive.

"Abby—"

"I asked you to leave," I said, my heart hammering in my chest. I opened the door.

"I'm not comfortable with you staying here alone," he said.

"Well, I'm not going to off myself," I said. "I'm the killer, remember?"

"Abby—"

"Forget it," I said. "Of course the killer knows who I am, where I live. He or she is in my midst, right? And I'm not a target." Although I do keep breaking my own heart.

"Promise me something," he said, stepping over to me. "Promise me you won't put yourself in a dangerous situation. If you want to run something by me, just call me."

"I'm not promising you anything," I said. "I'm not a liar, Ben. I'm not going to tell you that I'm going to sit around and do zippo while everyone I know thinks I'm a murderer."

"Care to fill me in on what you will be doing?" he asked.

"Nope."

"Don't do anything stupid," he said.

Too late.

It rained during the night, and a branch kept knocking on my window, scaring me to death. Around three in the morning, I'd gone to the door and peered out the peephole, expecting to find the bogeyman, aka The Killer.

And there was Ben, sitting against the wall across from my apartment door, his notebook balanced on one knee. He was awake and reading and tapping his pen.

I want to invite you in so badly. I want to invite you into my bed.

I slid down against the door and sat there for a while,

and the next thing I knew the daylight was streaming in through the living-room window and I was stiff all over.

I got up and peered through the peephole. Ben was gone.

Chapter 18

How I wanted to call Jolie and Rebecca and Shelley and talk endlessly about Ben and how hurt I was. It was so hard not to pick up the phone. To keep it all in. I needed a pet. Maybe I'd go the animal shelter today and adopt a cute pug of my own.

A week had passed since the night the note had been slipped under my door. An entire week and no new developments. Except for Veronica calling to apologize for "things getting out of hand" at the party.

I worked on a new Best Of column and watched Roger very closely. He was all I had. I trailed him a few times, but it was the same story. A coffee-shop run. The grocery store. A bookstore. A glance up at my apartment. I'd been so freaked out by it the first time that I'd forgotten how many times I'd done just that over the years. When I was a teenager, I'd walked past Ben's house countless times.

Walked by his classrooms, just to get a glimpse, making myself late for math. I'd pretended to be waiting for a friend in front of the club Slade used to frequent. And once or twice in the past week I'd walked past the Portland Police Department, hoping to see Ben, even from afar.

I missed him so much. I stared at the phone on my desk, willing it to ring. Willing it to be Ben just so I could hear his voice.

"Abby, you must be upset about something" came Roger's voice instead. "Your reader letters were riddled with typos. You always misspell when you're upset."

I froze. "I'm not upset. Really. Happy as can be." Could I be a worse actress? Natural, Abby. Natural.

Ben had already questioned Roger twice and had said he had no reason to think he was guilty of anything but a big crush on me. He'd been asked where he was the night of the murder and had said he was home alone, which wasn't an alibi. He'd been on vacation to the Grand Canyon when Riley had been attacked. But you never knew. To use Ben's logic, he *could* be the killer. Which meant a little detective work of my own.

My big plan was to drop a little false clue about my love life. I'd tell him I'd started dating someone new—no names, of course—who'd dumped me in a really mean way over the weekend. If Roger were The One, he'd very likely hound me for the name. So he could go and pummel the guy into the ground.

★ ★ ★

Roger insisted on taking me out to lunch once he learned that a guy had something to do with my inability to concentrate on my spelling. This was perfect. Shelley was out sick today, so it seemed completely natural that I'd go out to lunch with Roger alone. Especially because I was "so down in the dumps."

"I didn't even know you were dating," Roger said when our waitress arrived with our burritos. We were at Mamba Margarita's, my favorite Mexican restaurant. Roger bit into his beef burrito. Beans oozed out the other end.

"Well, I just needed a distraction from everything that's going on," I said, popping a tortilla chip into my mouth. "I'm about to crack from all the pressure."

He nodded. "I can imagine. I'm really sorry you're going through all this. It's so ridiculous that the police think you could have had anything to do with any of it."

"Well, a lot of people think I could have," I said. "Including our coworkers."

"Shelley doesn't," he said. "And I'm sure some others, too."

I was about to tell him that my family thought I was guilty, but then realized that if he was the killer, I didn't want to send him to their homes with a machete to make them pay for thinking less than pure thoughts about me.

"I guess I just keep picking the wrong guy," I said, shaking my head. "I thought I was being careful, that he was a great guy, but he turned out to be a super jerk, just like the rest of them."

"Is it that detective?" he asked.

"The detective! Of course not. Why would you think that?"

"Well, it's just that you're together a lot," he said. "I saw you going into your apartment building together last week."

Because you're standing around outside, watching.

"He wanted to check the locks on my door," I said. "He couldn't believe I didn't have a dead bolt. I do now."

So don't even try breaking in, buster.

"So who's the guy you were seeing?" he asked.

"You don't know him," I said, shrugging.

"Maybe I do," he said. "From around."

To distract him, I asked the waitress for more salsa, then said quickly, "Do you have any good dating advice for me? I keep picking the wrong guy."

He took another bite of his burrito. A shred of lettuce stuck to his chin. "Well, I couldn't really give you any advice from *experience*."

"You don't date much?"

He blushed. "I would, but the woman I like isn't interested."

"Who's that?" I asked, knowing full well it was me.

"You know," he said, deeper pink creeping into his cheeks.

"So what kind of boyfriend are you?" I asked, hoping

I wasn't veering into unfair territory. Roger had only ever been very kind to me, and he was innocent until proven guilty (I, of all people, understood that), so I needed to be very careful with how I proceeded. Careful of his feelings.

"Do you want to know a secret?" he asked.

I nodded.

He glanced around, then leaned forward. "I've never had a real girlfriend."

"A *real* girlfriend?" I asked. As opposed to blow-up dolls? Or…corpses?

"I've gone on a few dates," he said. "But I don't seem to be anyone's type. Like yours."

"It's not that you're not my type," I said. "You're a fine type. It's just that dating a coworker is really dangerous. Don't you think?"

"So if I quit *Maine Life,* you'd date me?" he asked.

Whoa, there. "Well, then there'd be the friendship thing," I said. "We're good friends. And I don't have a good track record, Roger. Given my past history, we'd be broken up within a month, and there would go our friendship."

"We might not break up," he said, his mud-brown eyes so hopeful. "I could be the guy you've been looking for all along."

"That's possible, Roger." I highly, highly doubted it, but it was possible. "I guess with this latest heartbreak, I just can't even think about dating for the foreseeable future."

Ah. Anger. There it was. He stabbed the remaining half of his burrito with his fork.

"That jerk!" he said. "He just ruined my chance!"

I sat back in my chair. "I need all the friends I can get, Roger," I said. "Friends?"

His face softened. "Friends." He sipped his Coke. "So what's this guy's name again?"

"I'm trying to forget it, okay?" I said with a smile. "Anyway, it was just a couple-of-weeks kinda thing. Nothing serious. It's more my ego than my heart."

"Good," he said. "The ego heals a lot faster."

That was probably true. Also true was that Roger had gone from suspect to prime suspect. At least in my notebook.

I needed to hear his voice. And I needed to let him know that Roger did need a more in-depth look. So I called Ben. Voice mail. Good. That meant he was out looking for Ted's killer.

My cell phone rang two minutes later. "Abby, I'm one hundred percent sure that I told you not to bait anyone."

"Those weren't your exact words. And I'm one hundred percent sure you said exact words were very important in your line of work."

"I don't think he's our guy, Abby," Ben said. "We've got Henry Fiddler under twenty-four-hour surveillance. He's the logical target now that he's seeing someone new. We can only wait."

"I can't wait, Ben. My entire life is falling apart."

"I wouldn't say that at all," he said. "You got promoted. You've got a lot of good friends. And you're invited to Opal's bridal shower this weekend."

"I guess that means you are, too."

Who needed a day planner when I had Ben to keep such good track of my social calendar?

"Should I get a gift from the two of us?" I asked.

"Is that a joke, or are you serious?"

"I don't know."

"You can sign the card from Abby and Detective Orr," he said.

Chapter 19

Ben didn't stick out like a sore thumb at Opal's bridal shower because the shower was coed. Jackson's fellow surfer-dude friends were there, one of whom I'd been fixed up with on a blind date years ago.

"Dude, good thing you didn't think she was hot or else you'd be six feet under by now," I heard someone say to him.

"She's hot now," he whispered, eyeing me up and down.

Interesting how being a murder suspect added sex appeal. As though I might cross and uncross my legs to show my lack of underwear like Sharon Stone in *Basic Instinct*. I always wore underwear.

Ben and I had arrived separately. He'd offered to pick me up, but I'd declined. He'd offered to stop by to "talk," but I'd declined that, too. There was nothing to say. My plan was to solve his case for him. Find the killer so I could go back to my former life—not that my former life was so great. And he could go solve a new murder. Or take a vacation. He needed one.

Opal and Jackson's wedding shower, held in the private room of a posh restaurant, had a theme, of course, which was Gorgeous Couples. Between the time the invitations had gone out and today, several of the celebrity Gorgeous Couples had broken up.

"You two make a gorgeous couple, you know," Opal said to me and Ben as we stood around like statues, not talking to anyone else or to each other.

"We're not a couple, Opal," I reminded her. "Detective Orr is my police chaperone."

Five different people called her name and she flitted away.

"So what did we get the happy couple?" he asked.

"Candles and holders from Opal's favorite little shop in the Old Port."

He nodded. "How have you been?"

I realized that he was wearing the same suit he'd had on that very first day in my office, when he'd told me that Ted was dead.

"Just fine. You?"

"Just fine, too."

Our scintillating conversation was interrupted several times by hellos from Veronica and Olivia and various other relatives. Every time Ben and I were separated, I searched him out. I felt his eyes on me more than once, too, and when I would glance over, he would be looking at me.

This was so frustrating! What did he think? How did he feel?

"You're next, I know it," my aunt Marian said to me.

"If next is a hundred years from now, maybe," I said.

"What, dear?"

I forgot that Aunt Marian blinked in and out of lucidity. "I said I hope so."

"You said you wanted some more pie?" she asked, tilting her head.

"Yes," I shouted.

That she heard. But off she went in the direction of the bar.

"Do you hope so?" came Ben's deep voice. He was behind me, eating a mini empanada from a tiny plate.

"It would be nice to stop dating," I said. I glanced at Opal, who was beaming and showing pictures of her veil to her cousin. "If I'd found The One long ago, I wouldn't be in this mess."

But then I wouldn't have met you, and you're The One, so it's all the same.

"Any luck tracking that little note I received to a particular computer?" I asked. "I was watching a *Law & Order* rerun last night, and they were able to pinpoint the printer to a specific high school."

"The printer was standard issue. The kind you have at *Maine Life*. The kind we have at the Portland PD. The kind countless businesses use."

"I didn't write it, Ben. I know you don't necessarily believe me, but it's the truth."

He stared at me for a moment, then took my hand and led me to the far end of the room. "I do believe you, Abby," he whispered.

I was so startled, I almost spilled my champagne flute. "You do?"

"I believe in means, motive, opportunity, forensics, evidence. Tangibles. But I've also learned to go by my gut. My gut has long told me that you're not our perp."

I glared at him. "And you weren't planning on mentioning this?" I asked. "This is only the most important thing in the world to me."

"I know. And I'm sorry. But you *are* still the prime suspect, Abby. That hasn't changed. What has changed is that where I was focused on you as the killer, I'm now ninety-five percent focused on your circle of friends and family."

"Why aren't you one hundred percent focused on Roger?" I asked.

"Because Roger was away for Riley's pit bull attack," he said. "He has credit card receipts from gift shops in Arizona to prove it."

"So we're back to square one?"

He shook his head. "You were square one. We're getting there, Abby. We've kept the pressure up. You think you've felt it? The killer has felt it double."

"So you think he or she is about to crack? I know I sure was."

He nodded. "We'll get him. Or her."

I took a long sip of my champagne. "Do you want to hear something really, really, really crazy?"

"Sure."

Say it before you chicken out. "I sort of missed you this past week."

"Well, we have spent a lot of time together," he said. "That makes sense."

Yeah, it makes sense because I'm in love with you.

The jazz trio started to play, and Opal and Jackson went out on the dance floor, then couples began following suit.

Ben took my half-empty glass and placed it on a passing waiter's tray, then took my hand and led me onto the crowded little stage. He put one hand at my waist and held my other. Finally I was *thisclose* to him. If we had been anywhere else, I would have lifted my chin and kissed him.

And then Veronica was jangling her little bell and announcing it was time to sit for lunch.

"Thanks for the dance," he whispered into my ear.

That sent a little shiver up my spine. And not in a good way. A little too out of character for the good detective. Was he playing me? Was the *I believe you* just a trick to get me to confess? Or to give up the killer? Did he think I might know who it was?

The people closest to you can surprise you, he'd said. I'd do well to remember that he was included.

★ ★ ★

When I was utterly confused by life, I tended to go visit my dad's grave. I would sit there for an hour and think; sometimes I'd talk to him. Once I saw Veronica there, her mouth moving, and I darted away fast. She'd been a little more humanized then. Who knew what went on in her mind or heart? Ben's theory about her made so much sense. Fear was such a control freak.

No one was there today. There was some snow left on the ground, but it was a strangely warm day, in the high forties. I sat on a dry patch of yellow grass to the side of his headstone.

George Foote, beloved husband, beloved father.

"Dad? It's Abby. If you have any words of wisdom to impart about what's going on, now would be the time."

I waited, in case some flash of insight overtook me. Nothing. So I just sat there, staring up at the cloudy sky. I took my Moose City snow globe out of my purse and watched the snow twinkle down over the mini moose, then shook it again.

Chapter 20

After work on Monday I followed Roger, as usual. If he didn't do something bizarre tonight, like, say, stalk Henry Fiddler or ask my friends for the name of the guy who broke my heart, I'd give up on him.

He was heading down Exchange Street, his hands stuffed into his pockets. He made a left onto a side street and walked a few blocks, then looked behind him as though he sensed someone was following him. I ducked into a doorway. I didn't want to follow him much longer. The wind was picking up, and this area was pretty desolate. I was about to pop out of the doorway when I spotted Shelley coming out of a bar and grill across the street. She wasn't wearing a coat. And she looked as if she was crying. I almost called to her, but she started running and rubbing her arms. Had she and Baxter gotten into a fight and she'd run out? Had she left her coat inside?

I darted across the street and went into the pub, surprised that Shelley would choose such a place. It was a dive, an "old man's" bar. Not her style at all. There was the requisite old man nursing a beer at the long bar, his eyes on the basketball game on the TV perched on the wall. A few tables dotted the place, and menus inside triangle-shaped Lucite holders offered hamburgers and fish and chips.

I glanced around; maybe Baxter was in the restroom.

"Help you?" asked the bartender, an old man himself.

"Um, I was just seeing if my friend left her coat," I said. "Young woman with long brown curls? She just left."

"She was sitting right there," he said, gesturing at the table closest to the pool table.

There was Shelley's green wool coat around one of the chairs. And two glasses. One untouched bottle of beer and one half-drunk glass of red wine.

Ah. She'd ordered for him but he never showed? Or they got into a whopper of a fight and he left just as their second round was delivered?

"Sad girl," the bartender said, wiping glasses. "Comes here twice a week and sits at that same table and orders a red wine for herself and a bottle of Beck's, no glass, which she directs to be placed at the seat across from hers. But here's the thing—no one ever shows up to drink that Beck's."

What? "Wait a minute. How long has this been going on?"

He shrugged. "Long time. Months now. Maybe even a year."

"She's been coming in alone twice a week for *months?* Ordering a beer for someone who never shows?"

He nodded. "Strangest thing. Sad story, I gather."

I gnawed my lip. "I gather."

"Yeah, I guess things didn't work out with that guy. Or maybe she was hoping to run into him again or something."

"Baxter?" I asked.

"Don't know his name. British guy. I remember him because of his accent. Just like the royal queen's. Well, Prince Charles, I guess. They were getting hot and heavy at the pool table one night, and since then, she's been back alone, ordering what he ordered that night."

Oh, God. Shelley. Baxter must have broken up with her months ago and she didn't have the heart to tell anyone. Still, what about all her grandiose stories? *"He wants me to move in, but why not just get engaged? We're going to his mother's birthday party this weekend.... Baxter and I had the best weekend skiing at Sunday River.... He drove me down to Boston to surprise me for my birthday...."*

Lies? All if it?

I took her coat, thanked the bartender and left and waited a reasonable time for Shelley to get home before calling her. No answer. From the bar and grill, the direction she'd headed would also take her back to *Maine Life,* so I figured I'd try her there. Before we'd left work tonight, she'd been frustrated by an article she'd been fact-checking. Maybe she went back to work to finish?

Nope. The offices were dark. Only the cleaning crew was there, vacuuming and emptying the trash cans. I draped Shelley's coat around the back of her guest chair. My cell phone rang as I was heading back into my cubicle.

Ben.

"Are you going to be there for another half hour?" he asked. "I want to show you a couple of photos and see if you recognize anyone."

"Photos? Of who?"

"Fargo found a witness, an amateur photographer, who'd been taking pictures for a holiday photo contest that the *Portland Press Herald* was sponsoring. Guess who's just visible in the shot? Tom Greer with his hands full of shopping bags."

"This is great! This is our first break!"

"It's our first break if you recognize anyone in the photo," he said. "And it's a sort of artsy shot, at a weird angle, so I'm not getting my hopes up too high."

"I'll be here, Ben," I said. I hung up, elated. *Please, please, please* let me recognize the person behind Tom! Although if Ben hadn't, that wasn't a good sign. He was all too well acquainted with everyone I knew.

My shoulders slumped. So much for elated.

I tried calling Shelley's house again. No answer. I was too worked up to actually do any work, so I just waited for Ben. This could be it. The end.

He called my cell from the reception desk to let me know he'd arrived. I ran to let him in.

He looked so tired. Just the hint of dark shadows under his eyes.

"Ben, if you didn't recognize anyone in the photo, why would I?" I asked him as we headed back to my cubicle.

"Maybe it's someone we overlooked, someone not in your daily world. It could be anyone, Abby."

I turned on my strong overhead light. He handed me three photos, all the same one, but blown up to different sizes. I stared at them so hard that the faces blurred together. "Damn it! I don't recognize anyone! And that tall guy doesn't even look like Roger!"

"I noticed that," he said.

"Let me get my loupe." I searched my desk and top drawer, full of junk, for the little magnifying cube, but I couldn't find it. "Let me see if Shelley has one."

I darted next door to her cubicle. No loupe. I opened her top drawer, where she kept her desk supplies. The photograph of Baxter was face-side down. Huh. I wondered what had happened. The photo had been out on her desk for months and months until just a few weeks ago. If they broke up long before that, why would she have had it out? And why suddenly put it away? Had they gotten back together and then broken up again?

"Find one?" Ben asked from the doorway.

"Nope. But I found where Shelley put her ex-boyfriend's picture. This situation is so weird. She's been supposedly dating this guy for over a year, but I found out tonight that he broke up with her months ago. Maybe even a year ago. But she's been acting like they're still a couple."

"Sounds like she couldn't face it," he said.

"I just feel so bad that she felt the need to keep up the pretense. That must be so hard. Why not just tell everyone about the breakup and get comforted?"

"People get wrapped up in fantasies sometimes," he said. "Abby, trust me, I've seen it all. Before you know the facts, don't jump to conclusions, though."

"Like you do?" I shot back. "It's your job to conclude things from circumstantial evidence."

"People are convicted on circumstantial evidence, Abby."

"Great. I'll see you on visiting day," I said. "I look awful in orange," I added. "Even if you really do believe that I didn't kill Ted, does your boss? Does the prosecutor?"

"You're not under arrest, Abby. There is nothing connecting you to any of the crimes except for the individuals involved. That's not enough."

"Shelley doesn't have a loupe, either," I said, so tired of this. "I'll get one from the art director's office." I glanced at Baxter's face again, then went to slide it back facedown, as I'd found it."

"Wait a minute," Ben said. "Let me see that."

I handed him the frame. "You know him?"

He studied it. "I don't know. But I've seen him before."

I shrugged. "Around Portland, maybe?"

His eyebrows furrowed. "I can't place him, but I've definitely seen that face." He thought for a moment, then shook his head. "Go get the loupe and take another look at the photos."

"Okay." I slid Baxter's picture back into the desk and then ran to the art director's office. Aha. He had all the loupes. Four were lined up on his desk.

I ran back to my cubicle and studied the photos with the loupe. The faces were magnified, but I still didn't recognize anyone.

"It almost looks like someone is behind Tom," Ben said. "But it's just an arm. Tom's so damned tall himself that he's obscuring half the people behind him."

I looked for the arm. There was just a hint of it. "Looks like whoever it is wears a black coat and black gloves."

He took a deep breath. "I'm going to see what else I can dig up from the *Herald*'s contest. It might take all night, but if I find anything, I'll need to come by whether it's 2:00 a.m. or 7:00 a.m."

"That's fine, Ben."

"Walk you out?" he asked.

"I might as well finish up my Best of South Portland column," I said. "It's due tomorrow afternoon. Plus I have a slew of reader mail to answer. I'll be here for another hour, then I'll head home. But I'll keep my cell on, okay?"

He nodded. "We're close, Abby. I feel it."

I nodded. I didn't feel it. The only thing I felt was alone as I watched Ben leave.

I turned on my computer and got to work.

Dear Best Of Editor, Where do you think the best place to break up in Portland is? I need to tell my girlfriend it's over, and someone said I should do it in a restaurant so she can't make a scene, but then I'll be stuck paying like fifty bucks for dinner. Would a park be good? Thanks,
Mike F., 32, Portland, ME

I heard the elevator doors ping open in the reception area. Ben? I glanced out. It was Shelley. She was staring down at the carpet. And she was crying.

"Shell?"

Her head shot up. "I didn't know you were here."

I gestured to my computer. "Ton of work due tomorrow."

"Me, too," she said, though her eyes were so red-rimmed from crying I doubted she'd get any work done.

I took a deep breath. "Shelley…" I went into her cubicle and opened her desk drawer and took out the picture.

"What the hell are you doing?" she asked, grabbing the picture. "Since when do you just go into my drawers?"

"Shelley, I saw you come out of that pub tonight. I was trailing Roger, and all of a sudden there you were, running out without your coat."

She stared at me, her expression hardening. "So?"

"So I went in to see if you left your coat…."

"And?" she said.

Ugh. Why didn't she just tell me the whole story right now? Why was she pulling it out of me?

"And you did leave your coat. And your gloves."

"Did you get them for me?" she asked.

I nodded and gestured toward her guest chair.

"Thanks," she said. "Baxter and I got into a huge fight. I think it might really be over this time." Tears came to her eyes.

What was I supposed to do? Tell her I knew? Go along with her charade?

"Shelley, the bartender told me."

Again the same stare. "Told you *what,* Abby?"

"That you come in twice a week and order a wine for yourself and beer for Baxter." I walked over and took her hand. "And that he never shows up."

She burst into tears and sank to the floor. "He dumped me."

I knelt beside her. "Shelley, it's okay. Who's been dumped more than I have? It's okay to talk about it."

"I feel like such a fool," she said. "I just got so tired of being the only one without a boyfriend. You had a new boyfriend like every week, and I couldn't even get past one date. I just liked the fantasy so much better than the reality."

"I understand, Shell."

"You'll have a new boyfriend by next week, Abby. You always do. You can't possibly understand what it's like for me."

"I know what it's like have your heart broken," I said. "I know what it's like to be in love with someone who's just using you."

"Riley Witherspoon is old news, Abby. How many boyfriends have you had since him?"

"Shelley, my last boyfriend ditched me in a department store."

"Yeah, but he didn't break your heart. It's not like you were in love with Henry Fiddler."

"I'm in love with Ben," I said. "Trust me. I know what it's like to love someone for whom you're just a means to an end. Once he catches Ted's killer, that's it."

She stared at me. "I didn't know you and the detective were fooling around."

"We're not. We've never even kissed."

"So how did he use you?" she asked.

"Forget it," I said. "He really didn't. He was just doing his job and doing it well, and I got caught in the crossfire of that. I fell in love with another guy I can't have. Talk about old news."

"So maybe you do understand, Abby," she said, wiping at her eyes. "Could we get out of here?" she asked. "Maybe go for a drink?"

"You bet," I said.

The phone at my desk rang. I started to head for it, but she grabbed my wrist. "You don't want to talk to him. He *is* just using you, Abby. He's just going to break up with you. Like they all do."

"Break up with me?" I said. "Shelley, I just told you that we're not dating."

"Yes, but you're in love with him. Why are you such an idiot? He's just going to break your heart and dump you."

I whirled around and stared at her.

Why are you such an idiot? The cop is just going to break your heart and dump you. And then I'll have to kill him, too....

Oh, God. *No, no, no, no, no.*

Stay calm. Don't let her know that you know. Just get out of this building. Alive.

"Where do you want to go for drinks?" I asked, striving for natural. "Moxie's? Maybe Mamba Margarita's?"

She didn't respond. She just stood there, zoning. And then her expression changed. Softer. Sweeter. Like the usual Shelley.

"I wish I could, hon," she said. "But I'm meeting Baxter for dinner. Rain check?"

Huh? Was she totally psycho? Split personality?

"So you two are back together?" I asked. "You worked things out?"

She smiled. "He finally proposed! We're getting married."

"That's great, Shell. Really great." She was blocking the entrance to her cubicle. There was no way I could get past her.

"Where are you meeting Baxter?" I asked. "Maybe we could go have a celebration drink until he arrives."

Her expression changed back. Hardened. I'd said the wrong thing. Intruded on her fantasy world?

She reached into her tote bag and started digging around. "Where is it?" she muttered. "Shit!"

"There's only one place you can meet Baxter" came Ben's voice. "The John Doe cemetery."

We whirled around. Ben held a gun trained on Shelley.

She dug in her tote bag again. Frantic. "Where is it? Where!"

"This?" he asked, holding up an evidence bag containing a small handgun. "You left it in the bathroom at Runion's Bar and Grill."

"I was going to shoot myself in the head," she said slowly, staring at the floor. "But I couldn't do it."

Ben motioned for me to run past her, but Shelley grabbed my hair.

"You're so stupid!" she yelled at me. "He's just going to dump you. They all do!"

"Is that what Baxter did?" Ben asked. "He dumped you?"

"We're getting married," she screamed.

"Baxter Coe is dead, Shelley," Ben said. "I saw that photograph of him, which I assume you put away because there were cops nosing around *Maine Life,* and I finally remembered where I'd seen him before—among photographs of unidentified murder victims. He was from England, here to hike the Appalachian trail. His family reported him missing after he failed to check in at a promised stop, but they had no idea where to start looking for him, where on the trail he might be. People he came across had different recollections of when they'd met him.

They resigned themselves to thinking a bear had gotten him, or a bad fall."

"He almost made it, too," Shelley said. "The entire trail."

"But then he met you," Ben said.

She nodded. "He decided to visit Portland one night, and he picked me up as I ate alone in a restaurant. Me. Do you know that's never happened to me? And then he sweet-talked his way into my apartment, where he used me. Had sex with me, and then snuck out in the middle of the night. Jerk. He was a jerk just like Abby's boy-friends. He didn't even say goodbye."

I held my breath. Ben waited, not moving a muscle.

"And so I took my gun down from the high shelf in my closet," she continued, "and followed him down Commercial Street. He was stumbling a little because he was still drunk. He stopped to piss, right in the water, do you believe that? And I confronted him. 'You didn't even get my number,' I said. He stared at me and laughed. *Laughed.* 'It was just good sex, okay?' he said. 'Let's just leave it at that.' And then he started to walk away. So I pulled out my gun and shot him in the chest. He fell back into the water."

"Is that what you intended for Ted Puck?" Ben asked. "For him to fall back into the water? So he wouldn't be found right away?"

She rolled her eyes. "That idiot grabbed on to a post when he went down," she snapped. "I would have kicked him off the pier, but I heard voices and so I hid for a while. But it was so cold and I heard more voices, so I just ran off."

I closed my eyes. This was crazy.

"You pushed Tom Greer in front of a truck?" Ben asked.

"I heard his bones crack," she said with a smile. "I'm so petite no one ever looks twice at me. A crowd full of people and no one noticed me. It's always like that. I guess being little and unattractive has its advantages. He was my first. Baxter dumped me, and then a few months later that drippy therapist dumped Abby. Minutes before our holiday party. How dare he embarrass her like that! Well, I got him back. My little secret, too. I can't tell you how good that felt. So good that when the next loser hurt my good friend Abby, I got even with him, too."

Ben stared at her. "And you let a pit bull loose in Riley Witherspoon's house?"

"I hid nearby to hear him scream. Pansy. He was screaming, 'Help me, help me.'" She laughed. "What a baby."

"Shelley Gould, you're under arrest for the murder of Ted Puck and the attempted murders of Riley Witherspoon and Tom Greer. You have the right to remain silent...."

My ears felt as if they were stuffed with wet cotton. My legs gave out and I dropped hard to the floor, which thankfully was carpeted. Ben called for backup, and within minutes the offices were full of police.

"You were there for me, Abs," Shelley said as an officer led her away. "So I was there for you."

I stared at her. She was out of her mind. She stopped and turned back. "I would have gotten to that sniveling little tax lawyer, Henry, but he was such a baby and kept himself surrounded. I couldn't get him alone. But don't worry. I'll put a hole in his head. Little shit."

I gasped. Answers, questions, *why* would come later. But there was one thing I had to know. "Shelley, what was so different about tonight? Why did you get so upset tonight?"

She burst into tears. "Because Baxter told me it was over this time. For good. I really loved him, Abby."

Ben nodded at the officer at her side, and she was led away.

"Wha—" I started to say. But I had no idea what question to ask. My mind was racing with questions.

Ben put a bracing hand on my shoulder. "You okay?"

I nodded. "I need to lie down."

"I'll have an officer take you over to Urgent Care," he said. "I want you checked out. And then an officer will drive you home."

An officer. Because the case is closed. I waited for him to say his famous *I'll be in touch,* but he didn't.

Chapter 21

I spent the rest of the evening at home alone, uninterested in being with anyone but Ben, and who knew where he was? Not here. He'd called a couple of hours earlier to tell me that Shelley had signed a confession, that she slipped in and out of lucidity and was being evaluated by a police psychologist.

How could someone seem so normal on a daily basis for over a year? How could someone have committed Shelley's crimes, lived in her dream world and functioned at work? Finch had often praised her as *Maine Life*'s best fact-checker. How was that possible? Jolie and Rebecca couldn't believe that the tiny, seemingly cool woman they'd met a few times, most recently at my apartment the morning we found out Ted had been murdered, could have been behind it all.

Once people started hearing the news, my phone rang

off the hook. Roger was beside himself and so trauma-
tized by the turn of events that he was planning to give
Finch his notice and thinking about signing up to become
a park ranger, to work in the wild. That sounded pretty
good to me. I thanked him for being my friend and
silently apologized for doubting him.

Oliver called personally to apologize, but informed
me that Olivia had demanded he call or she'd leave him.
That got a tiny smile out of me. Opal called to say she
knew all along it wasn't me and that I'd be like a celebrity at her wedding, but that I'd better not steal her
thunder. Veronica left a message that she was thankful
this "messy business" was all over and that things could
go back to normal. But of course they couldn't.
"Normal" had changed.

Ben's partner, Frank Fargo, had stopped by the E.R. to
"thank me for everything." And then Finch and Marcella
surprised me by coming by my apartment to see how I
was. For great work under pressure, I was being promoted
to features editor and moving to a real office on the other
side of the hall, as far away from Shelley's cubicle as
possible. Finch had already asked the building crew to take
out Shelley's cubicle and get rid of her furniture.

The sucking-up e-mails continued and all said the same
thing. *I never believed you did it for a minute!*

The strange thing was, the only person I truly believed
had known I was innocent from the get-go was Ben. I
was one hundred percent sure he'd known. And that he'd

thought if he stayed glued to my side long enough, I'd lead the killer right to him. And I had.

My cell phone rang. Ben.

"How are you holding up?" he asked.

"I'm totally shell-shocked," I said.

"Up for a visit?"

My heart leaped. "Sure."

"Good, because I'm in front of your building."

I ran to the door and opened it and waited, needing to see him. When the elevator pinged open and there he was, it was all I could do not to fling myself into his arms.

"Her lawyer said she'll plead guilty by reason of insanity," Ben said. "She'll probably be found incompetent to stand trial and turned over to a mental hospital for the criminally insane."

"But how can she be insane and function at work every day?" I asked. "Do her job so well? As a fact-checker, no less! And conduct normal conversations? I don't understand this at all!"

"I don't, either," he said. "But I am glad it's over."

"Me, too." Except for the part where you have no reason to trail me around the clock.

He smiled and didn't say anything else, and my heart squeezed painfully in my chest. "Well, I'd better get going," he said. "I've already been assigned to a new case."

Do not cry. Do not cry. Do not cry. "Well, we'll always have Moose City," I said, and then burst into tears.

"Abby, hey," he said, squeezing my hand. "I know it's

going to be tough for you to just go back to your old life after everything you've been through. If you ever need to talk, I'm here for you, okay?"

So that was it? Thanks for your help and call me if you need a friend?

"Will you be okay here alone?" he asked. "If you want to call someone to come over, I'll wait till they get here."

They're already here, I thought. I shook my head. "I'll be fine." And I would. I knew that, as a graduate of the school of bad breakups. I'd been okay and I'd be okay. And it wasn't as if Ben was breaking up with me, since there was never even a *we* to begin with.

"You take care, Abby," he said. And with one last look at me, he smiled and was gone.

Chapter 22

Two weeks later I walked down the aisle of Opal's wedding as a blonde. It was wonderful to not be me for a night. No one recognized me with my long blond hair, so there was very little "That's her—that's Abby Foote, the one who was suspected of murdering her ex-boyfriends!"

I did get a lot of "Want to dance?" from male relatives who didn't recognize me. Of course, the minute I said, "It's me, Abby, blond for a day," the whispers and questions started.

The telephone version of events again made its way around the chairs set up for Opal and Jackson's ceremony and then at the reception. I was seated at the family table—me, my lack of date, Olivia and Oliver, Veronica and her lack of date, and Opal and Jackson.

My wig itched, but Opal refused to let me take it off.

I sat at my table in my pretty pink dress and sipped my white wine, watching Opal and Jackson slow dance to a Frank Sinatra song. On the other side of the dance floor, Olivia and Oliver were chest to chest, cheek to cheek, looking happy for once. Veronica was deep in conversation with an attractive fiftysomething whom I'd never seen before.

Good for you, I thought. I wasn't so sure I agreed that it was all about letting go when you wanted to hold on. I wasn't so sure that hanging on until you were ready to let go was such a terrible thing. It was in Shelley's case. But it wasn't always. I wouldn't be ready to let go of Ben for a long time. And who said I should? When my heart, mind and soul were okay again without him in my life, I'd know it.

Out of the corner of my eye I thought I saw Ben in a tux, but of course it wasn't him. *Do not think about him,* I ordered myself. *He is not in bed with another woman right now. He is out solving crimes. He is chasing bad guys. He is—*

Right next to me. I almost jumped out of my chair at the sudden sight of him. It was as though wishful thinking had conjured him up, looking more gorgeous than ever in a tuxedo.

He held out a hand. "Dance?"

I couldn't speak. So he smiled and took my hand and led me to the dance floor. The band played a Norah Jones song, but the singer was no Norah.

He touched my hair—my wig. "I meant to tell you that day in the bridal salon that I liked you much better as a brunette," he said, his arm slipping around my waist.

I smiled. "Good. You didn't need to come, you know."

"I know. But I'd already RSVP'd, and you know how brides get about head count. I would have made the ceremony, too, but I got tied up with a new case."

I laughed. "You were always very polite."

"Abby," he said, serious again, "I wanted to thank you once more for all your help with the case. I know it was tough on you. And I'm sorry for what I put you through."

Oh. So that's why he was here. Opal or Veronica had probably reiterated the invitation to the wedding, despite my no longer requiring a chaperone, as a thank-you for saving their lives when they thought they were in need of saving. He'd likely make his rounds, shake some hands, thank me again, take a token bite of his chicken or fish and then leave.

"You were doing your job," I said. "I get it."

"There's something I want you to know," he said, his hand squeezing mine.

"You won't forget me this time?" I asked, trying to smile.

He laughed. "What I was going to say is that I wouldn't have solved the case without you. You're an amazing woman, Abby. Stronger and tougher than you know."

If he said *I hope we can be friends,* I would drop dead. *So tell him how you feel. Don't let him walk out the door without knowing.* Be bold. You have nothing to lose. You will not have to deal with the embarrassment factor because you will probably never see him again anyway, unless your next boyfriend ends up dead, so just *say it*.

"Ben, there's something I want *you* to know," I said.

"What's that?" he asked.

"I want you to know that…that I was hoping you were going to say something a little more romantic back there. A little more romantic than 'I couldn't have solved the case without you.'"

I held my breath.

"How's this?" he said. "Have I ever told you that I like your perfume?" He leaned closer to me. "Hmm."

"That's not bad," I said. Not exactly the declaration of endless love I was hoping for, but it was something. "You've never told me you like anything about me."

He smiled. "I like your perfume. I like a lot of things about you."

"Oh yeah? Like what?"

"Like your brain. Your mind. Your heart. Your face. Your body."

I froze and stared at him. "What about my feet?" was all I could think of to say.

"Those, too. I like the whole package, Abby. In fact, I was going to say something romantic back there, but you didn't give me a chance. Actually, I wanted to say something romantic two weeks ago, when I came to see you the night Shelley was arrested. But I needed some time to sort everything out. Think things through."

He could top what he'd already said?

He squeezed my hand again. "I was thinking that since we know each other so well, we could skip dating and go straight to a serious relationship."

My heart flipped. I laughed. "You know what I think?"

"What do you think, Abby Foote?"

I think that even though I love you to death, we need to go back to the start.

"Since we got to know each other under such crazy circumstances, I'd like to start from square one," I said. "From the beginning. I want to go back before the badges flashing in my cubicle. I want to go back to 'Hi, Ben! It's me, Abby Foote. We went to high school together!'"

"I think that's very wise," he said. "Abby Foote, well, well! I remember you. I had a mad crush on you," he added, those dark, dark eyes twinkling.

I narrowed my eyes at him. "No, you didn't."

He smiled and took both my hands. "I do now. So, how about for our first date I treat you to the best lobster in Portland?"

"Where?" I asked.

"My place."

I smiled. "Opal says that everything you need to know about the man in your life you learn on your first date. She'd say this was a blinking neon sign that you were moving too fast." *So when you propose to me six months from now and I accept, she'll say, "See, he was in love from date one!"*

"She'd be right," he said. "But I have ten years to make up for," he added, pulling me close.

And then he kissed me. A fireworks kiss. Worth the wait.

★ ★ ★ ★ ★

Look for another Abby Foote mystery
next January.

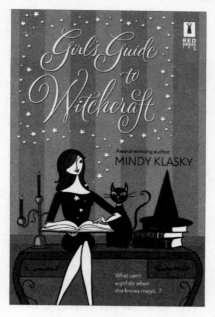

New from the author of *The Thin Pink Line*

Lauren Baratz-Logsted

HOW NANCY DREW
SAVED MY LIFE

On sale September 2006

When Charlotte Bell takes a job as a nanny in Iceland,
she's determined to be courageous, just like her favorite
heroine, Nancy Drew. But when Charlotte stumbles
upon a mystery of her own, she'll need some of
Nancy's wisdom to keep her from running for home!

NANCY DREW is a
registered trademark
of Simon & Schuster, Inc.

*Available wherever
trade paperbacks
are sold.*

RED
DRESS
INK
™

RDILBL591TR

Are you getting it at least once a month?

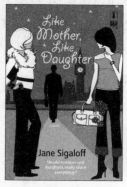